Utopian Literature

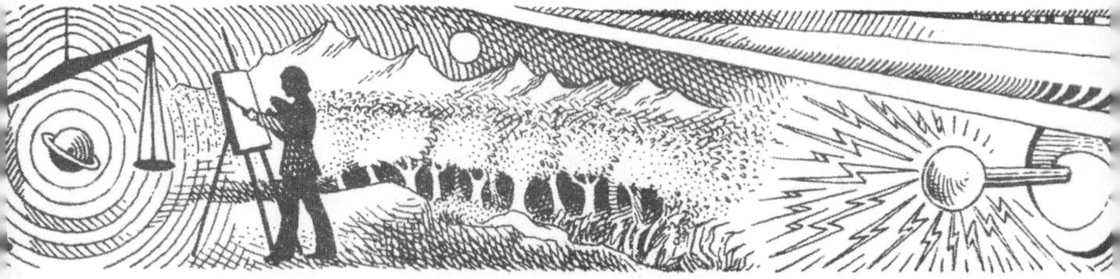

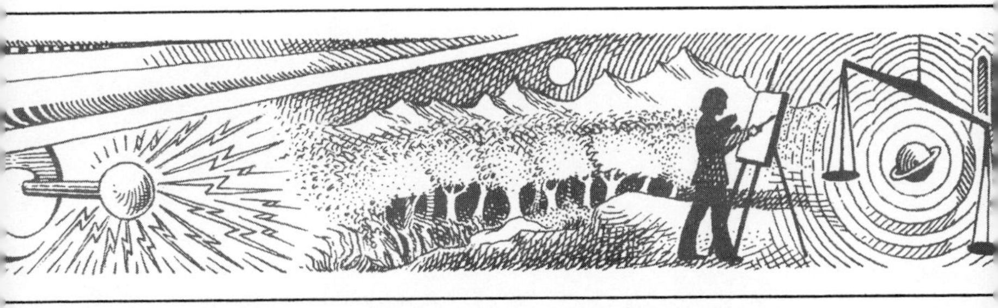

President John Smith

Frederick Upham Adams

ARNO PRESS & THE NEW YORK TIMES
NEW YORK • 1971

Reprint Edition 1971 by Arno Press Inc.

Reprinted from a copy in The Pennsylvania State University Library

LC# 72-154428
ISBN 0-405-03511-X

Utopian Literature
ISBN for complete set: 0-405-03510-1

Manufactured in the United States of America

Publisher's Note: This edition was reprinted from the best available copy

54337 1-30-86 Ayer Co. 24 41

Sign in the heavens. (See page 23.)

PRESIDENT JOHN SMITH

The Story of a Peaceful Revolution

BY

FREDERICK UPHAM ADAMS

CHICAGO
CHARLES H. KERR & COMPANY
1897

PREFACE.

THE following chapters were written in the autumn of 1893, just after the close of the great Columbian Exposition. The panic of that year has passed into history, though at this writing the nation has not yet emerged from that enervating depression which surely follows an industrial or financial collapse.

It was the intention of the author to rewrite this book; to bring it up to date; to eliminate all reference to certain events which then seemed strange and portentous, but which now are accepted as a matter of course, and to insert in their places others of more recent date, which seem to have a significance to students of our commercial and industrial development. Not many years ago such an event as the legislative theft of a great franchise was regarded with public horror. A decade ago a national bond steal would have aroused vast indignation. But a nation, like an individual, can become accustomed to almost anything. In view of the complacency with which the American people permit themselves to be deceived, swindled and robbed, and their evident enjoyment of the operation, the author is sometimes of the opinion that he was unduly excited over the events of 1893, and that perhaps general bankruptcy, distress, poverty and national decadence are matters of small consequence.

Yielding to the advice of friends, the author submits "President John Smith" to the public practically as it was written three years ago. In the original manuscript, John Smith was nominated against William McKimbly of Ohio, and as a gentleman with a name somewhat similar was recently elected president, it has been deemed proper to substitute the "Hon. Mark Kimbly" for the former fictitious character.

The author is not vain enough to regard this book as a prophecy. In common with all who have made even a superficial study of the existing social system, he knows that vast changes are impending, and is sincerely desirous of adding some thought or suggestion which may be deemed worthy of consideration in the discussion of this—the grandest subject which ever demanded the attention of mankind.

In the recent presidential campaign the author was an earnest advocate of the free coinage of silver; not because—in his humble opinion—the consummation of that end would have finally solved any great problem, but because the battle between organized greed and the people was fought on that issue.

Silver should not be the great issue in 1900. It is not worthy in itself of the struggle made in its behalf. More than that, the people cannot win. They might succeed at the polls, but that would avail them nothing. They would eventually be defeated either by the corrupt use of money at Washington or by that last resort of an influential minority—the Supreme Court of the United States.

The great issue of 1900 will be: "Shall the Constitution of the United States be so amended or revised that the rights of the Majority shall be preserved? Shall the Majority rule?"

To-day the majority has no right which a fortified minority is bound to respect. The people of the United States are powerless to enact legislation for the redress of their grievances. Instead of wasting their time in an attempt to pass a free silver bill—which the Supreme Court will promptly declare unconstitutional—

they should turn their attention to a crusade, which, when successful, will make constitutional any enactment passed by a majority vote of the free citizens of the United States.

The United States is not a republic. The Republican party is not republican. The Democratic party is not democratic. Does the Supreme Court represent the people? Are its members elected or appointed by the people? Are they responsible to the people? Can the people by any legal process remove or discipline them when they have trampled under foot some law which the people have passed after a victorious struggle with their oppressors? No.

What modern monarch is vested with such a power as this? Has Queen Victoria, the legitimate successor of King George, from whom our forefathers wrested independence in war, only to sign it away in convention —has Victoria any such power? No. Does Emperor William dare disregard the recorded verdict of his subjects as expressed at the ballot box and voiced by the representatives of the people at a session of the German parliament? No.

As one who believes that the majority of the people of a republic is right; as one who believes they should be permitted to make and unmake laws without an appeal to any higher body; as one who believes there is and can be on higher authority than the majority, and that they can be safely entrusted with the regulation of their affairs and the shaping of their prosperity and happiness, the author dedicates this book to the American people with this sentiment:

"The rights of the Majority shall no longer be abridged."

FREDERICK U. ADAMS.

See yonder poor, o'er-labored wight,
  So abject, mean and vile,
Go beg a brother of the earth
  To give him leave to toil;
And see his lordly fellow worm
  The poor petition spurn,
Unmindful though a weeping wife
  And helpless offspring mourn.

BURNS.

INTRODUCTION.

AMERICAN indifference to misgovernment must end or the republic will cease to exist. American ignorance of economic problems must be dispelled or a great nation will miserably perish. The United States will survive the panic and depression of 1893-94, but it cannot long exist under the industrial system which made that panic inevitable, and which menaces the nation with a never-ending train of industrial depressions and financial calamities.

As these lines are written, millions of American workmen are and have been idle for months. These idle workmen are honest, faithful American citizens, who have committed no offense against their former employers For eighteen months enforced idleness has been general from one end of the country to another. Thousands have been waiting in vain for the opening of the cotton mills in Massachusetts and Rhode Island; thousands are idle in the iron industries of Pennsylvania and Ohio; starvation has stalked among the hills of northern Michigan, and 60,000 of her people have been dependent on charity; in the great city of Chicago nearly 200,000 workmen have been unable to find employment; in the far west whole towns are destitute, and the people are fleeing from the stricken districts into the poverty-infested east, glad to reach a country in which even charity is possible. Vast stores of money are piled up in the banks awaiting the coming of the investor or the manufacturer. In the warehouses are quantities of manufactured goods sufficient to carry on a war, but no purchaser calls for them. Industry is paralyzed. The manufacturer is helpless. The capitalist is helpless. The banker is helpless. The workman is helpless. The statesman is—but there are no statesmen.

The most remarkable fact is that the American people seem to regard the existing state of affairs as something natural, a thing to be expected. Certain stupid reasons are advanced for this wholesale poverty, this stupendous waste of capital and wealth. We have become accustomed to the presence of this vast standing army of the idle, and charity is now a science. We seem unable to realize that this condition of affairs is an awful mistake, a colossal and unnatural crime, an atrocious and unparalleled outrage. The dark pages of history, reciting the cruelties of barbaric ages, tell no tale which can match in horror the awful tragedy of 1893-94—15,000,000 innocent people condemned through the long months of winter to idleness, pauperism, suicide and crime in a free country, under the stars and stripes of a republic.

We have been schooled to expect a recurrence of these periods of hard times. The majority of our people believe that such periods have always prevailed, that they cannot be averted, and that it is patriotic to submit patiently to such seasons of sufferings.

A certain class complacently declares that everything is all right and that people who do not like the way things are run in this country are at liberty to get out of it.

There exists another class which imagines that this is a matter in which workmen alone are interested. They declare that the rich oppress the poor, that wealth is unequally distributed, and that capital is reaping great rewards from the depression of industry. All of which is false. The rich, as a class, are not oppressing the poor; on the contrary, the world has never witnessed such generosity as has recently been displayed by the wealthy people of America. Wealth is not fairly distributed, but if it were the situation would not in the slightest degree be permanently improved. We would all be poor. Capital reaps no financial harvest nor gains any advantage from hard times. This is not an issue between capital and labor. Both are sufferers from existing conditions, but capital is in the greater danger and has sustained enormous losses.

This is not a question of sentiment or of patriotism or of bombast. It is a plain matter of business. It is a question of facts and figures. The United States cannot exist under the present industrial system. Capital cannot make profits and workmen cannot obtain employment or wages. The system is inoperative. The industrial machine has locked itself. After a while it will start again,run for a shorter interval than before, and again lock itself. And in this process capital will be destroyed and labor will starve. This is no prophecy of things to come. It has already happened. The country is poorer than it was a year ago. National wealth has decreased. We are forced for a time to consume more than we produce. We are compelled to remain idle because there is no work. There is no work because we have already created more than the people can buy. The people cannot buy because they have no work and no money. The manufacturer and merchant fail because there are no customers.

That is our industrial system. Clear your brains a moment and take a calm, dispassionate survey of it. It does not seem possible that intelligent human beings would consent to exist under such an idiotic system. We are poor because we are rich; we are in distress because we have created more than we know what to do with; we have invented machinery so perfect that we are about to perish for lack of employment; the unhappy day has come when there is no work.

Who gains by the continuance of this system? No one. It entails a direct loss on every citizen of the republic. It has no intelligent defender. It survives because the American people have been too indifferent or too ignorant on economic questions to make a change. The business men of America must become politicians. They have a problem in government to solve They must take a few lessons in political economy. They must take immediate steps to forever abolish hard times; if not, hard times will abolish them.

Millions of men are idle in the United States to-day. They are miserably existing either on charity or from the scanty hoard saved from times of employment. The majority of them are being supported by the community. Who defrays the greater part of this enormous expense? The rich. They pay it in public charities, in private charities, and in added taxation. They cannot escape it. Society will not permit the starvation of these idle millions and their dependent families. In periods of severe industrial depression the masses may suffer from hunger, but the financial loss falls upon capital.

The waste of production is enormous. The loss to capital is almost incalculable. At a conservative estimate, 3,000,000 men have been idle in the United States for over a year. Reliable statistics place the average producing power of workmen at $2,000 per year. Six billions of dollars a year—$20,000,000 a day. Cut these figures in two; quarter them if you will, and they yet remain beyond comprehension. And every dollar of this is forever lost. That $20,000,000 a day represents the value of food, clothes, comforts and luxuries which 3,000,000 men would have created had they been given a chance. Their labor would have created this value, but society shackled their arms, sentenced them to idleness, and at a vast expense supported them as paupers. Every man at work stands as an asset in the trial balance of national wealth and production; every idle man must be scheduled as a liability and a loss. He is an incumbrance. He must be fed and clothed and provided for. No system which forces men into idleness is practical, nor can it long exist.

Unless this book shall shock many good people it has been written in vain. As an American citizen who can trace his ancestry back to a time when no citizen was idle except from choice, to a time when the American nation was a nation of freemen, patriots and fighters, the author has assumed that he has the right to criticise and even denounce any of the so-called American institutions as they now exist, not excepting the constitution of the United States and the Standard Oil trust.

It is time to discuss these matters. It is time to consider practical remedies It is time for plain talk. It is time for the flag-waver and professional patriot to stand aside and permit the business men, manufacturers and workmen of the nation to agree upon a plan of action.

In the chapters which follow, the author has been rash enough to criticise and attack some of the sections of the constitution of the United States. Americanism is older than the constitution. Patriotism had not its birth with the framing of that document, and patriots may breathe the free air of America when the constitution as it now exists is discarded forever. If our form of government is perfect it can withstand the feeble attacks of deluded would-be reformers. If it is faulty in any respect the stupid veneration which is attracted to any antiquity cannot long stand in the way of common sense. If the American republic has outgrown the constitution it is the first duty of its people either to alter or abolish it. All knowledge of government did not perish from the earth with the death of the founders of the constitution.

If it is visionary to suggest that in a republic the majority should be permitted to rule—this book is visionary.

If it is Utopian to urge an industrial system in which a willing man shall not be denied the opportunity to work, obtain wages, and support himself instead of being an expense to the community—this book is Utopian.

PRESIDENT JOHN SMITH.

CHAPTER I.

THE ANARCHIST CONSPIRACY.

THERE was nothing to indicate impending trouble that beautiful spring afternoon. The streets of Chicago resounded with the accustomed roar of traffic, and hurrying pedestrians dodged truck and cable cars heedless of aught but the immediate cares of life. The afternoon papers contained no hint of threatened danger, and the afternoon of May 23, 1899, drew to a close as uneventful as thousands which had preceded it.

It was the afternoon before the anarchist riot—the last demonstration of force anarchy in America. A prolonged period of industrial and commercial depression with its train of poverty and suffering had revived the anarchists' groups, scattered and dismembered since the Haymarket tragedy of years before. Of the extent of this movement the press and public knew little, but it was an open book to the police department.

Chief of Police Sullivan was alone in his private office. The din of the street came in through a half-open window, but the chief heard it not. Intent on the study of a strangely marked map, he hardly noted the approach of his secretary, who announced the name of a well-known detective.

"Tell him to come in," said the chief. A slightly built man entered the room, saluted his superior, and drew a chair up to the desk. Sullivan eyed his officer curiously and waited for him to break the silence.

"They make the attack to-night," the detective said.

"To-night?" repeated the chief, slightly astonished. "Why have they changed their plans?"

"They are suspicious that spies are at work. I had to knock a red down last night, who made a sort of insinuation that I was not all right."

The chief pressed a button and a clerk responded. He was instructed to send messengers to all the captains and inspectors for a meeting in the chief's office a 4 o'clock. An earnest conversation followed.

"Have you the signal which has been agreed upon?" asked the chief.

"'Watch the sky at about 11:30,' is all the instructions they have sent around," replied the detective. "Johnson expects to get the details before night, but the signal is known only to three or four men and I am afraid he won't get it. We know as much about it as the reds do, and can 'watch the sky' and them too."

"The big parade of the unemployed comes off to-night," said the chief. "I am sorry now I issued a permit for it, though the poor devils are harmless enough if let alone. I have an idea that the reds are calculating on assistance from the men in the procession. We will see about that."

Every detail of the conspiracy, excepting the signal, was known to the police. The anarchists had enrolled 1,200 desperate men in the various groups, and for several months had been planning a revolution. The time was ripe for trouble. They expected to blow up the police stations, rout the police, and capture the city hall and the various armories. They anticipated that their temporary success would bring to their support the thousands of idle workmen, who for weeks had been, whenever permitted, parading the streets with banners and transparencies demanding work. The anarchist plot was sheer folly, and even had they succeeded in defeating the police their success would have been short-lived As it was they were walking into a carefully laid trap, to almost certain death. For a week the police stations had been guarded at night by detachments of militiamen and volunteers, carefully selected and sworn to secrecy. With great caution Gatling and other rapid-firing guns were transferred from armories to the police stations. The arrangements were all completed, and at the 4 o'clock conference Chief Sullivan issued final instructions to his officers.

"Don't shoot before they show themselves," he said. "Tell your men not to be afraid of any dynamite bombs which may be thrown through the windows. They won't hurt anything. Our men made the bombs themselves, and they are filled with as fine a brand of sand and sawdust as you ever saw. The reds have plenty of guns and will use them. Warn your men not to expose themselves until after the first volley. Have them keep on the inside of the building. The men in the surrounding buildings will take care of the reds when they break and run. Don't shoot to kill after the first volley."

At 9 o'clock that evening 1,200 officers and 2,000 armed citizens were massed in and around the police stations, awaiting the coming of the anarchists. It was a merciless arrangement, but it was a fight in which neither side gave or accepted quarter. The anarchists were longing for revenge. They had not forgotten the execution of Spies, Parsons, Engel, Fischer and Lingg, and the police had not forgotten the dead and mangled officers who lay bathed in blood on the cold pavements of the Haymarket that eventful night of May 4, 1886. The anarchists had lost all patience with the labor movement, and denounced the men who were marching the streets in parades of the unemployed as cowards and weaklings.

In the streets along the river hundreds of idle men lounged away that beautiful spring afternoon. They leaned against the walls of buildings on the sunny side of the street and sullenly regarded the well-dressed passer-by. Some were looking for work, waiting day after day for some one to come along with the glad offer of employment. Others were loafers. There may have been a time when they wanted work, but that time was forever past. They were tramps, some of them, and others were far more dangerous than the shiftless vagabond tramp. The bridewell knew them well, and the frowning walls of Joliet only awaited them.

Chief Sullivan and his officers met in conference at 4 o'clock. Fifteen reporters met in an adjoining room. The conference lasted for an hour. At its close a reporter for an afternoon paper stepped up to the chief and the following interview ensued:

"What was the meeting held for, chief?"

"We met to make arrangements about the labor parade."

"Are you going to stop it?"

"No."

"Do you anticipate any trouble?"

"You need not print this," said the chief, lowering his voice, "but confidentially, I do expect a disturbance. The entire force will be massed along the line of parade until after midnight. We are reliably informed that there will be a large number of anarchists in line prepared to make trouble. If you say anything about it warn the people to keep off the streets and remain at home. It is the innocent spectator who always gets hurt, you know."

The confidential interview with the chief appeared in the extra evening editions of the papers. The anarchist leaders read them and chuckled. Chief Sullivan and his inspectors read them and smiled. Timid people stayed at home, but thousands remained downtown and watched the great demonstration of the unemployed.

One hundred thousand men marched in parade that evening The vast army of the idle massed on and around the lake front and, headed by a detachment of police, swept through the city It was a strange and impressive demonstration. Twenty years ago it would have been regarded as phenomenal, but in those later years people had become accustomed to such manifestations, though never before had idle labor made so grand and awful a showing. No bands of musicians marched in their ranks; no banners or transparencies fluttered over their heads. Pinned over the breast of each man was a large paper card, on which was printed in plain type the word

IDLE.

There were thousands of bricklayers, carpenters, stonemasons, plasterers and others in the building trades; iron molders, machinists, printers and scores of other trades and occupations. Eight thousand retail clerks marched in a solid body. Immediately following the police were over 100 idle reporters, who were cheered all along the line. It was interesting to listen to the comments of the thousands who crowded the streets along the line of march. Here are some of them:

"I would like to see myself in that kind of a crowd."

"Bet there ain't fifty men in the whole lot who would work if they got a job."

"Tramp, tramp, tramp, the bums are marching."

"Guess those fellows wish they'd saved some of the money they've spent for beer."

"There ain't that many honest idle men in the country."

"That fellow there looks as if he needed a bath more than he does a job."

It was 7 o'clock when the parade started and it was after 11 o'clock before the shoemakers, who formed the last division, paced wearily past the city hall. There was not the slightest approach to disorder. No one seemed to notice the gradual disappearance of the police.

It was clear early in the evening, but the sky became overcast about 8 o'clock. Great masses of fleecy clouds overhung the city, and in the west an occasional flash of lightning betokened an approaching storm. The thousands of spectators and marchers paid little heed to the warning and the downtown streets were yet crowded. The theaters poured additional throngs into the multitude. It was nearly 11:30 that evening when

Sergt. Morse of the signal service bureau left his office in the eighteenth story of the Auditorium and in company with a reporter climbed the iron stairs and landed on the top of the great tower. Morse was busy recording some indications registered by the signal apparatus when the watchful reporter uttered an exclamation.

"Look at that! What in thunder do you suppose that is?"

To the north a stream of light came from the roof of the Masonic Temple, a huge pile of masonry at the corner of State and Randolph streets.

"That's the searchlight on the Masonic Temple," said Morse, regarding it intently for a moment. "What is it burning at this time of the night for? Look at it now."

From their watch-tower the signal officer and his companion witnessed a peculiar sight. Nearly 300 feet below them lay the city of Chicago, half buried in a sea of steam and smoke, from out whose billows came occasional flashes of electric and gas lamps. To the south long rows of lights on Michigan boulevard gleamed brightly in the foreground and faded away until swallowed up in smoke and fog. In the western sky masses of clouds were occasionally illumined by lightning flashes, while low scudding clouds heralded an approaching storm. But their eyes noted none of these picturesque features of the scene before them.

From the roof of the Masonic Temple, which lifted itself above all surroundings, a powerful flood of light swept out over the lake, focused at first on the north government pier. For a few seconds it remained stationary, growing in volume. The fluttering and flickering incident to the adjustment of the carbons ceased, and under the manipulation of a skilled operator the great shaft of light shot across the lake and burned a disk of pure white light in the low-hung clouds in the eastern sky. It rose rapidly until the shaft pointed upward at an angle of 45 degrees. Against a bank of clouds was a white disk of twice the apparent size of the sun.

As the startled watchers gazed over the lake the light vanished for an instant, and when it reappeared in the center of the white disk was the word

"STRIKE"

in letters of red. With a majestic sweep the disk, with its red and portentous inscription, traversed the southern and western sky, passed to the north, and then slowly increased its altitude until it stood stationary in the heavens, a threatening, malignant midnight sun, burning almost directly overhead. A broad sheet of lightning played angrily across it. Mingled in the thunder which followed, came the unmistakable rattle of musketry to the north. In the west the red glare of a fire illumined the sky.

"Hell!" said the reporter, "I must go to work."

The anarchists had struck, and with frightful results to themselves. Betrayed by their associates, they plunged recklessly into a trap which had been carefully laid, and from which there was no escape. The scenes at East Chicago avenue were repeated at seven other police stations. At the signal 120 desperate men who had been massed around the building for an hour dashed down the street and hurled themselves against Winchester rifles and a Gatling gun. One dynamite bomb was exploded by a daring "red," whose life went out with the crash of the bomb, which caused no further loss of life and only nominal damage.

Four men were shot down while attempting to blow up the waterworks and two were captured while trying to destroy the city hall.

Three hundred rioters were killed and wounded and over a hundred arrested. The anarchists were successful in starting several fires, which were extinguished with little difficulty and small loss. In spite of all the preparations of the police, the man who manipulated the searchlight made good his escape. As the anarchistic electrician adjusted the great light so that it pointed high in the western sky, two officers advanced toward him. Stepping quickly to one side, he raised a trap door and disappeared, the door closing with a snap. He was never captured. The dead and imprisoned anarchists received little sympathy from the thousands of unemployed trade unionists. A small defense fund was raised and expended in a trial which resulted in imprisonment for terms ranging from three to twenty years for twenty-eight of the rioters. Such was the tame and unromantic ending of what was the last anarchist conspiracy in the United States.

CHAPTER II.

SOME HISTORICAL FACTS.

How came anarchy on American soil? What inspired the anarchist conspiracy of May 23? Where and when was planted the seed which ripened into the Haymarket riot of May 5, 1886? Why did vast armies of unemployed men skilled in their several crafts parade the streets of New York, Cincinnati, Chicago, St. Louis and other great cities in the fall of 1893? These are pertinent questions, and it is the duty of the historian to answer them These were new experiences in America. There was a hint of industrial revolt in 1877, but it was smothered only to break out in 1886, and to assume new and more dangerous forms in 1893. There was something majestic and pitiful in the silent protest sent up by hundreds of thousands of men marching through the streets of cities, past granite walls whose impressive fronts guarded the wealth their now idle hands had helped to create.

It was a new thing in America—America, whose proudest boast it was that upon her soil were work and welcome for the nations of the world; America, whose sovereigns were the men who earned their bread by work, and whose laws were framed for the protection of her wage earners. For the first time in history the admission was reluctantly made in the latter part of 1893 that there was no work for willing hands, idle through no fault of their own. A most remarkable situation. Perhaps a study of the past may afford some clew, which, closely followed, shall solve the mystery of American poverty and American idleness.

Away back in 1787 a number of distinguished gentlemen met in Philadelphia for the purpose of forming a general government. The several colonies had just emerged from a terrific struggle with England, and had hardly recovered from their surprise and joy at finding themselves the victorious and undisputed possessors of what promised to be the greatest country on earth. It may be well at the start to mention that the majority of the gentlemen present at this momentous occasion had had but little experience in founding great countries The commonwealth of Massachusetts, with a constituency fewer in numbers than her principal city has to-day, was, perhaps, the most powerful sovereignty with which they were closely identified. It is hard for us at the present day to realize the conditions which then existed, and the author has not the slightest desire to disparage and belittle the work and efforts of the estimable gentlemen who convened in Philadelphia for the purpose of forming a constitution which would last all time and should read to future generations as an inspiration.

To tell the plain truth, these gentlemen had no such idea when they met in Philadelphia. A great many of them did not know what they had come together for, and when Mr. Randolph and others told them they threatened to put on their hats and go home and allow Mr. Randolph, Mr. Madison, Mr. Hamilton and their friends to ascertain how the people who lived in 1896 should be governed. They were finally prevailed upon to remain and, as a consequence, the constitution as adopted was probably different in many respects from what it would have been had these gentlemen not been placated. It was a strangely composed convention, a mingling of broad statesmanship and narrow and bigoted partisanship. It adopted a compromise dictated by the representatives of the weaker states, and by the aristocrats, Hamilton and others, who feared the people.

The constitution as adopted was fairly well fitted for the people of that generation. They would have prospered under any form of government. It remained for certain of the people of 1870-96 to discover that the compromise constitution of 1787 was the final embodiment of all earthly wisdom, and that all knowledge of government ended with the death of the men who formed it. They refused to open their eyes to the palpable fact that the constitution of 1787 was, in many important respects, as absolutely unfitted for their government as if it had been written to regulate the affairs of the people who are supposed to inhabit Mars.

It is not strange that the primitive people who lived in 1787, many of whom yet held allegiance to England and considered the revolution a crime, were unable to agree upon a constitution suitable in all respects to the demand of the people of 1887. The remarkable historical fact is that the constitution as adopted at Philadelphia survived the close of that century.

When the original thirteen states had ratified the constitution and it stood adopted as the organic law of this great country there was not a mile of railroad in existence. There were no steamships, no telegraph lines, no adequate means of communication and exchange. Invention was in its swaddling clothes. There was no Chicago, no Cincinnati, no St. Louis, no San Francisco, no St. Paul. The greater part of that magnificent empire, the Mississippi valley, was down on the maps as a desert. There was no Standard Oil trust, no Tammany, no solid south, no bloody chasm, no Vanderbilt, Astor, Pullman, or Carnegie. Messrs. Randolph, Pickering, and their associates, not being gifted with prophecy, foresaw none of these. It is but fair to assume that if they had there would have been mention of them and certain remedies adopted in the constitution as finally drafted. These last-named men lived and died before the birth of modern civilization.

Measured not by time, but by achievements, the constitution of the United States as it existed in 1893 was an antiquity, the cherished heirloom of a vanished age; a venerable, doddering old document whose senile second childhood was taken advantage of by those whom wealth and influence thrust into position.

The founders of the constitution did not attempt to rear a government which would survive unaltered through the ages. They knew better than to attempt it. When they had finished their labors and adjourned to their homes they did not think much of what they had accomplished. Several of the states represented in the constitutional convention took two years' time for deliberation before adopting the constitution, and came into the fold then only because they were forced to by circumstances and environments. It was nearly a hundred years before the discovery was made that the constitution was an inspired document, a summing up of all earthly wisdom pertaining to government. After amassing $40,000,000 under its munificent regime and having successfully engineered a reduction of wages among his 6,000 employés, Andrew Carnegie made the discovery that ours was the greatest government on the face of the earth. He embodied his ideas in a book labeled "Triumphant Democracy" and inflicted it upon a helpless world.

The founders of the constitution evidently had a most wholesome fear of or contempt for the people. They certainly succeeded in so molding the document that the majority of the people had limited legal redress for their wrongs. With the avowed intention of founding a government of, for and by the people, they established a system in which the majority of the people often had no power to shape or direct their affairs. The only national officers the people were permitted to directly vote for were members of the house of representatives. They were not trusted even with a direct vote for president or vice-president, but were compelled to vote for electors. As a result several presidents were inaugurated and served their terms who received many votes less than their defeated opponents. This was considered "representative government." The house of representatives was not trusted with representing or deciding anything. A senate, founded upon and copied after the English house of lords, was elected by the several state legislatures—two senators from each state, regardless of its size, population, wealth or importance—and delegated with power to defeat anything which might emanate from the house.

Even this precaution was not enough for the monarchists, who controlled the constitutional convention. For fear the voice of the people might prevail despite the cumbersome machinery of the house and the ever-threatening hostility of the senate, the president of the United States was clothed with the power to veto any bill after its passage through both bodies. It could then prevail only after receiving a two-thirds vote in both houses. So that the president could more easily sway both houses he was empowered to appoint 100,000 officeholders. Federal patronage in the hands of the president became a powerful whip and was used unsparingly.

It would seem that the aristocratic founders of the constitution of 1787 had removed the control of affairs so far from the people as to render their meddlesome interference impossible, or at least impracticable. But no. They want another safeguard. They proposed to take no chances. It was just barely possible that the fool people might pass through the house and senate and over the president's veto a law harmful to their own best interests The all-wise lawgivers of 1787 wished to make sure that the people would be governed. To their minds a government that did not override the people and that did not govern them was not worth having. So they established a Supreme Court. The Supreme Court was supposed to know everything. After the people had set their hearts on the passage of some measure and had overcome the stumbling-blocks placed in their way, had elected a huge majority of the House of Representatives and also of the Senate, and passed their favorite bill over the head of an unfriendly executive, the Supreme Court could calmly declare the bill as passed "unconstitutional," and that was the end of it. In 1894 this was termed "representative government," and a considerable part of the people fondly imagined that the United States had a government "of the people, for the people and by the people."

None of these matters, however, seriously affected those who lived in the happy days from 1787 to 1830 or even up to a time twenty years later. Poverty was unknown. There were no millionaires and the pauper was a curiosity. The greatest undeveloped country on the face of the earth was waiting for a free people to take possession of it. There were no foes more dangerous than Indians. Deadly competition had not yet fastened its grasp upon the throat of industry. Land was free. There were no great cities, with their pent-up populations of thousands of toilers struggling for a chance to work. Tired of the town, the toiler was at liberty to leave it and become a pioneer and the founder of a prosperous community in the seemingly inexhaustible west. Those were the days of homely lives and republican simplicity. They were living in an age which has now forever vanished and were standing on the threshold of a new era—the "mechanical age." There was no labor question in those days. There was work enough for all and the foreign immigrant was warmly welcomed. There was no struggle between man and man, no enmity between employer and workman, no banding of employers and no unions of wage earners. None was needed. All these peaceful conditions were swept away with the advent of the mechanical age.

The mechanical age had its birth and first development in the years between 1800 and 1840. Its influence was not severely felt until 1850-60, and it did not attain full sweep and sway until 1870. From that time for a quarter of a century everything was subordinated to the iron rule of the new regime.

The dawn of the present century found Watt working on the steam engine. Two years later gas was first used for illuminating purposes. America had begun to raise cotton, and in 1830 the invention of the spinning mule established a new industry. Fulton built his first steamboat in 1807, and in 1819 the first steamship crossed the Atlantic. America built her first mile of railroad in 1827, and telegraphing became possible in 1835. An industrial revolution was brewing but the people did not notice it, and the constitution did not recognize it. Factories reared their tall chimneys on every side. Bands of iron and steel bound the country together. The boy rested on the plow handle, watched the train rush by toward the great city, and his heart was filled with a strange longing and unrest. The next month he had left the farm forever. The great heart of the west was penetrated. Railroads were projected across the continent, and the government donated them land enough to found empires. While the government reserved some land, it permitted great corporations to grab millions of acres of forest and rich prairie, vast tracts filled with mines, property worth billions of dollars. All this was almost unnoticed. There was plenty left, the people said. Uncle Sam had a farm for everybody. This was in 1850.

In 1893, 300,000 people massed around the Cherokee strip, a barren tract of land the government had purchased from the Indians, and at a signal made a wild scramble for a home in the treeless wilderness. Many were killed. While these unfortunate people were fighting for a home millions of acres of choice farming land in New York, Pennsylvania and Ohio were in the undisputed possession of foreign syndicates and capitalists who were holding them for speculative purposes.

For over seventy years the people lived and prospered under the constitution adopted by our forefathers back in 1787. The country was so great, its resources so inexhaustible, and the opportunities for expansion so limitless that questions which vexed the statesmen of other lands never presented themselves to the favored people of America. It would have waxed powerful under a monarchy and its people would have grown rich had there been no government. The first severe test came in 1860.

The constitution had recognized slavery, and in after years the people almost came to war over the establishment of a line which should divide the slave labor of the south from the wage labor of the north. As the manufacturers of the north proceeded with the development of machinery the south learned with chagrin that it could not compete in open market even though it had the supposed advantage of slave labor. It was the first triumph for the mechanical age. Jealousy turned to rage when the political leaders of the south saw its national candidates defeated, and they decided to sever all connection with the government at Washington, found a confederacy of their own, and they undoubtedly contemplated levying a protective tariff against the machine-made products of the north.

South Carolina, Georgia, Virginia and the other southern states declared in their state conventions that they were sovereign states having full power to sever at will all connection with adjacent commonwealths. In support of the justice and truth of their position they quoted the constitution of the United States, and invoked history to prove that they entered the union as sovereign states and had an equal right to withdraw as such. They proved by the constitution beyond any doubt that they had this right, and thereupon seceded. The north whipped them into subjection and thereby demonstrated that it is better to have common sense and plenty of ammunition than to be a strict constructionist of the constitution and state patriot. But the war did not originate in any controversy over state rights; it was not waged by the north for the purpose of freeing the slaves; it was an inevitable outgrowth of the triumph of the mechanical age and resulted in a life and death struggle between the slave labor of the south and the wage labor of the north. That the latter won was logical. More that that, it was just. Any other result would have been an irretrievable disaster.

No man who reads history aright can make any defense for the position assumed by the south in that controversy. Sovereign states! They may have been sovereign 200 years before they seceded; they may have preserved some of that sovereignty up to the time they merged their fortunes in the Union, and the constitution undoubtedly affirmed that sovereignty, but in the seventy years which had intervened this country had become a nation in spite of a constitution framed by men, some of whom cared more for their political fortunes as officeholders in their respective states than they did for the glorious future of the republic. When it came right down to business the people of the north spent precious little time trying to find out exactly what Mr. Randolph and his associate constitution manufacturers meant. The north knew that this was the United States—poor grammar, but good patriotism—and they proceeded to shoot a little common sense into certain politicians who attempted, by quoting the constitution, to perpetuate colonies, petty monarchies and land grants founded by dead and almost forgotten European tyrants The government laid the constitution aside while this was being done and got along very well without it. It was a splendid time to revise or rewrite the aged document.

The progress of the war did not check the industrial and mechanical development of the country. On the contrary, it stimulated it. A few years previous to the war of the rebellion the country had experienced its first panic. There was a period of "hard times." Factories shut down, workmen were thrown out of employment, banks failed and a period of depression ensued. The wise men of that day did not appear to know what caused this phenomenon. Politicians accused each other of responsibility. After a time the factories resumed work, business revived, and the experience was almost forgotten.

Times were never better in the country than during the four years of the war. There was plenty of work. The more there was destroyed the better the times became. Wages increased. The government issued greenbacks and bonds, the former passing current as money, but not maintaining parity with gold. The nation was enabled, however, to keep up a vast army at enormous expense, and those who remained at home prospered as never before.

The war undoubtedly was a curse, but it created good times. The south surrendered and the war was ended. That certainly was a blessing. A million of the nation's defenders returned to peaceable avocations. No longer would the men who remained behind be compelled to support the soldiers in the field. This certainly was a matter for congratulation. A million men were added to the working force of the nation and new life was to be infused into the republic. Surely an era of happiness and prosperity was at hand.

Strange to relate, nothing of the kind happened. The advent of peace was followed by industrial depression. The men who had been making guns and ammunition to kill other men and destroy property were thrown out of work. A million men entered into competition with those already at work and wages fell. A strange phenomenon! The prosperity of the country evidently did not depend upon the perpetuity of peace, either inside or outside the country. The manufacturers had made a discovery. War was just the thing they wanted. Continued peace had a depressing effect on business. So they scanned the papers and smiled with joy when a war cloud darkened Europe. Stocks and provisions rose when war was imminent and fell when the cables announced that hostilities had been averted.

The depression following the war was short-lived. It did not take the country long to assimilate the ex-soldiers. To the west there were still tracts of land open for settlement. A period of marvelous activity in the invention field began in 1867 and continued without serious interruption for a quarter of a century. Under such a stimulus manufacturing establishments doubled their capacity. Old models were discarded and improved devices put in place. By means of automatic machinery hundreds of men were displaced for a time and forced to find other employments. The producing power of labor was rapidly increasing. The wages of the laborer remained stationary or fell. The price of products decreased. In every department of industry the inventor was at work. Farming was revolutionized by the creation and successful operation of planting, mowing and harvesting machinery. In 10,000 factories whizzing belts and pulleys sang a song of triumph for the mechanical age. Poets wrote of the wonders of machinery and foresaw a golden time when through its agency man should live without work.

There was a crash in 1873. A bank failed in New York. Securities on Wall Street tumbled down the scale. Great workshops closed their doors and surprised workmen came the next morning, but walked sadly home. The sheriff nailed notices on shop doors all over the United States. Money depreciated in value and gold was at a high premium. What was all this trouble about?

Why, it was a panic. Oh, yes; there was a panic away back before the war! What caused it? No one seemed to know. It was generally supposed to be something like cholera, which had a sort of license to sweep around the world once in so often. Good Christians explained it on the ground that the Almighty took this method of punishing the nation for some great wrong, not specified. The Democrats said it was caused by the Republicans, and the Republicans avowed it was caused by a fear on the part of the country that the Democrats would get into power at the coming election. During all this time business was at a standstill. Property depreciated and fortunes were swept away. Mortgages were foreclosed by unscrupulous money-lenders. Families were driven from their homes, and poverty stalked throughout the nation.

The panic of 1873, in common with all other commercial and industrial panics, or periods of depression, was caused by the overproduction of manufactured articles. There came a time one day when the manufacturer awoke to the realization of the fact that his warehouses were filled with goods for which the jobber and retailer had made no demand. He made an examination of his books and learned that the retailer had not paid for the last bill of goods. The retailer also had a store full of goods for which there was little sale. The word went out that this condition prevailed all over the country. Too much had been manufactured. The factories therefore closed. Banks called in loans and refused to extend accommodations. Over a million workingmen found their wages cut off entirely. Others had theirs reduced and were permitted to work part of the time.

All this happened because the people had produced more than they could purchase with their wages. Hence the panic; hence workmen discharged and homes impoverished.

It might be supposed that the people declined to patronize the tradesman and consumed his wares for the reason that they had already purchased sufficient quantities of such articles as they needed. This was not so. They had expended all or nearly all their wages and were still in need of the various things which the retailers had for sale. In 1873, as in other panics, the people needed shoes, but could not buy them. They had no money. The shoe manufacturers had buildings full of shoes, but could not sell them. The discharged shoemakers would have been glad to make shoes for the barefoot multitude, but there was no way to do so. So therefore the people went barefoot or stubbed along with their old shoes, the manufacturer held possession of his unsold shoes until the sheriff closed him out, and the shoemaker hired out as a farm hand or became a tramp until the panic was over.

This is not an overdrawn picture. It happened in this country in 1857, in 1873, in 1882, in 1889, and in 1893.

The situation was an extremely simple one, and it is difficult to understand why the people were at a loss to ascertain the cause of panics or to provide a remedy.

Production is limited by consumption. The manufacturers of the United States aimed to produce an

Held possession until the sheriff closed him out,

amount equal to that which the people consumed. To this should be added what was sold abroad, but, stated broadly, production was limited by what the people consumed. Now, the great mass of the people was composed of wageworkers or farmers. The great bulk of manufactured and other products was consumed by the workers and producers. Their capacity to consume was limited by their wages. Hence production was limited by wages. That was all there was to it, and that simple statement contains the key to the mystery of panics.

The people were unable to purchase with their wages that which their labor had created. They could not keep up with the machines they operated. They could come nowhere near it. Even when aided by the extravagance of the rich and independent they could not keep pace with the machines. A first-class conflagration which would destroy millions of dollars' worth of products helped matters once in a while, but a new machine would more than offset the blessings which followed a destructive fire, flood, or other calamity. So in the natural course of events a surplus or overproduction would be created and a panic ensue.

Now that we have reached a period in civilization when such a thing as a panic or financial depression is unheard of and impossible, it may be interesting to recall how the people of 1860-96 survived a panic and how good times were restored. This is how they brought about a "revival of business":

In times of panic or depression a large percentage of the factories was closed and others operated part of the time with decreased forces and decreased wages. The problem was to consume the already manufactured product. The unemployed were not in good shape to accomplish much in this direction, their purchasing power being destroyed, and the burden of absorbing this surplus fell upon the rich. Such of the discharged and discarded workmen as had saved money for old age or a rainy day spent it. When their scanty hoards were gone those who had homes placed mortgages on them at high rates of interest, money being a scarce commodity at such times, and usurers and pawnbrokers were more than usually exorbitant. Others of the unemployed were forced to depend on charity. The large cities would extend and enlarge the scope of charitable institutions, and enterprising newspapers did good work by supervising free-soup, free-bread and old-clothes distributions. A great many of the unemployed became thieves and tramps, and some of the more energetic embraced train robbery as a profession and were quite successful. All of these expedients reduced the surplus and hastened the advance of good times. The charitably disposed rich acted nobly in such times. They gave freely of their money, and kind-hearted ladies engaged in the work of relieving the distressed.

Father Time also did good work. He rotted the perishable articles which "good times" had produced in superabundance and laid his destroying fingers on costly products stored away in the warehouses of the manufacturers. Dame Fashion also came to the rescue and with an edict destroyed the commercial value of clothes, fabrics and wearing apparel which deft and dainty fingers had created and for which no purchaser came in time. During all this period the wealthy and independent classes were eating away at the surplus and after a time it vanished. All hail the prowess of good old Father Time, aided by Taxation, charity, Patience, Dame Fashion, and the rotund stomachs of those who lived without work! The panic was past, the depression was over, hard times were gone, good times were at hand.

The people who lived in those days must have been singularly lacking in an appreciation of humor. It was a side-splitting farce, a wildly hilarious national comedy, but the people did not seem to enjoy it and took it seriously. Some of them got mad and started riots and the militia had to shoot them. The whole situation growing out of a panic was full of comical complications, which were utterly lost on the people.

They had become so rich that they were poor.

They had invented a machine which sawed and split so much wood that they had to freeze in winter time.

They had reduced shoemaking to so fine a science and piled up so many boots that the whole nation had to go barefooted.

The unhappy day had come when there was no work. Poets had dreamed of a time when work should be banished from earth. Now that the day had arrived a million men fell on their faces and worshiped work as a god and begged that they might be his slaves. Everywhere the cry went up for work.

One day a man made a speech to a crowd of unemployed and half-starved men and told them that what they needed was not work, but something to eat. He advised them to kill off the rich and take possession of the things their labor had created. The speaker was not very logical and knew little or nothing of the cause which had produced the distress of his audience, but he had that rude eloquence which hunger and desperation inspires and his speech created a riot. He was clubbed and arrested. The next day some of the papers said he was an anarchist. Other papers said he was a socialist. Some said he was an anarchist and a socialist, which was as consistent as it would be to accuse a man of being an infidel and a Christian. Anyhow he was an enemy to society and had dared to attack the spirit of American institutions. More than that, he was not born in this country, and knew nothing about liberty. If he didn't "like things as he found them why didn't he go back whence he came?" This was a very popular expression and was supposed to contain a vast deal of wisdom. Even full-blood Americans who could trace their ancestry clear back to the time their forefathers burned witches in Salem, and who should have been running over with the spirit of American institutions, made themselves extremely unpopular by denouncing certain things they did not like.

As a result of all this it came to be understood that Americanism consisted (1) in submitting to everything which happened with sublime resignation, (2) an implicit trust in the government which was handed down from Washington and Jefferson, and (3) a childlike belief that everything was all right no matter how unjust it might appear. Any other mode of conduct was stigmatized as being un-American. And in these few years following the panic of 1873 the people were actually made to believe that it was un-American to protest against vested authority, when every school history in the land proved that the American people had advanced as a nation only by repeatedly battering down the laws which some one had made to govern them; by indulging in revolutions; by instigating rebellions; ignoring when necessary the constitution, and in short by fighting usurping power, and striking right and left at anything and everything which stood in the way of their progress. Up to 1873 the American nation was a nation of fighters; after 1873 any man who talked about fighting for his rights was branded as un-American, and there was always a suspicion that he was a foreigner.

Great was the influence of the machine. Strange were the forces which governed in the mechanical age.

The panic of 1873 was followed by a depression, which lifted toward the close of 1877. From 1877 to 1882 there was a period of activity, finally resulting in overproduction. Hard times again ensued, and the business and manufacturing depression culminated in the Haymarket riot in Chicago in 1886. A favorable reaction occurred in 1888 and 1889, but there was not much of a boom. New forces were at work. There was almost a panic in 1889-90, but it resulted in nothing more serious than general depression all over the country. The skies brightened in 1891, and under the spur of the Columbian Exposition a genuine boom set in. The bubble burst in 1893.

Note the shortening interval between panics. Nearly a score of years elapsed between the first panic and its successor. The people had forgotten there ever was a panic. Those who remembered it never expected another one. The third panic did not wait so many years, and shrewd observers had expected it and made preparations accordingly. After 1886 the forecasting of panics became a part of a business man's education. The intervals between became so short that periods of depression were almost continuous. What was done to check this awful waste of wealth and demoralization of industries? Nothing. What statesman, inspired by the perils of his countrymen, arose to sound a warning and give the nation a remedy? None. What was the result? The birth of American discontent; the planting on American soil of the seeds of anarchy and hatred; the fostering of a growing distrust in the justice of American laws; a hatred of the rich, a contempt for legislators, and a groping in the dark. Grotesque political heresies found eager followers, but elections were held, congresses met and adjourned without producing a statesman or a patriotic national policy. So the country drifted on.

CHAPTER III.

A COUNTRY WITHOUT A STATESMAN.

FROM 1865 to 1896 the United States did not produce a statesman.

It did not produce a man whose broadness of intellect and courage in execution could by any stretch of the imagination be construed as statesmanship. From 1865 to 1893 the United States did produce a crop of politicians who disgraced and well-nigh ruined the fairest country the sun ever shone upon.

These twenty-eight years produced business men, and the best business men this world has ever seen. It gave to civilization great generals of production; men skilled in the science of manipulating industries; men who could look into the future and surely read the events of the coming years and lay their plans accordingly. It produced men gifted with the genius of organization and vested with the power to so concentrate human endeavor as to achieve the highest possible commercial results. These men handled vast armies of workmen, each of whom became a part in a perfect working machine. For politicians and the counterfeit statesmen of the day they had nothing but contempt. No inducement was strong enough to tempt them to accept political positions. They declined to enter Congress and participate in its sham legislation. Whenever they desired anything at the hands of the lawmakers they paid for it like gentlemen, and made the proper entries in their ledgers.

The age of conquest proved great warriors; the age of letters gave to the world its philosophers, and the age of mechanics crowned as king the business man.

With the close of the war of the rebellion statesmanship became a lost art, and business established a code of laws for itself and brought the country to its feet. Competition and unlimited and unrestricted production precipitated the panics of 1873, 1884 and 1893. These stupendous object lessons were lost on the politicians. They were a mystery to the common people. They were plain as day to the clear-headed business man. He had learned that with free competition profits were uncertain, and ultimate business failure inevitable.

Take a single example; a shoe manufacturer. For twenty years he had been adding to his business and filling his factories with improved machinery. The panic found him with an immense stock on hand, which had to be sacrificed at a loss. This must not occur again, he declared. How was he to prevent it? There were fifty large shoe factories in the country which he acknowledged as competitors. Now, our friend, the shoe manufacturer, knew just about how many shoes the people of the United States used in a year. He had reliable trade statistics on that point. He knew how many he could make, He knew how many his competitors could make. But he did not know *how many he could sell.* He did not know how many his forty-nine competitors would sell. He did not know how close they would shave prices in the fierce competition which prevailed. He was therefore powerless under the free competition to protect himself against overproducing. He had made a discovery; competition was not the life of trade; it was the death of profits. He had ascertained that as long as manufacturers were pitted against each other in an open market ultimate bankruptcy was certain for the majority of them.

Our friend then proceeded to analyze the situation. There was no reason why the shoe business should not pay sure and steady profits. He was making better shoes, more shoes, and selling them cheaper than twenty years before, but at less profit. His competitors were in the same predicament. They were reasonable men, and he decided to confer with them. An idea presented itself. He addressed a circular letter to the shoe manufacturers of the United States and suggested the calling of a convention to consider mutual interests. The proposition met favor and was adopted. The great manufacturers met and talked it over. As a result of their deliberations it was decided:

1. That unrestricted competition meant loss or bankruptcy.

2. That combination was a good substitute for competition.

3. That there was no sense in manufacturing more shoes than the people could buy.

4. That there was no sense in selling shoes at less than cost price.

They therefore formed a trust. Their trust included nearly all the shoe manufacturers in the country. They regulated the price of shoes and took good care not to make more than the public demanded. They regulated wages. When the demand for shoes fell off they shut down some factories and reduced the forces in others. The trust was a success. It was a distinct advance in civilization. Several states passed laws against trusts. They had no more right to interfere with the affairs of two manufacturers than they had to pass a law forbidding two milk peddlers to consolidate their respective routes. The legislative bull had no effect and the trust survived.

Other trades followed the example set by the wise shoe manufacturers. In a few instances the attempts failed for a time, but in 1890 all the great industries of the country were merged into trusts, pools and associations. Their methods of procedure varied. Some industries embraced in their trust all of those engaged therein at the time of its formation. Others were formed on more selfish and cruel lines. The watch trade was an example of the latter. The Elgin National Watch Company and the American Watch Company, of Waltham, consolidated their interests. These two concerns had about $25,000,000 invested in machinery, and together practically controlled the trade. In three years they bankrupted the outside small competitors, with one or two exceptions, and then absorbed them.

The trust was the logical and inevitable outgrowth of competition in the mechanical age. It was made necessary by the fact that the output of the machine exceeded the capacity of the people to consume. The trust was a life raft for manufacturers and producers. It was a shield against an all-destroying competition.

To the thinkers and to the student of political economy the evolution of the trust had a deep significance. It foreshadowed the downfall of the system of industry and production which gave it birth. The fact that the trust was necessary proved that the prevailing industrial system was wrong. Capital had abandoned competition and embraced co-operation. It shrewdly urged competition among the wageworkers.

The trust became the political scapegoat of both great political parties. Their platforms, their orators and organs launched argument and invective against the trust. They demanded the passage of laws compelling the disruption of all such associations. This was done by people who also denounced paternalism in government, but they were willing that the strong arm of the law should step in and prevent two men from combining their resources for the purpose of cheapening production, systematizing business and thereby increasing their profits. Of course no such laws could be enforced, though several were passed. The politicians knew this; so did the orators, the press and the members of the trusts. But the people took up the harmless cry and the trusts came in for all manner of abuse. It did not hurt the trusts, it amused the people, and it furnished them with an excuse for being out of work.

Let it not be understood that the clear-headed and sagacious business men who founded that new school of commercial economy, the trust, were actuated by any desire to serve their fellowmen. Far from it. They formed trusts because they had to, and remained in them for the very good reason that they would perish on the outside. They were interested in the public only from the fact that it consumed their products, and the more prosperous the public the more the products consumed and profits accrued. They kept prices just as high as good business policy dictated. They paid their employés the lowest wages they would accept. That was business. That was what the society they lived in gave them a right to do, and they would have been fools to have pursued any other policy. They were in business for the money there was in it, and they had joined in a trust to increase their profits. Whenever the stockholders wanted to bestow a favor on the public they gave it in the form of charity, endowed a hospital or founded an educational institute.

The writer does not desire to be misunderstood about trusts. Trusts were not great moral agents of reform, and were not grounded on strict justice. But the trust was inevitable as an institution. It followed the dawn of the mechanical age just so surely as a bud opens in the morning under the warming influence of the sun. The trust as it existed in 1890 did not represent the ideal; it was not the final limit of human endeavor.

But the trust of 1890—the sordid, grasping, cruel and scheming trust—represented a distinct advance in civilization and in commerce. It was as great a discovery in commerce as that made by the old farmer in transportation, who learned one day that it was not necessary to load one side of his mule with bricks so as to counterbalance the weight of the wheat on the opposite side, and who revolutionized traffic by throwing away the bricks and loading each side of the patient mule with equal weights of wheat. The trust took a part of the load from that docile mule, the public, and put the increased profits from this innovation in its pocket. The financial interests of the mule were not involved. He had none.

According to most excellent authority there were in 1893 not less than 200 fully equipped, well-organized and capably managed trusts, pools, associations and federations and combinations of interests in the United

States. These organizations included almost every industry in which machinery played a part, with the exception of farm products before they left the hands of the producers. After the farmer sold his grain or corn it passed into the hands of railroad pools, elevator associations, milling trusts, produce associations, and from them to the more or less unprotected retailers, and from them to the absolutely unprotected consumers. Coal, iron, copper, steel, oil and other products of the earth had their production limited and their prices fixed by trusts.

The 170,000 miles of railroad were merged into three or four pools and associations, which fixed rates and prohibited competition. In order to make this more compulsory congress was prevailed upon to pass an inter-state commerce law. It would be impossible to name any important industry which had been omitted.

We have noted the generally beneficial effect of these combinations to the men financially interested in them. What was the economic effect upon that vast constituency—the consumers—the people of the United States?

The power to regulate production carries with it the power to say how many men shall work at any particular industry, when they shall work and—as a rule—what they shall be paid. The trusts had that power. They acquired it legitimately under the constitution and laws of the United States. They had not transgressed those laws and had proceeded under the letter and spirit of the constitution. There was little to complain of when good times prevailed. There was work enough for all who sought it, money circulated freely, and both manufacturers and employers prospered. But the time came when the demand for goods diminished. The trust thereupon exercised its undoubted right to manage its own property and accordingly discharged some of its workmen. The purchasing power of these dismissed workmen was curtailed and the depression of the community became more intense. It was no longer profitable to manufacture, and over the doors of its workshops the trust placed the sign:

CLOSED.

Why not? It was their property. It was not their fault that business was dull. They were not to blame because retailers were unable to sell stocks on hand, much less place orders for new goods. They were under no obligations to furnish work for men. They were business men, conducting business institutions on a business basis, and were paying taxes to a state whose duty it was to dispense charity, if any charity could reasonably be demanded.

But the people did not understand this. They wanted work and when it was refused them denounced the monopolies for not opening their workshops and manufacturing a lot of stuff that the people could not buy for the simple reason that they did not have the money. In this foolish position they were encouraged by certain foolish writers, and their passions were inflamed by blatant and ignorant demagogues whose entire stock of political economy consisted of a strong pull in some ward. Other causes as innocent as the "trusts and monopolies" were alleged. Foreigners were denounced and the government petitioned to check or prohibit immigration regardless of the character of the applicants for citizenship in the glorious free republic of the United States. Others declared that the protective tariff was to blame and were ridiculed by their opponents, who announced that the protected manufacturers were afraid to go ahead on account of the frightful specter of free trade. The truth was so apparent that it would seem the worst fool could have discovered it—factories were closed because more than sufficient products had already been created. The forces of production were greater than the purchasing power of the consumers. The workman could not buy back with his wages the product created by the machine he manipulated.

From 1865 to 1894 the United States did not produce a statesman.

CHAPTER IV.

GROPING IN THE DARK.

In a study of the political and economical literature of the period between 1870 and 1896 the attention of the historian is attracted by the widespread belief in conspiracies which existed at that time among many classes of people. Political parties charged their opponents with being conspirators against the prosperity of the republic. It would be equally reasonable to accuse a man of conspiring to depreciate the value or cause the ruin of his personal property. The poor charged their conditions to a conspiracy among the rich, to whom they attributed a desire to hold the great masses in subjection through poverty.

There were no such conspiracies. No political party sought the ruination of the country. The rich did not desire the impoverishment of the masses; on the contrary, the continued prosperity of the rich depended absolutely on the betterment of the conditions of the common people.

Of all the people of the United States the business men alone had accommodated themselves to the requirements of the mechanical age. They occupied vantage ground because they had pre-empted it. The mechanical age, wrapped in its swaddling clothes from 1800 to 1840, grew in strength with the years and reached manhood before 1870. The mechanical age had nothing in common with the period which gave it birth. It was governed by no ancient laws and controlled by no musty precedents. The sun which shone on Philadelphia in 1787 illumined a new civilization in 1887—a civilization further removed from that of the preceding century than 1787 was from the age which witnessed the birth of Christ. In that short century the world had lived thousands of years, measured by the chronology of progress.

What had kept pace with that progress? The business and commercial interests, and they alone. Statesmanship groped in the darkness of the past; labor, shackled in the bonds of wage slavery, was chained to the chariot wheels. Justice fumbled over the musty tomes handed down from the decayed and detested kings, and attempted to settle disputes among civilized men by quoting precedents which originated with savages.

A law handed down by a judge who never dreamed of a locomotive engine, and who lived in a day when the murder of human beings was regarded as the only scientific profession, was quoted as a precedent to settle a controversy arising between an elevated railroad and an electric light company. That evening a machinist addressed a company of distinguished guests at a legal banquet to which he was invited as a curiosity. He uttered an aphorism:

"The path of progress is strewn with broken precedents." The grand truth contained in that short line was appreciated by a few, but lost on the crowd. The next day a judge issued an injunction stopping work on an enterprise which affected the wealth and comfort of 700,000 people, in a decision based on something which occurred during the reign of Henry VIII.

The people who lived and died amid such grotesque social, judicial and political surroundings accepted the situation with remarkable complacency. They were strongly imbued with a belief which was generally expressed in these words: "What always has been always will be." Just who was the author of this remarkable statement will probably remain a mystery, but it contains as much untruth and stupidity as can be expressed concisely. It was, however, a great comfort to many ignorant people. It reconciled them to their poverty, their oppression and their wrongs. They

The teacher tells the scholar he may emulate Gould.

imagined that poverty was something absolutely necessary, that a certain percentage were ever doomed to be poor, that in some way or another poverty was a blessing.

There were other popular beliefs which were of great comfort to the people. With few exceptions every young person firmly expected and resolved to become immensely wealthy some day. A most commendable ambition, but difficult of realization. This thought was instilled into his very being in the public schools and became a part of his education. It generally took from three to ten years' steady, monotonous work as clerk in a great dry-goods house, or half a lifetime devoted to cutting threads on bolts in some big machine shop to disillusionize the victim

How often the story was told of how John Jacob Astor started in life as a muskrat trapper and by strict application to business became a merchant prince; how Commodore Vanderbilt started with a ferry-boat and eventually built and owned the New York Central Railroad; how Jay Gould peddled maps in New Jersey and in later life was able to wreck a railroad company every year; how Phil Armour walked into Chicago, grew up with that great city, and accumulated untold millions!

These glowing examples were held up before the young, and they were taught that by industry, perseverance and honesty any one could do likewise. But the boy who graduated in 1894 found all the muskrats killed off, and they were not in style anyhow; there was a surplus of railroads, and those in operation were going into the hands of receivers; there was strong competition in the Jay Gould school of financiering, and as near as he could learn there were no new Chicagos sprung up in the west. There was no new west. It had been absorbed before he was born. He did not know it, but the fact was he had started in fully fifty years too late. Messrs. Astor, Vanderbilt, Gould, Armour, and other highly successful multimillionaires began their activity with the birth of the mechanical age, and some of them became rich from the simple fact that it was impossible for them to remain poor.

The schoolboy eventually discovered these facts with some surprise and resentment, and was glad to accept a $60-a-month job as a Columbian guard at the World's Fair as a compromise. He never fully forgave the simple-minded school-teacher who deceived him.

A great many people took intense satisfaction from the general belief that most wealthy people sooner or later lost their fortunes. The man who carried a hod for a living would pick up his weekly paper and read with great glee that Henry Villard, the great railroad king, had had his fortune swept away on Wall Street, or that some speculator had lost a million dollars on the board of trade, by a sudden drop in wheat. That was great news for the honest hod-carrier. He imagined that in some way it helped the country and indirectly would benefit him. He was unable to see that the success or failure of any stock manipulator or gambler in no way concerned him or his pocketbook. It was not often that great millionaires lost their fortunes. If they did it would be to other and greater millionaires and not to the honest hod-carrier or his friend the bricklayer or carpenter. But the thought was a consoling one and he was happy in it.

The people took a deep interest in what they called "politics." Their "politics" consisted in belonging to either the Republican or Democratic party. Those who belonged to the Republican party proved their fealty by cursing the Democrats when the latter were in power, and by proving, or attempting to prove, that all the wrongs under which the country suffered were directly traceable to the legislation, or lack of legislation, of the Democratic party. The Democrats would stoutly deny this and "point with pride" to the fact that the country was in as bad or worse shape under the Republican rule. An election would be held and the Democrats defeated. They would then assume the offensive and rail against the Republicans. The "outs" generally had all the best of the argument, for the reason that the country was usually experiencing a panic, had just recovered from one, or was anticipating one.

Each party had one thing which it always bragged about. The Republicans declared that they saved the Union in the war of the rebellion and boasted about it. The Democrats denied this and proved that they helped, and then proudly declared that Thomas Jefferson, who wrote the declaration of independence, was a Democrat, and so was Andrew Jackson. This the Republicans admitted, but declared that both Jefferson and Jackson would have been Republicans if then living. This constituted a high form of political debate.

In membership the two parties were about equal. There was generally a third party—at different times a Greenback, Prohibition, and in 1892 a Populist party—the latter being the only one making any decided showing at the polls. Both of the two great parties, as they were called, were made up of strange and seemingly incongruous parts. Their respective memberships may be thus analyzed:

The Republican party was made up as follows, in the order of influence and numerical importance:

1. Manufacturers who looked to the Republican party to levy and perpetuate a protective tariff. In consideration of this the manufacturers paid a large share of the campaign expenses.

2. Ex-soldiers of the war of the rebellion, who believed that this Republican party saved the Union and who were in favor of a liberal pension policy.

3. Those who believed that the Republican party comprised the "better class" and who imagined that they belonged to that class.

4. Those who imagined, for some unknown reason, that the Republican party was opposed to foreigners and intended to prohibit immigration. This was a common belief, though there is no case on record where a Republican convention, politician or prominent orator ever dared say a word against foreign-born citizens or in favor of prohibiting immigration. They sometimes hinted at restricting it.

5. Those who imagined that the pope had designs on the United States and who believed that there were

more Catholics in the Democratic party than in the Republican.

6. The vast majority of the negro vote.

7. Young men whose fathers voted the Republican ticket.

8. Republican officers, their relatives and personal friends.

9. About 40 per cent of the men working in protected trades. This was strange but true. The party leaders assured the workmen that the tariff was levied for their protection, but few of them seemed to believe it and the majority generally voted against protection.

10. A scattering of free traders and others of varying beliefs and theories.

The Democratic party was made up as follows, in the order of influence and numerical importance:

1. The solid vote of the southern states; several millions of men who had always voted the Democratic ticket and who swore they always would; mad on account of being whipped in the war of the rebellion and more or less jealous of the commercial supremacy of the north; a highly prejudiced and often unreasonable lot of gentlemen who declined to allow the negro to vote in the southern states.

2. The "machine" in the larger cities, composed of the tough element, backed by the almost solid saloon interest, and prepared to go to any length in order to carry an election, regardless, when necessary, of law or decency. A tremendous factor and one which determined many important elections. The Republicans attempted to enlist the same element, but were mainly unsuccessful.

3. Sixty per cent of the men working in protected trades and a large majority of city workmen employed in unprotected trades.

4. Free traders and tariff reformers.

5. Young men whose fathers voted the Democratic ticket.

6. Democratic officeholders, their relatives and personal friends.

7. Mugwumps and others who were disgusted with the failure of the Republican party to accomplish promised reforms.

8. Protection Democrats.

What the latter were in the party for no one seemed to know. The foreign vote—so-called—was about equally divided between the two parties. The great bulk of the foreign-born population settled in the northern states, which usually went Republican. Carroll D Wright of the United States census bureau prepared statistics which showed an almost equal political division of this much-sought-after vote. The bulk of the Irish, Poles and Bohemians were Democratic and the majority of the Germans, Scandinavians and Italians voted Republican. So far as religions were concerned, the majority of Catholics were Democratic and the majority of the Protestants in the north were Republican. Many distinguished Protestants were Democratic and many eminent and influential Catholics were ardent Republicans. Religion cut no figure except in the minds of a few bigots on both sides.

It may be asked how two parties thus composed could unite their partisans on any issue. The answer is plain—they could not. What was more, they did not attempt to. There were no issues. From the time of the close of the war up to 1896 there was not a clearly defined national issue on which these two parties took sides. There were no statesmen to formulate issues. The people did not know what they wanted and the politicians did not care. The elections were waged for the prize of federal patronage and for that alone.

There was a pretended issue of protection and free trade, but it was a sham. There were ardent protectionists and equally ardent and honest free traders, but the politicians were indifferent to either theory. They wanted the offices and the patronage. As the struggle for work become more intense this kind of partisanship increased in bitterness. Once in power, an officeholder would turn his back squarely against the platform on which he was elected and devote his entire time to making as much money as he could out of his position.

Too ignorant to even attempt the role of a statesman, the officeholder would play the demagogue when another election day came around. He would talk about the old flag, how he loved it and would defend it against all its foes. The mere fact that the flag had no foes weighed nothing with the demagogue. A visit to all the saloons in his district, a little money left with influential barkeepers here and there, a subscription to the campaign fund and a final "rounding up" of the floating vote were details which all ideal candidates religiously attended to. The opposition candidate pursued a similar policy, and election day the voters exercised that grand prerogative of American citizens—the franchise—and elected one of the two to represent them for a term of years. The victors duly celebrated their triumph, and the vanquished calmly awaited the day when the successful candidate's official record became so odious as to render his re-election impossible. That day always came.

It is certainly doubtful if the average intelligence of the men elected to office under the political system which prevailed in these years, equaled that of the constituents they were supposed to serve. Great cities like New York, Chicago and St. Louis were represented in their common councils, and even in Congress, by men who could not pass a grammar school examination; men who could not converse intelligently and properly in the English language; men who were at home only in the slums from which they sprung. The people knew this and deplored it, but they were powerless. They had no voice in the management of the political machines, and were called on only to ratify one of the two sets of machine-made candidates.

Such was the much vaunted "representative form of government" as it existed in the United States in the later years of the nineteenth century.

CHAPTER V.

SOME SOCIAL PHENOMENA.

THIS history has slighted a movement which came into existence after the panic of 1873 had strewn the country with financial wrecks, and revolutionized the business interests of the nation. The trade union movement is the one referred to.

It is true that there were trade unions and labor organizations at an earlier date, but they played no important part in the history of the mechanical age until 1873. A previous statement to the effect that the business man was the only one to recognize that the mechanical age had made free competition impossible was perhaps too sweeping in its assertion. With the formation of trusts and the incidental curtailment and regulation of production a true vision of the situation dawned on some of the workingmen. They realized that it was to be a survival of those who took advantage of the weapons at hand. The business interests had taken possession of the high ground and fortified their position. The trusts proposed to furnish all the products the people could purchase. The workingmen decided to form themselves into trade unions and monopolize all the work. They also expected to regulate their wages and be in a position to dictate or to at least arrange terms with their employers.

There were many brainy men at the heads of these organizations, and as years gave them experience they developed marked qualities of leadership. They acquired a full and clear understanding of the situation, but insurmountable obstacles impeded their progress. It was one thing to mass a score or 100 factories into a compact pool or trust, but a far more difficult problem to organize 100,000 workmen, speaking several languages, into a union with a discipline equal to the emergencies thrust upon it. But these men persevered and accomplished wonders. They were confronted at the start with the united hostility of the press and the general public. The trusts had not escaped mild denunciation, but were in a position to ignore it.

Not so with trade unions. Workmen were taught to believe that trade unions were conspiracies against and inimical to the traditions of America. The workman was told that he forfeited his "individuality" and his liberty when he joined a union. The leaders were assailed in unsparing terms, but in spite of all this the trade union movement went on.

The earlier history is a tale of protracted and bloody strikes. The first great outbreak was in 1877, which culminated in the Pittsburg riots and a complete suspension of business all over the United States. This incident was a set-back for the movement, but it recovered and continued with alternate victories and defeats. The trusts pursued different policies toward the unions. Some of them, including the great iron and steel manufacturers and the glass factories, made contracts with the unions for a term of years, fixing a scale of wages at such a rate as the condition of the business seemed to warrant. Other trusts declined to recognize the unions or to hold any conferences with their representatives. Such action always resulted in a strike, with the honors about equally divided. The trade unions steadily progressed and many of them finally won favor in the eyes of their former detractors. The Brotherhood of Locomotive Engineers was often referred to as a model.

Whenever the trade union was successful it occupied exactly the same position among workingmen as the trusts did in the business world. It became a monopoly in the truest sense of the word. That was just what it wanted to become and was the realization of the hopes of its projectors. That was what the union was organized for. They named the minimum wage for which their members would work and would engage on no job which employed non-union men. Not a very liberal or philanthropic policy, but it was the only one which was fitted to the mechanical age. It was copied directly from the plan adopted by their employers, and it was the scientific and inevitable alternative of starvation. It was decidedly rough on the man who was out of work and who was willing to undertake the same amount of labor for less money. The same complaint was made by the small concern when the trust froze it out of business.

And so the trade union established itself, and slowly but surely extended its scope and power.

The author repeats that he does not desire to be misunderstood as having in the preceding pages made, or attempted to make, a defense for the principle on which the trusts and trade unions were founded. Both were essentially selfish in their conception and harsh and cruel in the execution of their respective policies. But they were not responsible. They were born that way.

The misshapen children of competition and greed had a hard schooling in the mechanical age and had learned their lessons well. They believed in the truth of the adage that self-preservation is the first law of nature and also in that Darwinian theory concerning the survival of the fittest. They believed they were the fittest.

There was not enough work for all and the trade union was formed to monopolize what there was and protect its members. There were more factories than the country needed and the trust protected its stockholders. If manufacturing concerns must fail for lack of patronage, due to a defective social system, the trust proposed that no such calamity should befall any of its members. They regretted that any concern should fail, but they did not frame the government and were only doing the best they could under the circumstances.

The trade unions felt the same way about it. They sincerely regretted that there was not enough work to go around, but under the circumstances felt compelled to reserve what little there was for their own members. Any one having the required dues and having been duly elected could join the union.

As it was inevitable that some must starve for want of work, the trade unionists declined to offer themselves up as martyrs. It was not an age of martyrs—it was a mechanical age.

And so it came to pass in the merry whirligig of time that the year 1893 rolled around and found the trusts and trade unions entrenched behind their respective breastworks, arrayed against the world at large and prepared to protect themselves against the panic-stricken, half-starved and undisciplined hordes outside their lines. Between the trusts and the unions there existed a sort of armed neutrality, each ready to take advantage of some weakness of the other without asking or expecting quarter.

Aside from their established and inflexible policy of monopolizing work—a purely selfish, but, under the circumstances, a justifiable policy—the unions did a magnificent educational work. They taught the workmen the much-needed lesson that they had nothing to expect from the government as it was then organized and managed. The trade union served as a preparatory school for that social and governmental substitute which every student, thinker and close observer of events regarded as inevitable. The charge was frequently made that the trade union was a socialist product, and the trade unionists were at times classed with socialists and anarchists by ignorant writers and speakers who did not even know or seemingly care to learn even the dictionary meanings of these oft-used words.

Of all the phases of ignorance, bigotry and prejudice which prevailed during the period under consideration, that concerning socialism was the most pronounced. Before 1870 the word "socialist" could hardly be said to be in the American vocabulary.

Well-read people before the war considered the socialist a harmless theorist who had a scheme for a paternal form of government in which the state should act as the employer and distributer of all products. This was a fairly accurate statement of the opinions held by the average socialist and did him no serious injustice. He was regarded in about the same light as a spiritualist, a greenbacker, an anglomaniac or any other person who entertained views not in accord with the majority. No one had accused him of a desire to wade in blood, and the newspaper paragrapher had not then discovered that the socialist never took a bath. The great mass of the people had never heard of one, or, if they had, gave the subject no thought.

At the time of the panic of 1873 it is doubtful if there were 500 avowed socialists in the United States. The country had been so uniformly prosperous that any proposition to make a social or governmental change would have received no favor. Even during the four years of severe depression following the panic of 1873 there was little or no talk about socialism. There was no socialistic agitation, and the few placid gentlemen who believed in socialism made little attempt to propagate their theories. Then came the big strike of 1877, which started among the railroad men, the vast majority of whom were Americans and not 2 per cent of whom even belonged to unions. The strike spread and embraced a hundred industries. The strikers took possession of property, and in Pittsburg, Buffalo, Chicago and other places riots followed in which scores were killed and millions of dollars' worth of property destroyed. Not until the government ordered the regular army to the front was the trouble quelled.

It was then and not until then that the American people heard of socialists and anarchists. They were the ones who did it—the terrible socialists and anarchists. Innocent people were almost frightened to death by stories of the plotting of the bloodthirsty socialists. Little children were told that socialists would catch them if they did not behave So it came to pass that for many years following the riots the word "socialist" was used as a general term to designate a rioter, a revolutionist,a plotter against good government, a worthless vagabond who imagined that the world owed him a living. In the vocabulary of those days "anarchist" was synonymous with "socialist," and the two words were used interchangeably

Later on it came to be generally understood that anarchy was a term used to designate something a grade worse than socialism. A man who instigated a strike or made a speech at a labor meeting or declared that something was wrong with the government was a socialist;but the man who physically assaulted non-union workmen or advised a crowd to hang Jay Gould or advocated the use of dynamite was an anarchist. Anarchy was the high school in the educational course of depravity.

It might be imagined that this confusion of terms existed only among the more ignorant and careless class. Not at all. Even in 1891, when the social democracy of Germany carried the city of Berlin by tremendous majorities and the socialists of that great empire held the balance of power in all Europe, not one-fifth of the alleged well-read people of the United States could give an intelligent definition of socialism. Even in 1893, when every magazine in the United States was discussing socialism in all its phases, when every literary man of any prominence on both sides of the Atlantic was an avowed socialist, when socialism was preached from the pulpit by socialistic preachers, and its principles explained in the great colleges and universities of the country by socialist professors, half the newspapers of the country, including the majority of the great metropolitan dailies, made—with evident surprise—the sober announcement that William Dean Howells was writing a book giving his theories on socialism and that "Mr. Howells was a socialist and almost an anarchist."

If they had announced that Mr. Howells was 42 years old and almost an octogenarian or that he had white hair, almost black, there would have been some surprise, but as it was the incident passed without notice. Mr. Howells was amused; those who knew what the two words meant were too disgusted to say anything, and the people speculated on when and where Howells would throw his first bomb. This description of the prevailing ignorance concerning socialism and what it meant is not to the least extent overdrawn.

There were then, as there are to-day, several schools and branches of socialism. There were anarchists of varying beliefs. But all socialists agreed on certain points, and all anarchists believed in certain doctrines, and the two were as widely separated as the east is from the west and as antagonistic as heat is to cold or light to darkness.

The socialist believed that the greatest average good to the human race could be obtained by the perfection of the government; the anarchist believed that these ends could only be obtained by the absolute annihilation of the government.

The socialist believed in the perfection of the law; the anarchist believed in no law and claimed that the people could take care of themselves without written law.

The socialist believed in paternalism; the anarchist believed that the individual could do more for himself than could any government, and only asked to be allowed to work out his own salvation.

The socialist believed in the justice of the rule of the majority; the anarchist held that no majority, however great, had the right to dictate to an individual; that the man was greater than the state.

The socialist believed in the supremacy of the state; the anarchist believed in the supremacy of the individual. The socialist had in contemplation a government made perfect through wise laws passed by a majority of the people; a government in which the state should be given supervision over those industries and methods of production in which the people had a common interest. The socialists pointed to the postoffice, the public schools and the municipal systems of waterworks as familiar examples of state socialism, and claimed that the state could with equal success manage other branches of industries.

The anarchists claimed that man was not made to be governed; that he needed no laws; that if a community were left by itself unhampered and unrestricted by laws it would get along splendidly; that men broke laws simply because the laws were on the statute-books and committed crimes only because they were unnaturally restrained. They declared that private corporations could render cheaper and more efficient postal service than the government did, and that the same was true with schools, waterworks, etc.

And Mr. Howells "was a socialist and almost an anarchist." What a state of mind he must have been in!

It is important that history should preserve the commonly accepted definition of socialism by those who claimed to have "read something" about its principles. Here is a faithful reproduction of what one of those philosophers would say when asked to define socialism: "I tell you what socialism is. A socialist is a fellow who has been too lazy and shiftless to work and wants to divide. Yes, sir, he wants to divide. Here is a man who has been saving his money all his life and has a little home, and along comes one of these socialists and says to him, 'You have got to divide up with me. We are all going to divide up and start over again.' That's socialism Now, of course, I don't think it's just right for Jay Gould and Vanderbilt and those fellows to have so much money, but suppose they did divide up? What good would it do them socialists? Gould and the rest of them would have it all back in a few years. There is no socialism about me. What I want is to have the government buy the railroads and some other things and run them so as to give us a fair chance. I don't want no socialism in mine."

How this conception of socialism originated will ever remain a mystery. There is no book extant containing any theory based on the desire for a general division of

The workingman and the employer.

property, and in all the writings, speeches, essays and newspaper contributions which expounded, explained and defended socialism as it was then understood there cannot be found a hint of any such foolish doctrines. There were several more or less distinct schools of socialism, but none of them advocated a division of property. They all protested because property was divided, and each school advocated some method by which certain classes of property could be combined, consolidated and merged under the control of the state. Some socialists desired the absolute abolition of private property of any kind and proposed that the state should have supervision even to domestic affairs. They pictured a Utopia in which greed, selfishness and vice had absolutely disappeared. This was a beautiful theory; had many enthusiastic but visionary followers, who were quite charmingly æsthetic and optimistic in their opinions of the state of the future. They indorsed most of the views expressed by Edward Bellamy in a book entitled "Looking Backward," which described a highly advanced civilization in which people had come to such a point that it was as profitable an occupation to serve as a waiter in a restaurant as to be the manager of a national system of railroad lines, and the social standing of waiters and railroad president was the same. There were no private dining-rooms; all ate at the great hotels, and all, of course, fared sumptuously. The abolition of selfishness had solved all problems. The most serious drawback to this system of socialism lay in the firm grip selfishness had previously taken on the human anatomy. However, these good people did not advocate dividing, and Mr. Bellamy was never arrested for manufacturing bombs or inciting riots.

Then there were other socialists who did not go quite so far as this, and they graded down to the man whose socialism consisted solely in defending the common schools and other existing state institutions against the attacks of avowed and unconscious anarchists.

On broad lines the people of the entire country were either socialists or anarchists. They were either collectivists or individualists. They either had faith in the value of government institutions and were in favor of extending the scope of the government or they considered the government only as a more or less necessary compact and held that "that government governed best which governed least."

In principle, theory and declaration the Republican party was emphatic in its espousal of socialism. In practice it was more or less so, but the trend was ever socialistic. Among the more conspicuous examples of Republican socialistic acts and legislation may be mentioned:

1. A united demand backed by force of arms to secure the perpetuation of the union of states. The claim of the south that it had the right to secede was a purely anarchistic declaration. They wanted to "divide," the socialist north wanted to unite.

2. The fostering of railroads and canals through gifts of subsidies in money and land grants. The government helped in a work which the individual was too weak to undertake unaided.

3. The levying of a protective tariff for the defense of American manufacturers and workmen against foreign competition was a form of socialism.

4. The payment of pensions to ex-soldiers and veterans of wars was a Republican measure and was socialism in the purest sense of the word. In a general way Republican speakers, conventions and audiences glowed in their praise of the government, shouted for the old flag, raved about the little red schoolhouse, denounced people for not being in accord with the spirit of American institutions, and went to that dangerous extreme of patriotism which defends a government, good or bad, and declines to listen to argument or logic. That subsidies, land grants, the protective tariff and the pension laws were abused, and that the people were robbed by scoundrels shouting for the old flag did not prove that these socialistic features of the government were wrong in principle. Whatever failure attaches to them may be directly traced to an anarchistic constitution, which successfully subverted the right of the majority to express itself and to govern.

The Democratic party from the time of its birth was saturated with the spirit of anarchy. Democrats, anarchists and monarchists inspired and dictated the constitution, and a man was never counted a good Democrat unless he was what was termed a "strict constructionist." He was able to defend and find an excuse for every blundering clause in the constitution, and seemed only to regret that its incorporation had not included some more stupendous piece of idiocy that he might prove his rock-rooted bourbonism by falling down and venerating it.

Democracy was anarchistic in that it denied the rights of the majority and affirmed those of the minority. It believed in state rights—that the state was superior to the government—that the association of states was merely voluntary—all of which was exactly in the line of the kind of anarchy which Parsons, Spies and Lingg preached in Chicago, and for which they were hanged.

Democracy was in favor of cutting down the powers of the government to the lowest possible limit, and hoped to finally reach the time when government would be unnecessary. That was also what the anarchists wanted. In the pursuance of that policy the Democrats opposed subsidies of all kinds, fought pensions, resisted appropriations of money on every possible pretext, and prayed twice a day to the spirit of Thomas Jefferson, with whom all knowledge of government ceased. Jefferson was a great man, and he may have had a prophetic vision of the coming republic, but he never conjured up the bourbon Democrat of 1893, except in a nightmare.

The anarchists had the best of the situation. The political game was being played on rules laid down by them, and so long as the constitution survived in anything like its original shape there was no danger of majority rule. There were but slight indications that the Republicans would soon dare breathe a word against the exact wording of the constitution.

And thus the country stumbled along under its load

of mortgages, its armies of unemployed, its trusts and its unions; a grand and magnificent country without a statesman; a country tied hand and foot politically by the traditions of the past, blinded by bigotry and bunkoed by patriotism, the majority helpless to voice a protest or right a wrong until the inevitable came—the panic of 1893.

CHAPTER VI.

A COMPLEX SITUATION.

CONFIDENCE figured largely in the panic of 1893. The daily records of that time gravely announced that the trouble was mainly "lack of confidence." Every one was waiting for a "return of confidence." The panic was "sentimental," so many writers said. It appears that this lack of confidence and sentimentality was all on the part of our old friend the business man. There were a great many reasons given in explanation of how the business man happened to lose that indispensable factor in production and prosperity—"confidence." Here are some of them:

1. The protective tariff and the McKinley bill.
2. The fear that the Democrats were going to repeal the McKinley bill and reduce the tariff.
3. The Sherman bill, which authorized the purchase of 4,500,000 ounces of silver a month. This had debased currency, so the gold monometallist declared.
4. A scarcity of money.
5. A lack of faith in the Democratic party.
6. Too many foreigners in the country.
7. The Columbian Exposition.

There were some who had another reason. They explained that it might be possible that the factories had shut down because they had enough stock on hand to last awhile and that the manufacturers could not afford to go ahead and accumulate an indefinite amount of stock with no purchaser in sight. The manufacturer, when asked, promptly confirmed this explanation and said he would start the shops as soon as the demand for its products warranted him in doing so. There being no politics in this explanation, the statesman of the day calmly ignored the stupid business man and spent several months in a discussion of the Sherman bill. They might better have spent their time in discussing the hydraulic paradox. The only valuable service was that rendered by the Senate, which called attention to the fact that it should never have been created.

An entire library might be devoted to the explanations given at that time of the causes of the panic. It certainly was a remarkable affair. It was entirely different from anything which had preceded it. Such bewildering and inexplicable things happened. There was no money to be had for a time and the greenbackers and silver men wildly proclaimed that the currency was so contracted that the people could not do business. They made a great ado about it until the United States treasury department made a statement proving that the aggregate circulation of money was $1,701,939,918, which amounted to $25.29 per capita on an estimated population of 67,306,000. This was the highest per capita in a generaticn and was nearly 50 per cent in excess of that immediately after the resumption of specie payment July 1, 1879, when the amount was $16.75. So it evidently was not a shortage in the total amount cf money somewhere stored or in circulation.

Laying aside for a time the further consideration of the muddled opinions entertained at the time of the panic, let us ascertain the exact facts. The time has come when an unimpassioned history can be written, uninfluenced by gold bugs, silver men, greenbackers and other financial combatants who called each other names and strove to save the country, each in his own way, back in that bewildering year 1893.

The close of the war found the Republican party so firmly intrenched in power that even the panic of 1873 did not depose it. The majority of the people expressed dissatisfaction and unrest by giving Samuel Tilden a popular majcrity of over 100,000 in the presidential election of 1876, but under the representative form of government which then existed Mr. Hayes was counted in. During his administration the country absorbed the overproduction of 1873, and the close of his term found a financial boom at its height and on that wave Garfield was elected by a tremendous plurality.

Another period of overproduction and hard times marked the close of his term, and even the magic of Blaine's name was not sufficient to carry the Republican party to victory.

Cleveland assumed the reins of power and he was in the saddle as a result of a general desire for a "change." The first two years of his administration were marked by failures, riots and strikes, after which the country recovered and entered on another era of boom and prosperity. In a message to Congress Cleveland declared in favor of radical tariff reform, so scaring the manufacturers that they contributed a great corruption fund, and Harrison defeated him, Cleveland carrying the country, however, by a popular plurality.

This was in 1888. Harrison found the country in fairly good shape, but in 1890 there were symptoms of trouble, and in 1892 Cleveland swept the country by the largest plurality ever cast for the candidate of any party. If there could have been a vote two years later Mr. Cleveland would have been retired by a still larger vote. What was the matter with the people? Did they not know their own minds? They were simply attempting to bring about good times by electing men and regarded any political "change" as an improvement over the one they had been compelled to endure.

Just before Mr. Cleveland was inaugurated the second time a decided boom set in. Factories were running full force and every one was busy. Money was so plentiful that the city of Chicago had little difficulty in raising $22,000,000 for the Columbian Exposition. The railroads were doing a good business, wheat was high, and everything was lovely. Cleveland had been elected on a platform which promised a radical reduction in the tariff. The people had declared overwhelmingly in favor of that policy and had carried for the first time both branches of Congress. The Democrats were in a position to redeem these promises. For years they had preached that the protective tariff was what was blighting the country; that it had prevented us from competing in foreign markets and kept our workmen out of employment. For twenty years tariff reform had been the great issue. In the election of 1890 the people had repudiated the McKinley bill and in 1892 they had arisen almost as a man against it. Some people imagined that with Cleveland's election on such a clearly defined issue every factory in the country would take alarm and quit. They did nothing of the kind and went ahead as if nothing had happened. Why? The manufacturers had decided that even free trade would not affect them, as they were then situated, and they were sick and tired of being bled by the Republican campaign managers, and compelled to pay all the expenses of the election. They figured the thing out as only good business men can, and found that the balance was in favor of free trade, foreign markets, and no politics, as against high tariff, home markets, and regular contributions for a corruption fund. And so they declined to "thaw out" in the "fat-frying process" and consequently the Republicans were almost swept out of existence in the political cyclone which followed.

So, therefore, to the great surprise of the high protectionists, the manufacturers contemplated with complacency the coming doom of high tariff and continued their factories as if nothing had happened.

This conclusively shows the falsity of the charge which was frequently made by Republican demagogues in 1893 and 1894, that the panic was due to a fear of a change in the tariff. Had that been the cause the panic would have started the 8th of November, 1892, the day after the election, and not have waited nearly a year for the manufacturers to take fright. Just after the election there was every reason to suppose that Cleveland would call a special session of Congress to go to work on the tariff. Nothing of the kind was done. When the panic did occur every word and line of the

McKinley bill was in force and effect and the discussion of the tariff had entirely dropped. When Cleveland did call Congress it was for the purpose of repealing the Sherman silver bill, which had nothing to do with the tariff.

With these facts so apparent that no one had any right to misunderstand them, every hide-bound Republican partisan shut his eyes and howled that Cleveland and the free traders had brought the wrath of God upon the country.

But the panic was on hand. It struck the country with full force in July and August, 1893, and left in its train 600 broken banks.

From all over the country came the reports of bankrupt business houses and ruined firms. Great manufacturing concerns locked their doors, put out their fires, and notified their men that the shops were closed for an indefinite period. Money disappeared as does a turtle's head on the approach of a foe. Banks drew in their loans and refused to extend any accommodations. Business men with assets amounting to $1,000,000 were unable to secure an advance of $10,000 on gilt-edge security. Nor was this appalling condition of affairs confined to the United States. Australia was in the throes of an even more severe panic, and Australia had no McKinley bill or other valid reason for plunging into ruin. England was suffering from severe financial depression, and from Germany, Belgium and France came stories of widespread business disaster. The devastating scourge of panic smote free-trade England, protected Germany and France with almost equal force. There was no panic in China. There was no panic in Japan or Java. It may have been a mere coincidence, but panics were always in the countries which had created the mechanical age. When a cog in the great machine became clogged in Australia or even in the Argentine Republic the whole civilized world shuddered. Then the wise statesmen and the smug-faced politicians of each country would tell their constituents just how it happened, and how it could all have been avoided had John Jones been elected in place of Bill Smith several years before, or had their party been continued in power, and so on *ad nauseam*.

How about our old friend the Trust? How did the Trust stand the panic? First-rate, thank you.

To tell the truth, the Trust was the fellow who first "lost confidence." He lost it along about Jan. 1, 1892, at which time some of the jobbing houses and retailers reported that they did not care to order any more goods for the present, as they were unable to dispose of stocks already on hand. The Trust proceeded cautiously, and when all the jobbers and retailers were in the same condition the Trust closed down its shops. It did not fail, it simply quit. The Trust had a small surplus of manufactured goods on hand, enough to fill all immediate demands, but it had no great amount of capital locked up for an indefinite period. Some of the trusts went to the extreme of conservatism in limiting production, and were compelled to resume work right at the height of the panic. A notable instance of this was the experience of the sugar trust, which miscalculated the consumption of sugar, and as a result there was a sugar famine all over the United States during the greatest period of depression. The trust reopened its refineries, called back its idle men, laid in a small stock of material, and again closed its works. The various trusts were also careful in their dealings with the retailers and jobbers, as all well-managed trusts should be, and as the panic progressed closed many of them up and sold their stocks at auction.

As the members of the trust looked back to 1873 and recalled the days when they separately went into bankruptcy they more than ever appreciated the blessings which accrue with trusts and an advancing civilization. In 1873 they were going it blind, piling up stocks in expectation of a coming market, cutting prices right and left, squandering money in advertising, trampling each other under foot, until the crash came and only the stronger ones survived to tell the tale. The more fortunate found themselves with enough surplus and depreciated stock on hand to last several years. Those were sad but profitable days to the man who in later years joined the trust.

A familiar newspaper item in the summer of 1893 read about as follows:

"CLEVELAND, O., July 28, 1893.—W. H. Hardluc & Co., the well-known manufacturers of harness and carriage-makers' specialties, have made an assignment to-day. The assets are estimated at $485,000 and the liabilities at $43,200. The assets consist largely of stock and material on hand, and Mr. Hardluc insists that every creditor will be paid in full if he is given a chance to dispose of goods already manufactured. Hardluc & Co. withdrew from the trust two years ago and in their present embarrassment have the sympathy and respect of the community."

Here was another common one:

"OMAHA, Neb., Aug. 3, 1893.—Rush & Co., the leading dry-goods house west of Chicago, was closed to-day on an execution for $21,382.50 in favor of National Woolen Goods association (limited) of New York City. The failure has created a sensation and was entirely unlooked for. Up to yesterday noon Mr. Rush fully expected to be able to meet the claim, but found it impossible to raise the money. The total assets of Rush & Co. will exceed $1,250,000 and the liabilities not more than $340,000. Dullness in trade and inability to make collections from retailers is ascribed as the cause of the failure. Mr. Rush hopes to make an arrangement with the creditors for an extension of time, otherwise the immense stock will be sold at a sacrifice."

In almost every failure or suspension the assets doubled or trebled the liabilities. The companies found themselves with immense stocks of purchased or manufactured goods on hand upon which it was impossible to realize a dollar. The banks were scared to death and would not part with a dollar. In the course of time bills came due and insolvency followed. In a speech before a bankers' convention held in the autumn of that year Comptroller Eckels said:

"It is no exaggeration to say that the happenings of the months past, from May to September, must be accounted the most remarkable in every phase of financial bearing ever experienced by the American people. Heretofore in our financial distresses the test of solvency has always been applied to store and factory, to great industrial enterprises and railway corporations, but within the period of these months an affrighted people, fearful of the resultant effects of a financial system vitiated by ill-advised and ill-considered legislation, became for the first time doubtful of the distinctively financial institutions of the country, the banks, and as a consequence a steady drain upon deposits was begun, until within the period of two months, from May 4 to July 12, from national banks alone had been drawn out more than $193,000,000.

"To-day so greatly has the situation changed that, having in mind the past, both in the severity of the strain undergone and the long continuance of it, it would be in the light of the present conditions both unfair and unjust to deny that the bankers of this country have exhibited masterful skill in coping with a situation rendered complex beyond anything heretofore known."

The bankers certainly showed great skill "in coping with a situation rendered complex beyond anything heretofore known," and as a result 5,000 business and manufacturing firms were strangled to death with a loss of only 600 banks. It was a glorious victory.

The gold reserve was what bothered the statesmen of both parties more than anything else. To their minds the eternal salvation of the country depended on the amount of gold stored away in the vaults at Washington, and under the idiotic system which prevailed they were half right. When the gold reserve rose their spirits rose, and when it fell they were cast into depths of despair. Had it all suddenly been wiped out of existence every man, woman and child in the United States would have quit work and starved to death. There was a rule or a tradition, custom or superstition, that there should be $100,000,000 in gold as a reserve, a sort of pocket piece for Uncle Sam.

In the summer of 1892 there were $120,000,000 in this fund and the boom was on and everybody happy. Now this reserve depended almost entirely on the volume of our foreign trade, and it was depleted from time to time by the redemption of certificates. If the balance of trade continued against the country to such an extent that the certificates could not be redeemed, why, that would mean a financial cataclysm in the opinion of the wise men at the helm. These financial Brahmins prostrated themselves daily at the feet of the $100,000,000 reserve pile of gold and prayed God to save the poor people who had nothing but several hundred million acres of fertile land to fall back upon.

Mr. Eckels was right when he said it was a "complex situation."

The gold reserve dwindled away and, to the horror of the holy priests of finance, fell below the $100,000,000 mark. More gold was going abroad than was coming to this country. The reasons for this were plain as day. In the first place a protective tariff against raw materials had limited the manufacturers to a home market. The shop and mill owners paid into the government treasury the duties levied against raw materials, added this amount to the cost of the product, and charged it to the consumers of the United States. The trade unions kept up the price of labor and the trusts also charged that up against the consumers. But the trust, powerful as it was, could not change or regulate the laws of international commerce, and, except in rare instances, could not compete in the markets of the world. The consumers paid all the taxes. The consumers had paid all the taxes since governments were instituted among men and they always will. Thus the most prolific country on the face of the earth found itself unable to sell its products abroad, and people went barefoot in England for want of American shoes, and shoemakers in America starved because there was no work in the shoe factory. Another "complex situation." Of course the balance of trade was either against this country or only slightly in favor of it. Foreign countries were selling us tea, coffee, cigars, woolen goods, and the hundreds of necessities that the common people must have, and the numberless luxuries that the rich could afford to buy, and we were paying for them out of the limited supply of gold. Wealthy Americans filled every stateroom on the great steamships in the summer and laid their gold at the feet of the British snobocracy.

On top of all that, production in the United States was regulated and restricted by the trusts, and from the very nature of things nothing else could be expected. The manufacturer who created a surplus paid as the price of his folly or boldness the penalty of bankruptcy.

The country was living from hand to mouth, cooking just enough to last one day ahead, engaged in light housekeeping on an extremely economical scale. What a spectacle! and not a statesman in Washington, not a man whose head rose above the dead level of sickening mediocrity.

The gold reserve decreased until, as it so happened, England was in a worse fix than the United States, and a few millions came across the Atlantic. This phenomenon was witnessed with great rejoicing. But the current soon set in the other way and despair again ruled.

Perhaps the most remarkable feature of this most remarkable period was the part played by the "wealthy poor." This may appear a contradiction of terms, but it is not. There was such a class, and they added not a little to the general condition of financial distress. When poverty had finally intrenched itself as an American institution the unfortunate victims received little sympathy. Those who emerged from the depression of 1873-78 in a half-starved condition were assured that it was their own fault. They were told that there was always plenty of work in the country—except, of course, during times of a panic, for which no one was to blame—and that any industrious man could support a family and save up money which would come handy in such an emergency as a panic.

Books were written instructing the people how to live economically. There arose a school of philosophy, whose central theory was that the one problem which confronted civilization was to support and perpetuate the race with the least possible consumption of food and the other necessaries of life.

Edward Atkinson was the founder of this school, and he invented a stove which he fondly expected was going to usher in a millennium in which a man could live upon an expenditure of not exceeding fourteen cents a day. Just what all the great factories and the stupendous mechanical plant of the country, with its almost limitless capacity of production, would do when all the able-bodied men in the country each spent fourteen cents a day, Mr. Atkinson did not figure out, and he had the reputation of being one of the greatest statisticians in the world.

People were told day after day and year after year to save money, and after going through two or three panics a great many of them took the advice. Savings banks became popular; building and loan associations sprung up in every large city; safety deposit companies catered to the general demand and furnished places to hoard money, and where none of these more advanced safeguards were handy the simple farmer and his hired man hid away the treasured dollars in trusty old yarn stockings.

Note what followed this general fad for economy. Note how the people were rewarded for their attempt to "save money."

The fame of the coming Columbian Exposition of Chicago added to the saving propensities of the people, and several million wageworkers began to save up from $20 to $200 each to visit the great show. They denied themselves former pleasures and theatrical companies became stranded. They bought fewer fine clothes and adornments and the sheriff closed out some dry-goods houses.

They stopped the daily paper, and the editor set up a howl about hard times and berated the idiots who were withholding money from circulation.

The panic came and the wealthy poor withdrew over $400,000,000 from the savings banks and $200,000,000 from the national banks. They would have drawn out more had not most of the banks failed. When they regained possession of this money a great many adopted the plan of the farmer and his hired man, and millions of dollars reposed in the carefully hidden but ever reliable and solvent sock, and thus did the wealthy poor add their mite to the "complex situation."

What had these people demonstrated beyond the possibility of a doubt?

They had demonstrated that the widespread practice of economy by the people under the prevailing conditions meant general ruin.

They had proven that the man who saved money was an enemy to his country, and that the spendthrift was a political economist and a patriot. That the more people spent the more they would have, and that the less they spent the sooner they would be in want.

The situation was certainly "rendered complex beyond anything heretofore known."

Production is limited by consumption. Consumption is limited by wages. Where wages are hoarded consumption decreases and production is curtailed. When production is curtailed the wage fund decreases.

Under the "complex situation" which prevailed in 1893 and the years preceding it the wageworkers best conserved their interests by spending every dollar in their possession and putting their trust in Providence.

CHAPTER VII.

THE UNITED STATES SENATE IN 1893.

FIVE millions of men were idle in the United States on the day that Congress met in Washington to solve the problems which were confronting the nation. The Columbian Exposition of Chicago was in all its glory. No words can paint the splendor of that great white city. It was a superb realization of the dream of the poet, and the world stood entranced in the court of honor, speechless and awe stricken in the presence of art and architecture surpassing that of ancient Greece or Rome. The Columbian Exposition was the crowning triumph of forty centuries of civilization. It may appear like sacrilege to mention figures, but the Columbian Exposition represented an expenditure of about $22,000,000. With this sum a marsh had been reclaimed, lagoons excavated, the architectural genius of the country invoked, the spacious grounds beautified, and hundreds of palatial buildings erected and dedicated to the service of the Columbian celebration. It surpassed with a bound the past, and the future may never reach to its sublime heights.

The 5,000,000 idle men whose eyes were fixed on Congress could have reproduced the Columbian Exposition by the work of two days! The wasted energies of these 5,000,000 men to whom work was denied could in two working days have delved the iron from the ground, hewed the timber from the forests, fashioned the steel at the forge, and shaped the lumber in the mills; they could have reclaimed the marsh and beautified it, and in all its unspeakable beauty and splendor could have built three Columbian Expositions in a week and taken a Saturday half-holiday!

This was termed political economy in 1893. Congress met and the Senate spent three months in discussing a rule which decreed that the majority had no right which the minority was bound to respect. This, dear children, was termed representative government in 1893.

The majority had not attempted to do anything desperate or revolutionary. Something had to be done to "restore confidence," and President Cleveland wrote a message calling for a repeal of the silver bill and convening Congress in special session.

There then ensued the most revolting farce ever enacted under the guise of representative legislation.

It was nothing more than could have been expected from a body constituted as was the Senate, but it was so insulting a disregard and contempt for the principle of self-government that even the apathetic freeman of America aroused from his stupor and actually hissed that venerated institution, the United States Senate. It had long been known that the Senate was a rich man s club, and it came to be understood that one of the perquisites of a state legislator was the money paid him by rival candidates for senatorial honors. There were a few honorable exceptions. The Senate represented nothing but itself, and up to this time had been a quiet, complecant body of men who had been tolerated for the reason that the members had seldom exercised their power to resist legislation imperatively demanded by the people.

Five million half-starved men, many of them the sole support of families, were waiting for the majority of the United States Senate to pass a measure which had been indorsed by 75 per cent of the people of the United States.

At the end of the tenth week of the revolting farce a man arose in the gallery. He was a plain American citizen, dressed in gray tweed. History does not give his name, but it is a pleasure to record his nationality and his contempt. The gallery had been guilty of applauding Senator Hill for making the statement that the majority should rule. Vice-President Stevenson threatened to clear the galleries. It was then that this plain American citizen, probably one of those to whom work had been denied, arose from his seat. He was a large, broad-shouldered man with a heavy voice. He looked down on that collection of aged idiots with immeasurable contempt and said:

"As one of the common people, Mr. President, who has sat here six weeks, I will leave the gallery now."

His voice rang through the hall like a warning. It was as if the spirit of the American people had suddenly taken part in the affairs of legislation. The senators shrank back in their chairs, half expecting a dynamite bomb. The American citizen turned his back upon them and coolly left the building.

For the first time a new light appeared. For the first time in the history of the country men of high standing in the community, editors, lawyers and brainy business men, perceived that there was something wrong, but none was bold or broad enough to tell the truth—viz., that the crime which was being committed—the suppression of majority rule—was authorized by the constitution of the United States, and that in no section or clause of that document was the principle of majority rule enunciated or its rights conserved. They confined their denunciations to the Senate and its stupid rules. The rules were stupid, but not half so stupid or unrepresentative as that section of the constitution of the United States which created the Senate itself. Here is the way some of the great editors wrote about the United States Senate crime of 1893:

Baltimore *Sun* (Dem.): "It is clear, as clear as the noonday sun, that no government can be carried on, no government is possible, upon the principles professed by Teller and practiced by Dubois."

Galveston *News* (Dem.): "Unless majorities can rule, rules or no rules, in this country our form of government is a failure. The Senate should be quarantined against so that its anarchy can't spread."

Indianapolis *Journal* (Rep.): "The adoption of closure in the Senate should be made a test question in all future senatorial elections until the end is accomplished The people should not stop until the principle of majority rule is immutably established."

Kansas City *Star* (Ind.): "If even after a hundred years of trial and amendment any feature of our governmental system is found to work hardship, to be in effect an absurdity, then it should be changed. No lapse of time should be allowed to sanctify foolishness. If in a legislative body it is discovered that a minority amounting to only one-fifth can nullify the action of a majority amounting to four-fifths, then a change should be made, no matter how long the injustice and stupidity of minority rule may have been perpetuated."

A Chicago paper: "Hang traditions! Let Democrats act like men who know what ought to be done under existing circumstances, and not like boys guided by traditions of what their grandfathers did under entirely different circumstances and conditions. The people don't care a copper for traditions. What they want is rational action, and if they can't get it from Democratic representatives, they will get it from somebody else."

Another Chicago paper: "The absolute tyranny of habit and of precedent never was shown more strongly than in the case of these senators. The chains which bind them are mere cobwebs, and yet they say they cannot break them. Evidently there is nothing left for the people but to refuse to re-elect each of these senile senators when his term expires and to put in his place a man who will pledge himself to reform the rules of the Senate so that the majority can rule and legislation be possible again. This will be a slow process, but it will be a sure one."

The Washington correspondents were even more radical in their denunciation of the Senate than were the editors. A. H. Lewis of the Chicago *Times*, a gifted newspaper writer, struck some telling blows for the rights of the majority in the following vigorous language:

"One might wonder what Washington would think

of these people, and how if the dead gentleman at Mount Vernon were to stroll in and ask for the personal history of these Senate do-nothings, what thrilling information he would reach. There's Papa Stewart, aforetime the central figure of the Emma mine swindle, who roped in Minister Schenk of the long ago. In the present pantomime of legislation Papa Stewart, the Emma miner, has the role of Pantaloon and gets in everybody's way maliciously, and tips over everything malevolently, and trots about from one gay villainy to the other with the usual string of some other fellow's sausages hanging from his pocket. There's Mitchell of Oregon, whose real name is Hipple—but let it all go. It's too late. They are all senators now and regularly sworn and qualified to assassinate the country's welfare and hold up a nation in its onward march as some masked cutthroats might hold up a stage with their Winchesters. Of course, being senators, these men are all grown very respectable and pure, and one must not dream nor even think, much less say, that the Senate itself is aught but a well-spring of public good and the climax of public blessing. Well, well, well; call it a green tree and a fountain. Maybe it is. But it performs like a gang of horse thieves.

"The great grandchildren of the present Senate a century from now will still be blowing in the doubloons which their progenitors grabbed off in the rise and fall of stocks occurring from the present Senate antics in the fight over the Wilson bill now raging.

"It has occurred to Mr. Cleveland, and will occur to the American people when they bend a thoughtful brow to its consideration, that there is neither common justice nor public sense in allowing five men to absolutely withstand the entire Senate in its rights and duties. It is a Senate's duty to vote. It has no right to refuse or fail to vote. It has no more constitutional business to pass rules which will block and obstruct and thwart the purpose of the Senate's construction than it has to commit suicide. The vanity of these gray old morrice dancers of legislation has led it to put into every senator's possession the power to poison public interest by a dose of filibuster. But it was wrong, illegal, and without the law to do it. The public would indeed be the idiot which some men deem it, if it sat quietly at its own assassination by less than a half-dozen senatorial criminals simply because this paresis club we call the Senate, in its vainglorious drivelings and maunderings, had assumed in those paragraphed and numbered imbecilities it calls its rules to endow this quintet of malefactors, the murderous power so to do. No such power can be conferred. The right of the country to preserve itself, the right of the majority to rule, the right of the dog to wag the tail, are any of them a sufficient reply."

Incredible as it may seem, the average voter of the United States had firmly believed that the distinctive feature of the government was majority rule.

He had been told so over and over again by campaign orators and professional patriots who rang the changes upon a "government of the people, for the people, and by the people."

For the first time in American history the fact dawned upon some thoughtful persons that the majority was powerless to express itself. The cool insulting contempt of the millionaire's Senate had brushed the cobwebs from their eyes and one monstrous wrong stood clearly revealed. The Senate idol was badly cracked, but not shattered. But even then they fondly hugged to their breasts the sweet delusion that the government was all that the Fourth of July orator had claimed for it, and that the Senate was the only offender, and that its offense consisted in setting aside the verdict of the majority.

Thomas Cooley, who has declared himself authority on all questions regarding the constitution of the United States, and the author of a book on constitutional limitations, made this statement when asked for an opinion concerning the alleged subversion of the constitution by the Senate:

"It is a fundamental principle of representative government that the majority shall rule. For a majority of the Senate to concede for any reason that a rule of practice in debate or of senatorial courtesy makes it possible for a minority to prevent legislation by indefinitely protracting debate is equal to revolution. It is as much revolution as though accomplished with arms and violence."

Mr. Cooley could not have been referring to the United States or its constitution when he spoke of "a fundamental principle of representative government that the majority shall rule." He knew perfectly well that the constitution contemplated nothing of the kind.

Mr. Cooley knew perfectly well that the election of Mr. Harrison in 1888 over Mr. Cleveland by a minority vote was constitutional and legal and that it was a defeat for a majority of the voters of the United States.

Mr. Cooley knew perfectly well that in 1890 people of the United States by a majority of 1,500,000 repudiated the McKinley bill, and that the Senate under the power vested in it by the constitution of the United States perpetuated that bill on the statute-books of the country against the votes and wishes of the majority of the people.

Mr. Cooley knew perfectly well that the spirit of the constitution of the United States had been incorporated in municipal governments, under which the rights of the people were bartered at the highest market price, public streets and franchises sold to private corporations against the helpless protest of an overwhelming majority of the people.

When Mr. Cooley said that "it is a fundamental principle of representative government that the majority shall rule" he was partially right, but if he imagined that the constitution of the United States guaranteed such a government or that such a government had been evolved from it he was mentally in Egyptian darkness.

The closing days of October, 1893, found 5,000,000 men still out of work, and the United States Senate yet in session. The Columbian Exposition, the crowning triumph of the mechanical age, went out in a blaze of glory, and with its close 50,000 men and women found themselves out of employment.

And Congress was still in session.

The Senate was finally cowed and bought by Wall Street into passing the bill repealing the Sherman silver law. Was the country saved? Did 5,000,000 men return to work as had been predicted? Did 10,000 factories resume operations?

No. Wheat dropped to the lowest point on record. Robbery became epidemic in large cities, and Chicago was forced to declare a condition approaching martial law to protect its citizens.

CHAPTER VIII.

HARD TIMES.

THE panic of July and August was past, and the winter of 1893-94 set in with the people in the agonies of an unprecedented business and industrial depression. In the great cities of the country idle workmen paraded the streets by thousands until the demonstrations became so threatening that the authorities felt compelled in self-defense to suppress them. No language can picture the sufferings of the people. The distress was by no means confined to the large cities. In the smaller towns the factories, which were the main support of the working population, were shut down. Public charities were swamped by applications for aid. The pages of the daily papers were filled with horrors such as the vivid imagination of Victor Hugo could not conjure up; recitals of murders, robberies, suicides, embezzlements, starvation of innocent children, wholesale pauperism.

The daily paper was a daily report of crimes. A curse seemed resting upon the people. The man with employment was regarded as being specially favored, and wistful eyes were turned to the workshops where a few lucky mortals were yet permitted to earn a living.

In October there were in Chicago by actual enumeration over 135,000 men out of work in the great factories alone. Concerns which formerly employed 5,000 and 6,000 men had reduced their forces to 300 or 400, and others were entirely suspended. Of the 120,000 men engaged in the building trades not more than one-third were at work. Retail stores and small shops, which in good times had scores of clerks, reduced their forces to the lowest possible limit, and it is safe to say that of this class 15,000 were idle. How this vast army of idle subsisted is a mystery. The papers of Chicago and of other cities did splendid charity work, and, with a few exceptions, told the exact truth about the situation. A committee of Chicago business men attempted to raise money for the purpose of furnishing work, and did collect $300,000, but this amount could not go far toward the support of 200,000 idle men, many of whom were the heads of families. The drainage canal commissioners were appealed to and found place for nearly 2,000 former artisans and clerks, who were happy to dig dirt in company with imported Italians and Poles. The work was severe, and some of these unfortunates were not able to stand the strain, and their surrender was witnessed with glee by certain human hyenas, who would be convulsed with merriment at a railroad horror.

The wealthy people of America, as a class, were more than usually generous as cold weather approached. The lie that had so many times before been told and believed—that there was plenty of work for any man who wanted it—had gone out of date. There was no work. The workman knew it; the business man knew it; the manufacturer knew it and regretted it, and even the professional hater of workmen was compelled to remain silent.

And this was in Chicago, at whose feet the world had poured a sum of money estimated at not less than $150,000,000, the cost of their attendance at the great exposition.

The banks were bursting with money, but the shops remained closed. The manufacturer did not want borrowed money; he wanted customers who had money, and his customers were out of work and out of money. The rich must eat up the surplus and the poor must accept what the rich and municipal charities afforded them.

The complacency with which some well-fed and good-natured persons contemplated the sufferings of others in the year of the Columbian Exposition is illustrated by the following editorial clipping from the Chicago *Tribune*. The writer was musing over the existing condition and prospects of the 150,000 unemployed. Thus he wrote:

"Some are on the drainage channel. Others have found something to do owing to the extra demand for labor occasioned by the World's Fair. Manufacturers who shut down during the panic have taken back a part of their men—as many as the market for their products would justify—and they will go ahead manufacturing as long as they can find a market. During the rest of this month there will be no lack of employment in Chicago. The pinch will come in November after the closing of the exposition Then the street railroad companies will cut down the number of men. Merchants will discharge the superfluous clerks. Many of the hotels will be closed, and not one of them will need the large force it does now. There will be a general retrenchment after the World's Fair guests have gone, which will make work hard to find during the winter months. But that can be endured providing there is satisfactory assurance of good times in the spring. If the conditions are such then that capitalists feel justified in putting up new buildings, that manufacturers are reasonably confident they can find a market for their goods, and that storekeepers are convinced they can sell their wares and get paid for them, there will be profitable employment for all."

A cheering prospect certainly. Any wageworker who would protest against remaining out of work all winter and subsisting on charity, when there was a possibility that the capitalists might decide to put up some new buildings in the spring and thereby give him a job, was certainly an enemy to society, if not a real anarchist. Notice the off-hand way in which the great editor assures his readers, "but that can be endured." He knew whereof he spoke. He knew that a people long used to hardships lose by degrees the very notions of liberty. There was little danger to be apprehended from this hungry multitude. They would live until spring and be glad to compete against each other for such work as the condition of the labor market afforded. In the meantime they might sack a few bread shops, but as for fighting—history never recorded a battle or a revolution won by hungry men.

For several years previous to that of the panic of 1893 many well-intentioned and amiable citizens became greatly concerned about patriotism. They had observed with growing alarm that the rising generation was not patriotic. Unable to solve this strange manifestation, they decided to propagate the spirit of patriotism in the public schools. To this purpose certain days at the public schools were devoted to the teaching of patriotism. The young people were taught to believe that theirs was the greatest country on the face of the earth; the only one in which the people had a voice in the management of affairs, and other glittering generalities more or less founded on fact. It must be admitted that this manufactured kindergarten brand of patriotism was a very inferior article.

What was the matter with the children and why was it necessary to cultivate patriotism as a house plant?

The fact was that there was nothing in contemporaneous history or happenings to make them patriotic. When the child went home the hard-working father, fatigued from a day's severe toil and harassed by the constant fear of no employment, did not take the child on his knee and tell of the glories of the republic. On the contrary, he complained of his lot, cursed certain politicians, but never praised anything. To his benighted mind there was nothing to praise. Then again there were no political idols, no giants of statesmanship for the boy to worship. General Grant was a popular hero and was pointed to as a model, but it was hard to enthuse the youthful mind by reciting the exploits of Harrison, Cleveland, Hill, Brice, Gorman, Butler, Peffer, Vilas, Stewart, and that miscellaneous crop of alleged statesmen who occupied the public gaze in that period.

The Republican orator's workingman, and another idea of the laborer.

There was no politics—nothing but a blind and ignorant partisanship, which fooled men, but made no impress on the truthful mind of a child into whose nature prejudices had not yet been planted. The experiment of teaching patriotism in the schools was a failure. Those who had faith in such artificial patriotism could not perceive the truth so finely expressed by a thinker who wrote:

"Patriotism is a blind and irrational impulse unless it is founded on a knowledge of the blessings we are called on to secure and the privileges we propose to defend."

They would probably have taken exception to the forceful statement of bluff old Johnson: "Patriotism is the last refuge of a scoundrel."

There was a growing clamor for the suppression of immigration. To this cause the average American-born workman ascribed all the ills under which he suffered. He claimed that the foreign workman had underbid him in the labor market and that so many of them had come to the country that there was not enough work to go around. Work was the god which they worshiped. There was never any complaint because there was not enough food, clothes and other necessities of life. Every one admitted that there were plenty of such commodities, but what the people wanted was "work." There being a great sufficiency of everything which labor produces already on hand, there was no work, and the foreigners received the blame.

The United States was then supporting—more or less by charity—a population of 67,000,000 people. The single state of Texas boasted that it could support in luxury 150,000,000 people, and there was no doubt in the minds of intelligent people that the entire country had productivity and resources equal to a population of 500,000,000. The foreign workman, therefore, was not entirely to blame for the prevailing distress. It was popular, however, to abuse him, and some of the most vindictive know-nothings voiced their hatred of the foreigner in accent and dialect so complicated that English-speaking sympathizers in the same theory had difficulty in understanding them.

These were but a few of the signs of an approaching "something" to the keen forecaster whose eyes roamed over the political heavens. There was a disposition to coddle and confer with the once despised trade unions on the part of men who a few short years before had denounced all such organizations as un-American and to whom a "walking delegate" was a hated and contemptible person.

A series of "economic conferences" were held in the palatial recital hall of the Chicago Auditorium, in which speeches were made by such distinguished people as Bankers Lyman Gage and Franklin Head, Ferd W. Peck, the projector and largest stockholder in the Auditorium, and many other wealthy representatives of Chicago's capitalistic world. These speeches were responded to by Mr. Schilling and the famous Lucy Parsons, Socialists Thomas J. Morgan, Aveling, and various champions of the single tax and other theories of social and political economy. There was little intolerance among these great captains of capital and industry and the economic conferences were productive of a better understanding all around. They made no impression, however, on the $15 a week clerk who worked in Mr. Gage's bank, who yet imagined that the socialists were planning to make him "divide up" the $75 he had saved up by denying himself an overindulgence in neckties and russet shoes.

In the latter months of the year an epidemic of crime swept over the country, train robbery developed into a profession, and the papers were filled with reports of barbarous lynchings from all parts of the United States. Ex-President Harrison in an address at the World's Fair, Indiana day, called attention to this growing disregard of the law and appealed to all good American citizens to stand back of the sheriffs in the performance of their duties. Out in Colorado Governor Waite proposed to secede from the Union and was ready with

150,000 western miners and mine-owners to "wade in blood up to his horse's bridle." In Kansas the Republican militia officers were relieved and the state guard reorganized with nothing but populists in the ranks, an ominous incident, and one unprecedented in the history of the country.

More significant than anything else was the attitude of the farmer. Proverbially conservative, the farmer had broken away from old-party allegiances and was a radical of radicals. He was ready to listen to any scheme for the betterment of his condition, and seemed more inclined to fight than anything else. Unsparing in his denunciation of the "gold bugs of Wall Street," the farmer had cut loose from all former partisan alliances and refused to listen either to the voice of the professional Republican patriot or to the pleadings of the constitutional Democrat, whose panacea for all earthly ills was a retrenchment in the expenses of the government. The farmer was satiated with patriotism and had lost money by it, and had become impressed with the idea that governmental extravagance and not retrenchment was the need of the hour.

And thus in the parade of the years, 1893, with its columns badly disorganized and its band playing discordant music, passed before Time's reviewing stand and vanished in the distance. Congress was yet in session.

CHAPTER IX.

THE GREAT BOOM OF 1898.

[Note by the author.—The reader is asked to imagine that a short period of years has elapsed between the months described in Chapter VIII. and the opening of Chapter IX. If singularly gifted with imagination he may conjure up incidents equaling in interest to the lake-front demonstrations of the starving unemployed, the strange march of industrial armies across the mountains to Washington, the arrest of an American citizen who desired to petition Congress and his subsequent imprisonment for the crime of "getting on the grass," the great railroad strike, the judicial promulgation of the edict that American workmen cannot quit work without the consent of their employers, the opening of the sugar bowl in Congress, and other events strictly in accord with the spirit of American institutions. A presidential election in 1896 retires the Democracy from power; a slight boom is followed by a panic and a succeeding period of depression. The thread of the history is taken up in the spring of 1898.]

THE advent of the spring of 1898 brought a return of better times. The keen edge of the long depression had worn off, and with a beaming face the good husband came home one afternoon and brought the glad news that the shop was going to start up the first of next week. How they had managed to live the workman and his wife could hardly explain. They were lucky in having a kind-hearted landlord, to whom they owed many months' rent, and they congratulated themselves that they had escaped eviction—the sad lot of a score of their neighbors. One of the boys had made a few pennies selling papers, and a good lady had called once a week, and, despite the protests of the proud and honest workman, had left groceries and on three occasions a small sum of money. It had been impossible to send the children to school; they had no clothes and no money with which to purchase books. Some days the family had suffered from the cold, and all were glad when the sun arose high in the southern sky and April ushered in the warmer days. And now the factory was going to start up. John told Mary all about how it came about, and the good woman listened with tears in her eyes. All that winter there had been rumors of a European war, and hostilities were now considered inevitable. One of the leading foreign powers had placed an immense order with the firm John worked for, and the men were sent for at once.

"And they say," said John, his eyes dancing with joy, "that war is sure to come and that when it does there will be more work than we can do. We may have to work nights. I wish they would declare war tomorrow."

"But just think, John," said Mary, a little sadly, "just think of all the men that will be killed and of all the poor women and children who will be made to suffer all the rest of their lives. Think of the homes that will be broken up and the property that will be destroyed. War is an awful thing and when I hear it talked of it makes me shudder."

"Yes, I know war is an awful thing," said John, "but it makes good times and gives the people work. The boss was saying the other day that the best thing that could happen to this country would be a good war which would kill off about 2,000,000 people and destroy a lot of property. He said that would make the best kind of times, and blamed if I don't think he was right."

"It seems to me," said Mary, thoughtfully, "that something must be wrong when nothing short of war, with its wholesale murders and crimes, can bring about the prosperity of the people."

"Women never did and probably never will understand anything about politics," said John good-naturedly. He was too happy to philosophize about the horrors of war. It had no terrors for him and was indeed his best friend. The situation was exactly as John had stated it. France and Germany seemed on the verge of another conflict, with Russia and England sure to be drawn into the whirlpool of European war. Active preparations were being made on every hand and the United States was already being drawn upon for supplies. Hard times were forgotten. Stocks bounded upward and grain of all kinds followed suit. Factories resumed work and in many instances the men succeeded in negotiating for an increase in wages. Money was plenty and the rates of interest high. It was discovered that the stock of manufactured goods had run low and a genuine boom set in.

Europe placed more contracts in America, and as the papers dwelt triumphantly on this fact the excitement increased until the country resounded with the roar of machinery. The demand for labor increased and wages were forced higher. New enterprises were projected and many were started. Workmen went about with happy faces and the panic and distress of 1893-1896 seemed only as an awful nightmare from which a people had awakened to the grandest prosperity in their history.

Not for a moment were old conservative business men deceived by the situation. The trusts were not carried away by the excitement. They were in a splendid position to make money and did so, but they went ahead on a conservative basis and kept a close watch upon the market and a steady finger upon the pulse of the consumer. By the middle of July it became generally known that there would be no war. The empire of Germany wanted war and so did the aristocracy and bourgeoisie of France, but they dared not declare war against each other. Back of Emperor William and his battalions was the portentous shadow of the social democracy of Germany, ripe for revolution and eager for war to be declared. More potent than the republican government of France was that socialism which had overlapped the walls of Paris, and found enthusiastic adherents among the peasantry The proletariat of France had no enmity against the humble wage-earning social democrat of Germany, and was waiting the day—the inevitable day—when the revolution should be declared. That was why France and Germany did not declare war, and that was why October found the United States in the throes of another panic.

There was great disappointment when it became certain that war was to be averted, but it had no immediate appreciable effect upon business. Stocks declined a little and so did wheat. The people paid no attention to these slight evidences. They had come to regard themselves as authorities on good and bad times, on panics and business revivals, and they argued that there was no danger of a panic for several years anyway. But they did not realize the changed conditions which came into effect with the panic of 1892-93 and were totally unprepared for what was in store for them.

In the early part of September the papers announced that several of the factories belonging to the shoe trust had been closed for "repairs." A few days later the great English brewing trust closed down its Cincinnati and St. Louis houses. There was an increased scarcity of money and the banks raised the rates of interest. It became more and more difficult to borrow money on good security. September 27 the press announced that owing to lack of demand the refineries under the control of the sugar trust would be shut down on the following Saturday until further notice; also that the trust had declared the usual 2 per cent quarterly dividend. Then came the panic, but one which but little resembled its predecessors. Some big failures were announced of firms which had plunged wildly into the market under the guidance of inexperienced managers. A few large manufacturing concerns were caught and a large number of small concerns failed, which had branched out in expectation of supplying all of fighting Europe with the sinews of war.

There were the usual runs on national, state and savings banks, but, with one or two exceptions, the banks did not fail. They had money for all who came, and the people soon became tired of drawing their money out and let it remain in the banks. Money was again plenty, but none who had good collateral desired to embark in new enterprises or to enlarge old ones. All ever the country shops and factories were either shut down or running on half-time. Winter was approaching. What was the cause of the panic?

It was called a panic, but the word was a misnomer. The trouble in 1893 was termed a panic, but it was simply a general suspension of production, more especially in the manufacturing line. The remarkable feature of the boom and panic of 1898 was the wonderful rapidity of its development. The short interval between the severe depression of 1893-1896 was followed by a business revival and quickly succeeded by returning hard times and an even more intensified depression. In the natural course of events the patient would have remained in a dormant state and regained strength only after a long period of convalescence. Such had been the history of the past, but history blindly follows no rule prescribing a sequence of events. The political doctors had wisely predicted a lingering illness and prescribed various nostrums supposed to have more or less value, but all their calculations were scattered to the winds by the European war-cloud.

The sound of the preparations for war came to the ear of the fevered patient. It was like water to a parched throat, as a glass of brandy to a famished traveler. The patient sprang from the sick bed, with one hand brushed aside the astonished political doctors, and with the other tipped over the carefully compounded and mysterious nostrums. "War! War!!" Every repetition of the word made the blood tingle. The invalid had become a giant, and from 1,000 chimneys the smoke wreathed, and from 10,000 forges came the music of industry.

War! War! Blood! Carnage! Sweet words of comfort and inspiration to a Christian nation. Cut loose the bloodhounds, and let Europe run red with rape and rapine that men and women and little children may live in America!

For the first time in history the mechanical age had an opportunity to test its capacity. Not at any time in the twenty preceding years had all the powers of production been placed in operation. There had been good times before, but not such times as these. In good and bad times the machine had been developed, but not until now was it possible for America to show the world her wonderful resources.

It was a superb exhibition of material greatness. It was as if a big, strong, but indolent and good-for-nothing boy, whose only thought in life had been to subsist by the least possible exercise of his muscles, had suddenly attained manhood, and with that manhood had cast away sloth and with every grand faculty of nature awakened into life, had set about the realization of some magnificent ambition. Thus it was with the United States of America.

Forty million willing hands manipulated the machinery of production and added to the wealth of civilization. Forty million sturdy arms wrested from Mother Nature those blessings which she so gracefully relinquishes to the persistent suitor. A nation was happy and prosperous.

But why do the wheels of industry begin to slacken and why do men grow pale?

Ask the mill-owner. He will tell you. There has been an overproduction. The people have worked so hard and accumulated so much that as a penalty they must go hungry and perchance some of them will starve for their folly.

In the six months from April to October, 1898, the people of the United States had produced more than had ever before been recorded for a year. Some of it had gone abroad, but vast stocks of supplies remained at home. The country had been deceived.

They had been "confidenced" into manufacturing for a market which did not exist. The price of all commodities fell, but the people had little money with which to purchase at any price. With their wages the people had paid off debts formerly contracted, and but few of them had been able to save up a dollar against that "rainy day" now acknowledged to be inevitable but for which it seemed impossible to prepare. Millions of workmen were discharged from the great factories.

They had committed a crime. They had created too much wealth. They had worked too hard. They must be punished by being forced into idleness. In 1893 or 1894 the workmen of America were capable of producing in a few months all the manufactured products the people could purchase in a year. The boom caused by the rumors of war gave the workmen a chance to give the world a practical illustration of the wonderful resources of production. They then proceeded to starve for a much longer period.

In the fall elections the Populists refused to combine with the Democrats and made decided gains and carried states and congressional districts in which they were not supposed to have the slightest chance for success. The adherents of the old partes were surprised and disgusted when it was learned that the third party held the balance of power in the House of Representatives and would be able to elect three new United States senators. In the excitement of the election the people forgot their sorrows for the time and many of them saw a ray of hope in the presaged success of the People's party, whose leaders now confidently claimed that they would sweep the country in 1900.

The increasing strength of the trade union movement in the United States had attracted the attention of the entire civilized world. Under shrewd leadership they had proceeded on strict trade union lines and had successfully avoided the political and other entangling alliances which so many times before had been the rocks on which the movement went to pieces. The great boom of 1898 had greatly strengthened the unions, and their success in obtaining advanced wages had brought hundreds of thousands into their ranks. The panic found these organizations in exceptionally fine condition, with money in their treasuries and the membership in good discipline. Carefully prepared statistics showed that fully 95 per cent of all the men employed in manufacturing, building and kindred trades were enrolled in the various unions. With hardly an exception, the unions were recognized by the employers, and wages were adjusted without difficulty, all disputes being settled by arbitration. In a word, the trade unions had obtained the position which the founders of the movement claimed as possible, and that which they so earnestly worked for and had predicted for years had come to pass.

Not less than 6,000,000 were enrolled under the banner of the American Federation of Labor, and affiliated with them were 2,000,000 members of the Farmers' Alliance and similar organizations. Numerically the trade union movement had achieved the fondest hopes of its projectors. How did the trade unionist and his proud organization confront the situation as it presented itself when the panic of 1898 paralyzed the business of the country? In less than two months more than 3,000,000 members of trade unions were out of work. Even in the face of this appalling problem the ranks remained fast. The president issued an address in which he said:

"Trade unionism expects every man to do his duty. Our splendid organization is in no way to blame for the disaster which has palsied the hand of industry, and the darkness of this night but precedes a brighter day when panics and the enforced idleness of armies of men shall live only as a memory. In the hope and expectation of the dawning of such a day I entreat you to stand firm. This is to be a test of unselfishness. If every man shall do his duty, his whole duty, trade unionism shall live and to-morrow shall triumph. The alternative is anarchy, a wild struggle for life in which all we have fought for shall be lost to us forever."

Not since the world was created and mankind given authority over animate and inanimate things was there witnessed so fine an illustration of unselfish and ennobling discipline as that displayed in 1898 and 1899 by the federated trade unions of America. There were a few weak ones, a few cowards and traitors, but the vast majority obeyed the common orders without question and without hesitation. There was on January 1, 1899, work for but half of the 6,000,000 trade unionists, and as the winter came on the number of men at work steadily decreased.

In December a special convention was held. The labor leaders met in solemn session and discussed the momentous problem which confronted them. By a practically unanimous vote it was decided that the work, or the wages paid for work, should be divided among the members. The various unions were instructed to submit to their employers the alternative of accepting one of two propositions—either that a double force should be employed half time, or that at the end of a month the men then working should be then laid off and a new force substituted. It was also provided that a liberal trade union assessment should be paid into the treasury for the purpose of sustaining certain trades in which work was almost entirely suspended.

This heroic remedy was grafted into a resolution and submitted to the various national trade unions, and by them indorsed without a single exception. The manufacturers met the men half-way and in many cases offered valuable suggestions, which were accepted in good spirit. Wherever practical the men alternated in working, and by this expedient from 2,000,000 to 3,000,000 men with their families were constantly supported in idleness The most rigid economy was absolutely necessary and nearly one-third of the people of the United States existed for months only by denying themselves everything except the actual necessities of life.

This exhibition greatly pleased certain people who imagined themselves political economists. They read the labor people long lectures, pointing out to them the fact that at last they had come to their senses and had acted as they should have years ago. The advantages of the new system over that of striking were lovingly dwelt upon and the labor leaders were congratulated upon their generalship.

The average well-to-do citizen saw nothing wrong in the situation. He viewed it with the same complacency as he had in 1873, 1884 and 1893. That the government, or the state, or the community, was in any way responsible; that it was under the slightest obligation to furnish employment; that poverty was anything more or less than a dispensation of Providence, he had never imagined, or, in fact, considered to any extent. Men were made to work—that is, most men were made to work. Some men had to be rich, and thus were able to give other men work. If there were no rich men there could be no employment. The employer was a great benefactor to society, and society was under obligations to employers just in proportion as the latter furnished employment. When the employers were unable, from the condition of the market or from any other causes, to employ workmen—why, that was the end of it. Nobody was responsible. It was the duty of employers and wealthy people to be liberal at such times, and any attempt to excite the working class, or to lead them to rebel against what was clearly inevitable, should be frowned down, and if necessary sternly suppressed by the law. Work was ennobling and the American workman was naturally the most peaceable and easiest satisfied of any in the world. Foreigners had no conception of the dignity of American labor, and if they did not like things as they found them in this country they were at liberty to return from where they came.

The preceding chapters have described the sequence of events which led up to the anarchist conspiracy of May 23, 1899, with which this history opens and which Chief Sullivan and his officers so effectually "nipped in the bud"—to quote the language of the new reporter.

CHAPTER X.

JOHN SMITH, NATIONALIST.

JOHN SMITH was born in Quincy, Mass., September 12, 1853.

On the Smith side of the family the ancestry can be traced "clear back to old Pocahontas John Smith," as his good Aunt Maria so often expressed it. To tell the truth, John never took the trouble to look the matter up. His mother was a Paine, proud of the revolutionary blood which she had transmitted to her son, and the good lady was never weary of dwelling upon the Paine ancestral tree.

The Smiths were well-to-do people, and at the proper age young John was sent to Harvard and acquitted himself with honor to his family and to himself. He completed the under-graduate course in 1872 and returned home in time to witness the bankruptcy of the elder Smith, whose entire fortune was swept away in the panic of the following year. This incident changed the whole current of Smith's life. He had expected, as the only heir to the Smith estate, to go into business with his father, and eventually come into possession of the property. But the property had vanished. Certain unfortunate speculations, the advancing of large sums of money to some promising manufacturing concerns, had conspired against the estate, and a great property was dissipated.

Denied by the stern mandate of circumstance a life of comparative ease as a capitalist, John embraced law as a profession and first established himself in Boston. Acting on the advice of friends, he moved to Chicago, formed an advantageous partnership and rapidly acquired reputation and standing and with it a profitable clientage.

John Smith had ever been a student of political economy. His education had made him a free trader, and he was born a liberal. There was no taint of Puritanism in his veins, and no one ever heard him boast of his ancestors. He was proud of the fact that he was an American, but his Americanism did not lead him to hate foreigners because they were not so fortunate as to have been born in America.

John Smith was an American, but his Americanism was not of that rabid, hysterical type which impels men to defend and praise every law, tradition, practice and institution upon which some one had stamped the trademark "American." Smith preferred to pass upon such matters himself. To his mind a thing was right, just or proper not because it was American, but because it was right, just or proper. He could conceive of how a thing could be American and yet be wrong.

History had not taught him that Americans were a race especially inspired of God and so constituted as to be incapable of making mistakes. He saw, or at least he imagined he saw, where the Smiths and the Paines who lived and died a hundred years before had made some blunders, and as an American citizen it was not only his right but his duty to discuss such matters, and, if possible, ascertain and apply remedies. John Smith had no patience with certain of his friends who would hold up their hands in horror at his declaration that the constitution of the United States was full of errors.

"Have you no veneration?" exclaimed Jones one day.

"Not a bit," responded Smith. "Veneration is a half-witted, obsequious brother to superstition, and I care for the companionship of neither. The man who is afflicted with the venerating habit goes through life in a graveyard, poking around among the tombs, hunting for antique monuments erected to the memory of the dead that he may venerate and revere them. The fact that a thing is old makes me suspicious of it. I believe in the present. I believe that the people who live to-day know more than any people which have preceded them. Therefore I have no veneration for the past and study it only to avoid mistakes. Its history is largely a story of wars, of cruel and revolting crimes, and a ceaseless tale of man's 'inhumanity to man.'"

The city of Chicago was an interesting study to John Smith. He became a citizen of the western metropolis at a time when the gigantic forces of the mechanical age were at work restoring the ravages of the great fire and of the panic, which had swept through the young giant of cities. He became a part of that seething center of modern competition--Chicago. He entered the lists prepared to give and receive blows, with his hand raised against every other man. At this time John Smith had no serious complaint to make against established institutions. He was young and strong and a firm believer in the justice of the "survival of the fittest." He believed, and often said, that there was room for all in the United States, and he had no patience with those who demanded protection or charity.

Ten years brings many changes. In 1885 John Smith had materially modified his views on many subjects. His law business had increased and so had his income. So had his contempt.

For ten years wealthy clients had whispered into his ears tales of wrong, crime and cunning; for ten years he had defended men against legal robbery and had aided others to take legal advantage of their competitors.

For ten years he had been buffeted around in a frantic mob, until his ears rang with the cry of "money," "money," and his very nature revolted against the knavery, plotting and swindling which passed current as commercial honesty He became convinced that any social system based on the principle which then prevailed was destined sooner or later to fail. John Smith then decided to make a systematic study of the situation and form conclusions based on his own observations. He had abundant opportunity for such a study and for years quietly pursued a philosophic investigation of the business, social and political phases of the civilization in which he was living and of which he was a part. He subscribed to no creed and was the adherent of no ism. He read all there was obtainable concerning socialism, anarchy, the single tax theory and other schools of political and economic thought, and dispassionately weighed and considered their respective merits and shortcomings. He was unable to classify himself under any of the recognized schools of thought, and in fact did not desire to do so. John Smith could see no reason why a man should blindly follow the tenets of any school, and therefore continued his study of social phenomena unrestrained by any dogmatic bounds. Among the few personal friends with whom Smith discussed such problems he was regarded as a sort of mild crank with socialistic tendencies.

"I have discovered what you are," said Jones one day, seated in John Smith's private office.

"Good. Allow me to congratulate you," rejoined Smith with a suspicion of sarcasm

"No offense intended, John, I assure you," Jones hastened to explain. "I was referring to your peculiar theories about government, labor and all that. Well, I was reading to-day that they have formed a club or a society in Boston and the members called themselves Nationalists. I didn't read the whole article, but went far enough to learn that they desire to nationalize certain industries. They say that the word socialism doesn't mean anything, and that the fools who discuss such questions have ascribed every crime and idiocy on the calendar to socialism, and forever ruined whatever utility the word did have. From what I could make out of the article, their platform tallies very close to your ideas as you have explained them to me."

"Then you have decided that I am a nationalist?"

said Smith with a smile. "It is a good word and an expressive one. If nationalism implies an abiding faith in good government; if nationalism believes that there are certain functions that the whole people—the government—can do better than any faction or part of the people; if nationalism subscribes cheerfully to the rule of the majority with a proper respect for the rights of the minority, then I am a nationalist. It is a matter of little consequence. A name signifies little. What are you, Jones?"

"Blamed if I know. I was a Democrat six months ago, but I am so disgusted with the Democratic Senate and the ranting of a lot of those southern brigadiers that I have a good mind to read myself out of the party. Trouble is, there is no place for me to go. The Republicans are owned by a lot of manufacturers, and as for the Populists—well, I should like to see myself training around with those fellows. Don't believe I'll vote any more. It does no good so far as I can see. Think I will investigate this, this Nationalist idea. I may find that I am a Nationalist; who knows?"

And that was how John Smith, lawyer and man of property, became known among his personal acquaintances as the Nationalist, and a newspaper friend wrote a sketch about it and headed it "John Smith—Nationalist." Popular among his fellows and in the business world, Smith was nominated by the Democrats for a judgeship and was elected by a large majority. He served with marked ability a term as judge and declined a nomination in 1898, which would have been equivalent to an election. Judge Smith's letter to the campaign committee declining the nomination created a widespread sensation and was unsparingly criticised and denounced by many of the leading newspapers. In this letter Judge Smith said:

"An explanation is due the many friends, political, social and personal, who have so loyally supported me in the past and who have so kindly urged me to seek a continuance of judicial honors. In justice to them and in justice to myself I must firmly and unreservedly decline to accept a position, the oath of office of which imposes obligations repugnant to my sense of justice, fairness and honor. I am not in sympathy with certain of the provisions of the constitution of the United States. I am unalterably opposed to many of the laws incorporated in the federal, state and municipal codes, and submit to their exactions only under earnest protest. Believing as I do that it is the duty of a judicial officer to construe the laws as he finds them, having ever been an earnest, and, I hope, a consistent advocate of the absolute divorcement of the judiciary and the executive, I shall no longer seek to maintain myself in a position where I am compelled by my oath of office to dispense injustice under the guise of law. I hold that it is the duty of citizenship to make laws and the duty of the judiciary to interpret according to the strict spirit of such laws. Holding such views, I shall return to the ranks of private life, and as an American citizen shall do what is in my power to repeal, annul and revise the statutes which now stand as laws for the government and welfare of the people, aiming to substitute in the place of the old such new laws as the changed environment of our people has rendered imperative. I have, with the highest esteem, the honor to remain very truly yours,

"JOHN SMITH."

This was in September. Judge Smith was accused of treason by some excitable people, and these patriots were not a little surprised to learn that there was no law against criticising the constitution, or, in fact, anything else in this country. This rabid class was not large numerically, and Judge Smith's letter created a profound impression throughout the country. He was a man of national reputation and a judge whose opinions had ever been received with the greatest respect. As a lawyer he had amassed a considerable fortune and was a familiar figure in the best social circles.

When Judge Smith left the bench he resumed the practice of law, and declined repeated invitations to make public addresses and positively refused to be interviewed on economic subjects

The excitement following the anarchist conspiracy in 1899, soon died out. There was a slight improvement in business, but not enough to give employment to any great number of men. Under the constant strain of poverty the people grew more restive. Thousands of small shopkeepers were driven out of business and added to the ranks of the unemployed. In New York City a procession composed mostly of ruined tradesmen and discharged clerks marched down Broadway. Some trifling incident turned the parade into a mob, and in the fight which followed the stock exchange was wrecked, and many of the brokers' offices sacked and damaged.

As the condition of the country grew more desperate the hatred of foreigners became intense. From every section there came a demand that immigration should be stopped, and this culminated in a riot in New York City, the responsibility of which was charged to the Patriotic Sons of America, a secret society composed exclusively of Americans, and pledged to vote for and support none but native-born citizens. A mob drove a thousand newly arrived immigrants back to their ships, and several of these unfortunate people were killed and others badly injured. This affair was both applauded and condemned It was by some compared to the Boston tea party, and by others it was denounced as an unmitigated outrage on a people who had been taught to believe that America was a free country and a home for the oppressed.

September witnessed the famous Belgian, Holland and English railroad stock speculation, by which American capitalists lost millions of dollars and the foreign syndicate vastly increased its holdings. A powerful syndicate, composed of wealthy English, Belgian and Dutch financiers and speculators, successfully manipulated the American market and precipitated a Wall Street panic September 27. The Vanderbilts were pinched for about $8,000,000, and many of the best-known brokers in the country were ruined. It was estimated that the syndicate made $60,000,000 in the decline and subsequent rise in stocks. During all this period of depression the foreign capitalists had been heavy buyers of American securities, and reliable authorities placed their holdings at over one-half of the total values of the roads. The successful coup of the syndicate aroused general indignation. Some conservative papers even hinted that the time would come when foreign capital would be glad to let go of American railroad stocks, while others proposed increased taxation of foreign holdings and similar radical methods of retaliation.

The excitable temper of the people was strikingly illustrated in the October riots in New York, instigated by that erratic and grotesque person, George Francis Train. In ordinary times little or no attention was paid to Mr. Train's movements, and his picturesque individuality served only to amuse the public. But these were not ordinary times, and one of Train's practical jokes was the spark which spread into a conflagration, which at one time amounted almost to a revolution.

In a characteristic letter George Francis Train declared himself dictator of the United States, and called upon the people to hold a mass meeting in Madison Square, New York City, the afternoon of October 1, 1899, at which time he announced that he would formally assume the dictatorship and lead the people out of their distress. Train circulated thousands of circulars printed in red, white and blue, advertising the meeting and proclaiming his intentions. At first the public regarded the affair as a huge joke, but as the day approached for the meeting an undefinable feeling of apprehension pervaded New York City. The afternoon and evening preceding the Madison Square demonstration Train flooded the cities of New York, Brooklyn and Jersey City with these circulars:

LONG LIVE THE PEOPLE!
DEATH TO MILLIONAIRE STOCK ROBBERS, TRUST BARONS
(CARNEGIE, PULLMAN, GOULD)!
LONG LIVE THE PEOPLE!
HAIL TO
DICTATOR GEORGE FRANCIS TRAIN!
Formerly citizen, psycho, globe trotter, philosopher, orator and capitalist.
($200,000,000 in Omaha).

George Francis Train will proclaim himself dictator of the United States of America, at Madison Square Garden, Saturday afternoon, Oct. 1, 1895. Police and regular army dare not interfere! I will crush them! Down with the Byrneses, Pinkertons, murderers and assassins!
CITIZEN GEORGE FRANCIS TRAIN.
(Citizen Train to-day only. Dictator Train to morrow and forever.)

Shortly after 3 o'clock Saturday morning Train was arrested at the Continental Hotel by two officers. The old gentleman did not surrender until after a terrific fight, in which he successfully resisted the officers, one of whom had laid his hand on Train's shoulder.

"Don't lay a finger on me," shouted Train in a voice of frenzied rage. "I have not touched man or woman in thirty years, and no man can lay his hand on me and live. Stand back and I will go peaceably, but by all the powers of Psycho, I will kill the first man who comes near me!"

The officers, who had emerged from the scrimmage in a bruised condition, were undecided how to proceed. Train was finally permitted to have his way, and, after flatly refusing to ride in the patrol wagon, walked to Ludlow Street jail and entered a cell with the air of a conqueror.

"I have been in jail thirty times," he informed the reporter, "and I'll be damned if I don't enjoy it. Damn, you know, is Malayan for banana. If I say damn, you think of banana and you won't slip up on it. Went through anarchist trial in Chicago when I expected to have a bomb thrown at me by police every day, but never saw anything like this. Shall burn New York City to-morrow. Tell Depew to get out of town.

He is a friend of mine and I don't want to see him killed."

The police took possession of Madison Square early Saturday morning. The morning papers had no account of Train's arrest, but the noon papers were flaming with headlines. As noon approached small crowds of workmen, curiosity seekers, and the general riffraff of a great city gathered around the square. By 1 o'clock not less than 20,000 people blocked Broadway and Fifth Avenue. Few of them knew that Train had been arrested, and the papers containing the news were eagerly read. At 2 o'clock not less than 100,000 men were massed around Madison Square.

An unknown orator mounted the Wolff monument opposite the HoffmanHouse and commenced a harangue denouncing the police for arresting George Francis Train, whom the speaker lauded as a "true friend of the masses." Wild cheers greeted the orator and the great mob closed in around the monument Superintendent Byrnes decided to take action and charged on the crowd and ordered them to disperse.

A hand-to-hand combat ensued. Some one fired a revolver and an officer fell badly wounded. The commanding officer ordered another charge and the 500 police pressed forward. The crowd did not run; it could not retreat. For blocks there was a surging mob of men, and those in front were shoved ahead against their will. The officers clubbed right and left and those in front in sheer self-defense plunged into the ranks of the police and a fearful scene followed. The policemen were overcome by force of numbers and terribly beaten. Several drew their revolvers and fired, eight of the cowd, some of whom were idle spectators, being wounded and two killed. Superintendent Byrnes and seventy-five men forced their way through the crowd at the south end of the park and called for reenforcements. The unexpected victory of the crowd had its effect. They had smelled gunpowder and blood. They had whipped the police. From a curiosity-seeking gathering of men it became an unrestrained mob.

The storm broke when an unknown man gave the cry:

"On to Ludlow jail!"

Fifty thousand men took up the cry, and the resistless wave of humanity swept down the street. All manner of men were there. Barroom loafers and thieves jostled against honest mechanics who had not worked for months; jabbering foreigners from the back streets tramped beside pale-faced clerks whose former employers had been ruined in the panic; loud-mouthed toughs and rowdies from the Bowery joined with small tradesmen, and the seething mass of humanity rolled along with the uncheckable power of an avalanche.

A crash of glass! Five hundred men gave a wild yell and dashed into a jewelry establishment. A pale-faced proprietor makes a vain show of resistance and the few clerks mingle in the crowd, glad to lose their identity. One brave clerk—the proprietor's son, perhaps—pulls a revolver and points at the mob. They laugh and a burly brute wrenches the weapon from the boy's grasp and hits him over the head with it. In thirty seconds the store is turned inside out. Thousands of dollars' worth of diamonds, watches and adornments have been crammed into the pockets of the rioters, who fight among themselves over the spoils.

A bakery and a meat market meet a similar fate. The mob has become a monster. The smell of blood and the sight of spoil has aroused the demon which ever sleeps in the breast of man. A small detachment of police attempted to check the devastating march, but was swept away.

Above the deafening roar could be heard the occasional crack of a pistol. Down the street frightened merchants were locking their doors and putting up the iron shutters. Not all of the mob was bent on rapine. A few endeavored to check it, but their efforts were of no avail. The great mass kept up the cry of "On to Ludlow Street jail."

The police were prepared for the coming of the mob. Nearly 1,000 officers were massed in and around the jail, and the front rank of the mob received a volley which dropped sixty men and created a momentary stampede.

But only for a moment.

Every other man in the crowd seemed to have a revolver and the fire of the officers was returned. Thousands of men took possession of the surrounding houses, and in comparative safety poured a deadly fire into the ranks of the police. The experience of Madison Square was repeated. The front ranks were pressed forward by the pressure of the rear, until, with a wild yell, the mob charged on the jail. It was all over in a minute. The doors opened to receive the retreating officers and the mob poured in after them. In the desperate hand-to-hand conflict in the corridors which ensued thirty-two officers were killed and as many more of the mob were shot. The cells were battered down and the prisoners released.

George Francis Train was found in the keeper's private living-rooms. He had keen kindly treated, and on his promise to make no attempt to escape had been given the privileges of a "trusty." He had been a spectator of the fight, but not until the crowd captured the jail did Train show himself. As the mob swarmed through the hallway Train opened the door, and, stepping jauntily forward, raised his red fez and shouted:

"Are you looking for me, boys? I have been expecting you. Let's go back to Madison Square. Don't hurt these policemen; they can't help it. Some of them are good fellows, but damn 'em, I don't want them to put their hands on me."

The white-haired old eccentric was tumultuously cheered, and as he crowded his way to the front of the jail tens of thousands of men yelled themselves hoarse A carriage was procured and Train seated inside. A hundred men with a long rope pulled the carriage back over the route of the mob and took possession of Madison Square. Surrounded by an enormous multitude, few of whom could hear a word he said, Train delivered a rambling speech announcing that he would go to Washington the next day and assume charge of the government. The crowd slowly disintegrated. At 7 o'clock Train was still speaking, when eight companies of officers and nearly 500 members of the Seventh Regiment marched into the park. The mob broke and ran without a shot being fired. Train gracefully surrendered and that night was taken out of the city. He was subsequently tried for inciting a riot, acquitted on the ground of insanity, committed to an asylum and released shortly after on a writ of habeas corpus.

This remarkable riot entailed a loss of nearly 100 lives and the destruction and loss of several millions of dollars' worth of property. But for this feature it would have been ridiculous. With Train it was nothing but an erratic joke, and he heartily enjoyed the sensation he had created. The significant feature was the reception given by the people to Train's bombastic proclamation. Many of them were deeply in earnest, and thousands of desperate men embraced the opportunity for lawlessness and plunder which was given.

Had a daring, resourceful and brainy man been in command of such a mob, New York would have been powerless and the incipient revolution might have spread until it embraced the country.

This incident aroused an agitation in favor of increasing the regular army. At the next session of Congress a bill was passed increasing the army to 100,000 men, but the President vetoed it.

CHAPTER XI.

HOW SUPREME COURTS PROTECT THE PEOPLE.

GREAT things were expected from the Congress which met in December, 1899. In a stirring message the President reviewed the condition of the country and recommended some radical legislation. He urged an increase in tariff duties for the protection of manufacturers and of workmen. He also urged the passage and rigid enactment of laws prohibiting the formation or operation of trusts, combinations and all agencies designed to regulate and curtail production and competition. The President also recommended the appointment of a commission to inquire into the management and working of trade unions and to ascertain to what extent they were interfering in the free exercise of competition.

The Congress of 1899 did pass a stringent law against trusts in the spirit indicated by the President in his message. All such combines were declared illegal and a number of ways provided by which state, county and municipal officers, on the petition of a small number of citizens or of their own accord, could proceed against a trust and insure its disruption. The law was carefully drafted and conferred upon the attorney-general of the United States such additional power as would enable him to more easily crush out the monopolies. This bill was passed by a large majority of both houses and signed by the President. None of the trusts made the slightest opposition to the bill, and congressional callers on the trust magnates met a cold reception and went back and worked and voted for the bill. Congress handled the trade union question gingerly and adjourned without taking action. A presidential election was approaching and they dared not offend the unions.

The Supreme Court at the earliest opportunity declared the trust law unconstitutional. There was no dissenting opinion. Every sensible congressman and senator knew that the law would be set aside by the court.

In their written opinion, the court declared the law was an unconstitutional attack upon the right of contract and an unwarrantable abridgment of individual liberty. The court declared that two or more firms or corporations had the same right to enter into a contract, agreement or stipulation with a view of regulating prices and production as had two or more men to form a partnership for the same purpose.

In a word, the court plainly said that there was nothing in the constitution of the United States or in the common law which prevented any man or any number of men, firms, corporations or associations from controlling, if they could, any of the articles or commodities which entered into production. The trust had attained its position fairly and legally by taking advantage of the recognized laws of trade and competition and of supply and demand. If the court had the power to disrupt trusts and kindred associations, it also had the power to annul corporations and partnerships. This theory carried to its logical end would place every man on his own individual resources, restraining him from forming an alliance with his fellowman for any purpose, however useful. This was anarchy pure and simple, and directly opposite to the principles of any recognized system of government.

This decision had been anticipated by every man capable of making an intelligent analysis of the situation. The trust was plainly a legal and justifiable institution.

The cheap politicians of the day ranted about trusts and ascribed all the evils under which the country suffered to them. The fact was that had it not been for the trusts and the trade unions industrial anarchy would have been inevitable and civilization would have gone down in a series of bloody and fruitless revolutions. The trust was not inherently right or just, neither was the trade union. Both were fortresses behind which lay intrenched those forces of capital and labor which had been wise enough to fortify themselves against a state of society in which unrestricted competition meant general bankruptcy, misery and anarchy.

This decision of the United States Supreme Court recalls an interesting decision which was handed down by a Supreme Court of Illinois in October, 1893, which illustrated the extent to which the voice of the people was heard in the framing of laws. Illinois had become a great manufacturing state. Wages had been steadily reduced and the ranks of the unemployed increased. The workmen decided that they could do better with a weekly pay day. Many large firms had held back wages for a month. After a man had been idle for two or three months it was a hardship, after securing a position, to be compelled to wait thirty days before receiving the money he had earned. The weekly pay day was made an issue. The distinctively capitalistic papers strenuously opposed it, but the workmen elected two branches of a legislature and a governor favorable to the law, which was passed and signed. The Braceville Coal Company, an institution which for years was a member of a syndicate which had grown rich by starving men, women and children, and which had enforced by Pinkerton rifles a condition of slavery compared with which Siberia was an earthly paradise—this firm, with the blood of innocent children on its hands, went into court in 1892, and at its beck the Supreme Court of Illinois reversed the opinion of all lower courts and hurled back into the face of the people a law which they had passed in the face of combined capital and capitalistic influences of the state. Here is the substance of this opinion, written by Justice J. P. Shope, stripped of its citations of references back to the time of Charles II.:

"There can be no liberty protected by government

that is not regulated by such laws as will preserve the right of each citizen to pursue his own advancement and happiness in his own way, subject only to the restraints necessary to secure the same right to all others. The fundamental principle upon which liberty is based in a free and enlightened government is equality under the law of the land It has accordingly been everywhere held that liberty, as that term is used in the constitution, means not only freedom of the citizen from servitude and restraint, but is deemed to embrace the right of every man to be free in the use of his powers and faculties, and to adopt and pursue such avocation or calling as he may choose, subject only to the restraints necessary to secure the common welfare.

"One illustration of the manner in which it affects the employé out of many that might be given may be found in the condition arising from the late unsettled financial affairs of the country. It is a matter of common knowledge that large numbers of manufacturers shut down because of the stringency of the money market. Employers of labor were unable to continue production for the reason that no sale could be found for the product. It was suggested in the interest of employés and employers, as well as in the public interest, that employés consent to accept only so much of their wages as was actually necessary to their sustenance, reserving payment of the balance until business should revive, and thus enable the factories or workshops to be open and operated with less present expenditure of money. Public economists and leaders in the interest of labor suggested and advised this course. In this state and under this law no such contract could be made. The employé who sought to work for one of the corporations enumerated in the act would find himself incapable of contracting, as all other laborers in the state might do. The corporations would be prohibited entering into such a contract, and if they did so the contract would be voidable at the will of the employé and the employer subject to a penalty for making it. The employé would therefore be restricted from making such a contract as would insure to him support during the unsettled condition of affairs. They would, by the act, be practically under guardianship, their contracts voidable as if they were minors, their right to freely contract for and to receive the benefit of their labor as others might be denied them."

Note this judicial description of the economic conditions of 1893: "Employers of labor were unable to continue production for the reason that no sale could be found for their product." And it was to enable the hundreds of thousands of Illinois workmen to labor for a pittance sufficient to keep body and soul together that the kind-heartd judge repealed the wicked weekly pay-day law.

Read that decision carefully. It pictures a condition of grotesque distress more vividly than anything in the preceding pages. Look at the picture which Judge Shope presents. Factories and mines are shut down because they have produced so much that there is "no sale for their product." The unfortunate workmen who were guilty of doing all this wicked work are starving for the food they have created and freezing for want of the coal they have mined and the clothes they have woven. They beg to be allowed to work for "only so much of their wages as was actually necessary to their sustenance." They beg to be allowed to produce more stuff that they can not buy and for which there is no market. And in order that there may be nothing in the way of making such a contract Judge Shope, in the kindness of his heart, repeals with a stroke of his pen the weekly pay-day act. Such was the marvelous patience of the people who lived in 1893.

The author has refrained from any mention of the barbarous treatment accorded certain workmen and the outrages which were perpetrated in the development of child and female labor, for the reason that as a rule the American employer was kind and considerate to his employés. But there were exceptions, and as the fight for life grew more intense certain classes of labor were treated with a savagery which almost surpasses human belief. And the Braceville Coal Company belonged to a coterie of slave-drivers in whose company a cannibal would blush for his manhood.

It was the duty of the writer as a newspaper reporter to visit the Braceville, Braidwood, and Spring Valley coal regions and to spend several weeks with the miners and their families. This was in the spring of 1889, and while the introduction of this incident may be out of its proper sequence the author excuses it on the ground that it presents a true picture of mining districts as they then existed, and illustrates the depths of depravity to which competition and greed can descend in the pursuit of money.

The majority of the Braidwood workmen were Americans or Scotch and English coal miners who settled in Braidwood before the war. Most of them owned their homes. Then there was a scattering of recently imported German, Polish, Italian and some Irish workmen living in houses rented them by the company. The old miners had lived to see their wages decrease from $5 and $6 a day, until in 1889 $18 a month was considered fair pay. This decrease had been steady, and had all been accomplished under a protective tariff, the workmen steaily voting to perpetuate that system. Early in 1889 the coal company made another reduction and the men struck. The company made no effort to operate the mines in Braidwood, but kept open for a time those in Streator, Spring Valley and other points. No language can describe the suffering at Braidwood. The people had been unable to save a dollar in anticipation of a lockout—for that was what it was.

Little children starved in their mothers' arms, and hundreds would have perished had not the good people of Chicago, urged on by the newspaper accounts of the distress, sent car loads of provisions to the afflicted town.

Beneath a round hill near the town the skeletons of sixty miners repose under masses of rock and coal, in a flooded mine. The company decided that it would not

Occasionally there was a riot.

be profitable to attempt to work the mines or recover the bodies, and to-day these unknown and forgotten toilers sleep beneath the tons of rock and coal. In the dreary days and nights of that summer the children of these dead miners starved, while the millionaire members of the syndicate drove their carriages down grand boulevards and on Sundays lolled back in their church pews and listened to the teachings of Christ.

Every conceivable device was employed to rob these men. They were swindled in the weighing of coal, forced to patronize a robbing company, truck stores, and paid in vouchers which the banks cashed at a discount. After years of such treatment the company decided to restrict the production of coal, and the faithful miners were not given the consideration accorded swine and poultry.

Even worse was the crime committed at Spring Valley. Not in all the pitiful annals of the poor can be found a parallel to the outrage perpetrated in 1889 against 4,000 innocent people at Spring Valley. It was a new town built around several coal shafts. The company advertised for men, offering good wages. The company laid out the town, sold the miners lots and built them houses, taking mortgages on the same, and forced a contract stipulating that regular monthly payments with high interest be taken from their wages.

Five years passed. The wages had been steadily reduced until the monthly payments left but little for the growing family. But the workman smiled as he thought that the house and lot was over half paid for. Then came the news of the Braidwood strike. A few days later the Spring Valley men were notified of a cut in wages. They did not strike as the company had desired and anticipated. Thereupon the company closed certain shafts and locked half of the men out. The locked-out men and their families were on the verge of starvation. The men still at work held a secret meeting and agreed to divide their time with those out of work. Their wages did not exceed $16 a month. No greater unselfishness was ever shown. Two weeks later all the shafts were closed down. Spring Valley was isolated from the rest of the world. It was distinctively a mining town. There was not a factory of any kind in the vicinity. Spring Valley's starving people went into the woods and gathered acorns, which they ate ravenously. They begged farmers for half-ripe field corn.

Did the wealthy company give these honest people a dollar out of its abundance? No.

What did it do in this time of pitiful distress?

It foreclosed the mortgages on their half-paid-for homes and ejected weeping women and children from humble cottages, which represented the miserable savings of five years of the hardest kind of toil.

And the people who lived in those days marveled much that once in awhile a crazy man threw a dynamite bomb.

How did these people at Braidwood and Spring Valley accept their fate? As though it had been decreed by God. They made little complaint. They seldom talked violently. I saw men whose children were crying for food—great, strong men—stand around a truck store filled with groceries and closed because the company knew the people had no money. There was not enough manhood in the crowd to batter down the doors and take that which lay before them. Long years of oppression and enervating toil had effaced from their souls the very conception of liberty. Then, and not until then, did I realize that the spirit of liberty does not exist in hungry men.

People talked about a day coming when the people would become so hungry and desperate that they would rise in a revolution and sweep all before them. Such a day will never come. Hungry men may fight, but it will be for a bone—not for liberty. The perpetuity of liberty rests with those who eat three square meals a day.

CHAPTER XII.

THE PEOPLE HOLD A CONVENTION.

THE presidential campaign of 1900 was held under conditions which did not differ materially from those which prevailed in 1898. Manufacturing showed little change for the better. Shops would resume operations for a time and continue until they had supplied the limited demand, while others remained open and ran with decreased forces of men. New inventions created new industries, some of which thrived, while others failed, but the demand for employment ever exceeded the supply. The danger of overproduction was generally understood and with it the panic had evidently become a thing of the past, and in its place had come an era of constant depression, the concomitant of a carefully regulated method of production. The farming interests suffered even more than the mercantile from this cause. Every workman who could save enough money moved into the country in the hope that he could at least support his family upon the products of a rented farm. Wheat and grain of all kinds steadily decreased in price. The causes were simple enough. Production of grains had increased and home consumption had decreased. Wheat sold at 45 cents a bushel and except in speculative bulges seldom went above 55 cents

As the time for the conventions approached political excitement increased The Republicans made an aggressive campaign and charged the Democrats with the entire responsibility for the prevailing disaster. Mark Kimbly and Thomas Reeve were the rival candidates for the presidency, but Kimbly was the favorite. Kimbly was a typical representative of the protective system, undoubtedly the most idiotic heresy with which any considerable section of a people have been afflicted. Kimbly and his adherents believed, or claimed to believe, that the nation could become rich and prosperous by levying a high tax on imports. This was to "protect American labor." He did not propose to prohibit these imports, but simply to make a tariff so high as to "maintain American wages." Had there been a demand for labor in excess of the supply it is possible to imagine how an artificial wage scale could have been forced upon the employer by his workmen under the operation of a protective tariff. But there were two workmen for every position. Wages were thereupon regulated by two causes, viz., the surplus supply of starving workmen, and secondly, the strength of the trade unions. The trusts therefore manufactured under the tariff and sold their products at a sum a little below the market price of the foreign commodity with the tariff added. This did not stop imports, the foreign manufacturers supplying their products to American merchants, who paid the tariff, charged the amount up to their customers, and then disposed of the imported material to people who preferred foreign-made articles to those of home manufacture for one reason and another. The effect of the Kimbly and other tariff bills therefore was:

1. To increase the profits of the trust and to more strongly fortify the trust against competition at home or abroad.

2. To force the consumer to pay a duty not only on all imported goods, but also on all home products of a similar nature.

3. To limit manufacturers largely to a home market, it being impossible for them to pay duties on raw materials and compete in foreign markets. The tremendous natural commercial advantage which came from the development of American machinery was therefore lost.

4. It had not the slightest effect on wages, which were regulated by the iron law of supply and demand

and which constantly fell from the time high tariff was first adopted until they reached the starvation limit in 1893-96.

In 1896 the larger part of a high protective tariff bill was still in force and effect, and Republican orators were telling stupid workmen that the Democrats had brought hard times upon the country. These men had the brazen effrontery, in the face of facts so plain that any man with an ounce of brains could understand them, to openly proclaim that shops and factories were shut down for the reason that manufacturers were suffering from a "lack of confidence" in the Democratic party.

What of the Democratic party? What had it done?

Nothing.

That had been the consistent record of the Democracy for 108 years. The most timid factory owner in the country was not losing sleep over the prospective policy of the Democracy. It had no policy. The Democracy spent its time in venerating. It venerated the constitution. It venerated Jefferson, Jackson, and last but not least, it venerated the McKinley bill. When the Democrats came into power in 1892 they found the McKinley bill a part of the governmental furniture, and aside from removing some of the un-Democratic gewgaws and un-Jacksonian adornments the McKinley bill remained in all its glory under another name. It was the same old Democracy in 1900. It found all its ammunition in a denunciation of Republicanism for the passage of laws which it declined to erase from the statute-books. The Republicans were guilty of sins of commission and the Democrats of those of omission.

In 1900, as in 1892, the Republican party was marshaled by brilliant, brainy, but dishonest and unscrupulous leaders, who had no difficulty in controlling several millions of sentimetalists, bogus patriots, bigots and dupes, and other millions of well-intentioned people who could find no better company but desired to belong to some party. The Republican party was so tainted with corruption that many men naturally Republicans were forced into the graveyard of Democracy or into the Populist party.

The great middle class—the small merchants, tradespeople, the mechanics and workmen who had saved a little out of their earnings; the professional class—doctors, lawyers, journalists; that powerful, conservative body which lay between arrogant wealth and helpless, ignorant poverty, had lost all faith in the so-called Republicanism and Democracy of the day.

For half a generation they had been waiting for a leader who should disrupt old party lines; a Moses who should direct them out of the panic-infested and depression-haunted wilderness, but no such leader arose above the dull level of political mediocrity. No man prominent in the ranks of the Populists attracted the fancy of this dissatisfied but conservative army of voters, and as the campaign of 1900 drew near it became evident that the same old sham battle was to be again waged on the same dreary old lines.

The Republican national convention met in St. Louis, and after a bitter contest between Thomas B. Reeve of Maine and Mark Kimbly of Ohio the latter was nominated, and a platform adopted pledging the party to an increase in the tariff, a defense of the pension laws, and a strict adhesion to "honest money"—meaning a gold standard of monometallism. The convention was quite enthusiastic, and the orators made as much as possible out of the "hard times" issue, regardless of the fact that nearly every law of the country was passed by the Republican party and simply enforced by the Democrats when the latter were in power.

The Democratic national convention was held in New York City. The south demanded recognition, and presented Miles of Texas. Gorland of Maryland had some followers, and Boise and Pick had pledged delegations. It became evident that Miles could not win, and after a caucus the silver men decided to throw their strength to Hild of New York, who was considered not unfriendly to silver and was the stanchest kind of a spoils and partisan Democrat. He was not so strict a constitutional constructionist as the southern delegates would have liked, but otherwise he filled the bill. After a bitter contest Hild was nominated and Boise accepted second place on the ticket, the Republicans having nominated Thomas Reeve for that position. Reeve had accepted and pledged himself to put the Senate on a business basis, and was in popular favor on that account.

The Populist party promised to be a factor in this campaign, but it was badly handicapped by reason of a lack of organization, leadership or cohesion. It represented various expressions of discontent. In its ranks were found men holding such widely varying opinions that nothing but a common hatred of the prevailing conditions held them together. There were greenbackers, pure and simple, who believed that the country could be saved if the government would only issue enough paper money based solely on the credit of the country. Closely allied to these were the silver men, handicapped by the fact that they were led by the mine owners, who were alleged to have a selfish motive in urging the free coinage of silver. Their followers believed in an increased supply of money and were willing to enrich the mine owners if the country could in return be flooded with money. Then there were the farmers who wanted bonded elevators in which the government would store their products and issue them certificates with the wheat or grain as a security; a strictly selfish and limited remedy on the same plan as that of the gold and silver mine-owning syndicates. There was also an aggressive and influential body of socialists and nationalists who urged the governmental purchase and control of railroads and telegraph lines, a proposition in which the farmers concurred and in which the silver men had little sympathy and took no interest. There was also a smattering of woman suffragists and not a few free traders who had become disgusted with the Democratic party and had abandoned all hope of an overthrow of the protective-tariff citadel at the hands of the Bourbons.

Each of these factions had earnest, uncompromising leaders and followers, and at the party conventions it became more and more difficult to form a platform which would placate the conflicting interests. But with all these discouraging features the Populists survived, and with each election had increased their voting strength. In the south the Democrats lost by this defection and in some of the northern states the Republicans found their majorities cut down and ofttimes obliterated.

The People's party, or the Populists, as it was more commonly called, met in national convention July 1, 1900, in the Coliseum at Chicago. Every state in the Union was represented by a complete delegation. The great hall was filled to overflowing on the first day of the convention, and as the respective delegations filed in they were greeted with tumultuous applause. All the men who had become in any way prominent in the movement were present, and as the vast audience recognized some familiar character they cheered in that wildly boisterous way which marks the enthusiast.

Every shade of discontent was represented. The age which had forced this remarkable gathering had been a prolific breeder of selfishness. Each ism had its narrow representative, anxious to force to the front some remedy calculated to promote the renewed prosperity of the class or craft composing it.

Among the delegates of Illinois was Judge John Smith of Chicago. Judge Smith was known only by reputation to the majority of those present. Since his retirement from the bench he had devoted himself to law practice and had created somewhat of a sensation in the literary world by a series of articles in a leading magazine in which he boldly attacked the theory of representative government. He had also written articles on nationalism, in which he took advanced ground in favor of the nationalizing of railroads and other methods of transportation and exchange. These articles had attracted much attention, and among literary people Judge Smith was always spoken of as "The Nationalist."

After much persuasion Judge Smith had consented to become a delegate and was heartily welcomed by the old-time Populist leaders, most of whom he now met for the first time.

Judge Smith was in the full prime of a magnificent manhood. Six feet in height; a massive head covered with black hair and shaded with gray rested on a pair of shoulders of which an athlete might well be proud; a smoothly shaven face, keen but kindly black eyes, and nose and chin that betokened character and strength were the physical characteristics of Judge Smith. Judge Smith had none of the personal magnetism of the successful politician. He was described by a reporter on the day of the convention as a man who impressed one as "a cool, thoughtful, calculating investigator; a man of decided ideas, of hatred and contempt for the conventional; a despiser of shams and a lover of the truth; earnest in his convictions, but not a bigot or an enthusiast; a man conscious of his strength and confident of his power, but whose batteries were masked and held in reserve."

Judge Smith had all the bearing of an aristocrat. As one paper expressed it, "he looks like a banker and writes like a labor agitator." Few of the delegates present dreamed that around this quiet man vast forces would center and move irresistibly onward.

The convention organized, appointed its committees, and indulged in oratory while waiting for their reports. The expected and inevitable wrangle occurred over the platform. The committee on platform was unable to submit a unanimous report. The majority submitted a platform favoring the free and unlimited coinage of silver, the levy of an increased income tax, the governmental purchase of railroads, and the passage of a national eight-hour law.

The minority omitted all reference to silver and recommended the issuance of greenbacks, the establishment of government grain elevators and the issuance of grain certificates which should pass current as money, an increased income tax and governmental purchase and control of railroads and the establishment of a minimum scale of wages. Twenty delegates were on their feet at once demanding recognition. It was openly stated that the majority report had been inspired by money. The lie was passed and the convention was on the verge of a riot. Violence was prevented by the activity of the sergeants-at-arms and the police, and after a struggle the presiding officer secured something like quiet.

During this disgraceful proceeding Judge Smith had remained quiet. He had listened to the reading of the two reports and to the outburst which followed without giving expression to the honest indignation he felt. He addressed the chairman and was recognized. Judge Smith advanced to the platform and in a voice and manner which commanded immediate attention said:

"MR. CHAIRMAN AND DELEGATES OF THE CONVENTION: I move you, Mr. Chairman, that both the majority and minority reports of the committee on platform be rejected, that the committee be discharged, and that a new one be appointed, and on that motion I desire to be heard. You have mistaken the temper and spirit of the American people. They have not delegated to cheap politicians the right to use the sacred name of the people. They have made no demand for a party with a platform constructed of the political driftwood your committee has so laboriously collected and over whose comparative rottenness a conflict is now impending. There is no high place in American politics for a second-hand political junk syndicate. I do not believe that your committee reflects the patriotism and common sense of the convention or of the people of the United States.

"Why this stupid imitation of old-party methods? Has one generation of comparative poverty so stupefied the nation that the eyes of the representatives of the common people are blind to the weapons within their reach? What care you for the silver question? This is not a convention of bankers. What do you know about the money problem? Leave to the financiers for the present at least the discussion of monetary affairs. Open your eyes. Brush aside the crafty plotters who have muddled your brain and step out into the clear sunlight and let the free wind sweep away the cobwebs which custom and superstition have woven around you.

"Stand on an elevation and take a calm, dispassionate view of the country in which we hold citizenship. What do we see? A free people in slavery. A country without a king suffering from absolute despotism. A republic in which the majority is throttled by a minority. A land burdened with wealth, fields wavering with grain, warehouses bursting with manufactured products, and millions of people dependent on charity and at the verge of starvation. It is election day and they have ballots in their hands. The bands are playing in the streets, and the people seem happy and confident. Are these poor people voting to improve their condition? They think so. Are they all voting the same ticket? Oh, no. Some vote the Republican, some the Democratic, and some the people's ticket. What are they voting for? They are voting for men. These men when elected 'represent' them. They go to Washington, to the various state capitols, and to the city halls. What do they do there? As they please.

"Gentlemen of this convention, bravery is as essential to success in politics as it is to achieve victory in war. No successful political party was ever founded by cowards. Give the people an issue. The country is awaiting the formation of a political party that shall present questions in which the whole people is interested. They do not care for the silver question; they are not demanding greenbacks. They would like to see the government wipe out railroad monopoly and discrimination, but the national ownership of railroads is not what the people of the United States are now urgently demanding. They are interested in the success of trade unions and in just wages, but not all the people are members of such unions. They would desire to see the mortgage lifted from the home of the farmer, but all the people are not farmers.

"But all the people love liberty. Every man desires to be free. Slavery has few defenders. Let your platform declare for the political and economic freedom of the people of the United States. There are two great attributes of freedom: The right to live and the right to have an equal voice with all other men in the affairs of government. No man is a free man to whom these rights are denied or abridged.

"Both of these rights have been denied and are today trampled under foot in this country.

"Deny a man the right to work and earn a living and you have taken from him life, liberty and honor. You have made him worse than a slave. The slave earns his living. The man whom society denies work has a pitiful choice between suicide, starvation, the acceptance of charity, or a career of crime. Thomas Jefferson said that all men were endowed with the inalienable rights to life, liberty and pursuit of happiness. This trinity could have been expressed by the word 'wages,' signifying that which honest toil brings. Any country, any condition of society, in which by any combination of circumstances a man is refused an opportunity to make a living by honest work deserves to be swept into oblivion by a defrauded and indignant people. The first duty of the government is to protect the life of its subjects

"Man must live by work. In payment for that work he receives wages. That government governs best which assures to its subjects the largest share of the products of their labor. Any government which tolerates a condition under which a willing subject is denied work has denied to that subject all the inalienable rights which nature bestowed upon him. The United States is essentially a nation of workmen. It has been our proudest boast that honest labor is dignified and that the sovereigns of the republic are its toilers. Under our industrial system, with its introduction of machinery and the minute subdivision of labor, the workman has been stripped of his tools and his entire capital has become his brains, hands and muscles. Deny him the right to use these and receive compensation for this service and you have sentenced him to death, pauperism or crime. In the United States within the last four years not less than 5,000,000 men have been at one time sentenced to involuntary idleness, entailing misery on untold millions of dependent wives and children. No greater crime ever blackened history. The blame rests upon the government and can be traced directly to the constitution of the United States.

"Give the people an issue. Declare in your platform that:

"'The right of a citizen of the United States to demand and obtain work at wages sufficient to support himself and family shall never be abridged. It shall be the duty of the government to guarantee employment to all who demand it.'

"Radical and revolutionary? It may be, but it outlines the duty of the government of to-morrow, unless reason shall disappear from among men and anarchy prevail. Radical and revolutionary? Do you expect to check Niagara's flood with a mud wall? Do you expect to awaken the sluggish blood of the republic, vitiated and poisoned by a century of malpractice, with some such mild nostrum as an injection of diluted silver or an application of paper plasters? Do you believe in magic and wands? The knife of the surgeon and not the incantations of the magician will save the life of the government.

"Give the people an issue. Declare in your platform that:

"'The right of the majority to rule shall no longer be abridged. We denounce representative government as a failure and demand that the people be habilitated in the right to elect what laws shall govern them. We demand the absolute supremacy of the majority, from whose decision no appeal shall be taken. We demand the repeal of every clause in the constitution of the United States and in the constitution and laws of states, counties and municipalities, the language, construction and execution of which has nullified the will of the majority and made the United States a republic only in name. We demand that to the people shall be given a direct vote on all important legislation, and that all officers elected shall be the servants of the people, subject at any time to recall or dismissal and not, as at present, the masters of those who created them.'

"Such, Mr. Chairman, is my conception of a platform broad enough for a party which takes its name from the people. It is idle to waste time and energy in an attempt to work out political reforms with the machinery at hand. I have a great deal of respect for our friend the farmer, who is so numerously represented here to-day. He wants government grain elevators, and, being a peaceable citizen and a patriot, has faith in what we are pleased to term the republican institutions of the United States. He believes that his prosperity would be assured if the government would issue him grain certificates the same as it has issued silver certificates. He has a perfect right to that belief. He has been taught that this is the country in which the majority rules, and he has good reason to believe that the majority favors his proposition. Now let us see if this honest, law-abiding American citizen, with the majority of the people back of him, can place one law on the statute-books of his country. A good Republican or Democrat, he spends ten years in a fruitless attempt to have his party make grain certificates a political issue. He does not control the primaries, he was not built for a ward heeler; he has no political patronage; he is only a common voter against whose name the secretary of the campaign committee has marked R or D, as the case may be. The politicians laugh at his request, but he persists, and after ten years leaves the party he has served so faithfully and attempts to build up a new one which shall be in full sympathy with grain certificates. What is arrayed against him? The combined capital of the country, the federal, state and municipal patronage of two parties, and, more than that, the inbred conservatism of the people against a new party—a conservatism which often amounts to bigotry and ignorance. He makes a fight against these tremendous odds. The first campaign is a failure. Two years later a few congressmen are elected. Two years later and the new party is a recognized power, and at the subsequent election the farmer has carried the country by a popular majority and has captured the House of Representatives and the presidency. But the Senate blocks the way. The Senate has nothing to do with popular majorities. It was designed for the express purpose of defeating our friend, the farmer. It takes many years to dislodge an unfavorable Senate, but firm in his faith in representative government and in the rule of the majority, the farmer attacks the state legislatures and wins a majority of the Senate. By this time it is likely that the complexion of the lower house has changed or that an unfriendly President has been elected. But suppose that it has not, and that the grain certificate bill passes the House and Senate, and the President vetoes it? Perhaps the farmer may muster up enough votes to secure the necessary two-thirds. If he does, that is a happy day for the farmer. He celebrates his victory, which illumines the declining years of a life spent in overcoming a minority. In the midst of his joy and while preparing to enjoy the well-earned fruits of his victory, the Supreme Court of the United States declares the grain certificate bill unconstitutional, and that is the end of it. The political machine, the United States Senate, the President of the United States and the United States Supreme Court have successfully defeated the plainly expressed will of the people. I have assumed that no money had been illegally used. If the farmers of the United States had a majority of two-thirds of the people of the United States back of them to-day it would take them ten years to advance a grain certificate bill to a presidential veto, and from twelve to fifteen years of the hardest kind of work to obtain an adverse decision from the Supreme Court declaring grain certificates unconstitutional. The banking interests alone could and would defeat any bill inimical to their interests, no matter how great a majority of people favored it.

"Have you faith in the majority of the people? If not you should change your name. Do you believe in the rule of the majority? If so incorporate that belief in your platform. No reform for the good of the whole people as against active private greed is possible under the voting machinery and alleged representative system of government as provided by the constitution of the United States.

"Too long have the people of the United States been bound hand and foot by a false conservatism and by a slavish adhesion to obsolete precedents and out-of-date customs. You are Americans. Who shall tell you your duty as Americans? Beware the man who is ever prating of the patriotic duties and obligations of American citizenship. The first duty of a citizen is to his family and his home. Next to home and family a man should love his country. But love of country transcends a blind devotion to the written laws which may be ingrafted on the statute-books. I may love my country and yet patriotically hate laws which have survived their usefulness, and may despise enactments which corrupt men have passed for my government. The first duty of an American citizen is to batter down that which threatens the life, liberty and happiness of those who depend upon his labor.

"The people are in no mood to tolerate class legislation. They have had enough of it. They have witnessed the building up of monopolies as the result of class tariff legislation. They are not in a temper to foster trade unionism at the expense of the general interest. They will never consent to make grain or silver the foundation of a currency at the expense of any other commodity. It is not good politics to force such measures. You cannot win if you do force them. Even with a majority the undemocratic machinery of existing laws will defeat you. Attack those undemocratic and majority-defying laws. That is good politics. Unforge the chains you have aided in welding. In the name of the people champion the rights of the majority. You will be opposed by every man, every interest, every institution which has reason to fear the people. The aristocratic spirit which animated Hamilton and which impressed its hatred and fear of the people in the constitution of the United States still lives, and will be defended by argument, money and all the weapons that an existing plutocracy can command. It will be no easy task to overthrow the conspiracy against the majority, a conspiracy which had its origin among certain of the founders of this republic, men who had no sympathy with popular government, men who, though cowed and defeated in the war of the revolution, still loved the monarchial institutions of England and were powerful and crafty enough to force the hatred of popular rights into the warp and woof of the constitution which now governs us.

"Boldly attack every word and line bequeathed us by these conspirators against the people. Heed not the cries of 'treason' and 'traitor' which will be raised against you. If it is treason to advocate the rights of the majority in a republic, then I desire to be adjudged guilty of treason and punished as a traitor.

"Mr. Chairman, I move that the committee on platform and resolutions be discharged, their reports rejected, and that a new committee be appointed and instructed to draft and submit a platform which shall affirm our allegiance to the rule of the majority, our eternal opposition to all laws which aim to defeat the will of the majority, and our belief in the inalienable right of a citizen at all times to obtain employment and compensation."

CHAPTER XIII.

JUDGE JOHN SMITH IS NOMINATED.

THE opening sentence of Judge Smith's address was greeted with cries of disapproval. To this he paid not the slightest attention. As he proceeded the great audience paid the closest attention, and cheers greeted his declaration that every citizen of the United States was entitled to employment at honest wages. When he denounced the monarchists who inspired the unrepublican clauses of the constitution and closed his speech with a bold appeal for radical action the delegates and the great audience gave cheer upon cheer. The silver men did not abandon the fight without an effort, but they were no longer in a majority. Judge Smith had given expression to a thought which awoke a response in the heart of the convention. While there were delegates who yet favored a patchwork platform, composed of various selfish planks, the great body of the convention swept them aside and Judge Smith's motion was carried by acclamation. The chairman appointed Judge John Smith and a committee of seven to prepare a platform. In less than an hour the convention ratified a platform in accord with the views so clearly expressed by Judge Smith. The afternoon of July 4, 1900, Judge John Smith of Chicago was unanimously nominated for President of the United States by the People's party. In a conference with a committee Judge Smith was tendered the nomination, and in the course of the conference said:

"Gentlemen, you have asked me to accept an honor which no true American can refuse. If you believe that I am qualified to make the campaign, if you are willing that the People's party shall stand sponsor for the radical and even revolutionary opinions I hold and shall fearlessly express; if I am guaranteed your earnest support and unselfish aid, you may present my name to the convention. If nominated by a substantial majority I will accept the honor and the responsibility and to the best of my ability will work for the triumph of those principles laid down in our platform."

Fifty thousand people were massed around the Coliseum the closing day of the convention. Inside the great hall other thousands filled every available space and even encroached on the section reserved for the delegates. In an eloquent speech General Warker presented to the convention the name of Judge John Smith and amid tumultuous applause said:

"I present to you an American of Americans, in whose veins flows the blood of an ancestry which fought for American liberty before the days of Washington. Born in the state of Massachusetts, almost beneath the shadow of Bunker Hill, and reared from boyhood in an atmosphere of Americanism, John Smith grew to manhood and entered upon the duties of citizenship. His life has been that of an American. In early years he became imbued with an intense American hatred of shams and of hypocrisy. He has lived long enough to witness the birth and development of a moneyed aristocracy, an insolent, domineering plutocracy, with a cry of patriotism ever on its lips and its hands ever in the pockets of the people. He has lived to see the fair acres of his native country confiscated by alien corporations, syndicates and speculators. With pain and humiliation he has seen the majority of his countrymen defrauded by the ballot box and the voice of the people stifled by organized rapacity. Into his life has come a day when the door of the workshop has been closed against the mechanic and when the little children have pleaded to their parents in vain for bread And this in America, a land favored of God, the home of the free and a haven for the oppressed of all nations. To Judge John Smith the distress of an American community, the impoverishment of a people by panic or financial depression, is not an economic phenomenon to be calmly studied and diagnosed, but an outrage to be condemned, a crime whose perpetrators should be apprehended and punished.

"A scholar of splendid attainments; a lawyer of national fame and honor; a jurist whose decisions have never been questioned, but whose sense of the just impelled him to retire from a place where practice directed the dispensation of injustice; a man of business sagacity and of a considerable fortune honestly acquired; a gentleman in the truest sense of the word; a philosopher whose breadth of mind is bounded by no contracted horizon; an uncompromising opponent of bigotry and prejudice, a searcher and defender of the truth—Judge John Smith is an ideal American citizen. Higher praise can be given to no man. On behalf of the people of America and in the name of the People's party of the United States I present the name of John Smith of Chicago and ask that the nomination be made by acclamation."

A hundred men seconded the nomination, and in a voice of thunder the entire convention and audience swelled the chorus of "ayes" when the chairman put the question. Judge Smith was seated with his delegation. He had smilingly declined to conform to the usual custom of retiring to some convenient place and greeting with feigned surprise the committee charged with breaking the news. Escorted by the Illinois delegation, Judge Smith marched down the aisle and to the platform. When the cordial ovation had ceased Judge Smith addressed the chairman and said:

"Early American history is a tale of hardship, a story of peril, successive chapters of suffering, and a struggle against seemingly insurmountable obstacles, from which struggle a sturdy people emerged victorious. In these colonial days the young nation was ofttimes menaced by secret and open foes, but not since the pilgrim fathers landed on American soil has so great a danger menaced the people as that which confronts them to-day. The fathers of America, the pioneers whose ashes now peacefully rest in the beautiful valleys of New England, had escaped from despotism and their veins thrilled with that exhilaration which comes with newly acquired liberty. They were free men, and they transmitted to their children a heritage grander than that bequeathed by kings. That heritage has been lost.

"I have sometimes thought that only the slave can appreciate freedom. I have sometimes thought that the king-ridden peasants of England who fled to this country were the only Americans who ever tasted and appreciated liberty. What does the child of to-day know of freedom? What has become of the heritage left by the pioneer founders of America?

"The history of America is a history of the decadence of liberty. Its pages tell the story of how a birthright was lost. Its chapters mark the annals by which a republic faded into an aristocracy—an aristocracy not of position, title or heredity, but of money. The gloom of this history is relieved by pages which glow with the inspiring story of a re-awakening of the inborn spirit of liberty—a spirit which crushed for a time the strength of aristocracy in 1776, and which asserted itself again in 1861.

"The revolution of 1776 was inspired by grievances and abuses which would pass unnoticed to-day. But the people of 1776 had not lost the notion of liberty. The slow encroachments of England and the growing influence of a tory aristocracy had dulled their conception of liberty, but had by no means destroyed it. They were a handful of people skirting the Atlantic coast with few resources useful in war, but they defeated Great Britain, the most powerful nation in the world, and sacrificed their lives and property rather than submit to a few trifling exactions which to-day are tolerated without a murmur. They had been taxed without representation. Why, for years the American people have been taxed and robbed out of more money than the entire property of the thirteen colonies was worth—taxed billions of dollars for the benefit of home and foreign tariff barons, and the tax is imposed to-day in spite of the fact that in successive elections the people have declared by emphatic majorities against a continuance of this robbery. The men of 1776, with their peevish notions about rights and liberty, would be denounced as anarchists if they lived to-day. They would be invited to leave this country if they did not like it, and reviled in all manner of terms if they talked of fighting for such ridiculous things as they termed 'their rights.' Not so in 1776. They fought and they won. We are proud of the revolutionists and glad to trace our ancestry back to our fighting forefathers. What would Patrick Henry, Benjamin Franklin, George Washington, General Stark, General Warren and the patriots of 1776—what would that illustrious body of freemen think of a modern United States Senate, of a Carnegie syndicate, a Homestead riot, and a Hocking Valley, with thousands of starving families? What would they think of 5,000,000 men out of work? What would they think of a panic, of a period of depression on account of an overproduction of wealth? What would they think of a people who would tamely submit to corruption in high places, to the sale of their streets to the highest bidder, to the gift of consulships in consideration of checks for $50,000? Would they revolt because their children were starving or would they meekly accept the crust which charity offered them? These questions need no answer. The spirit of 1776 is dead. It did not survive the close of the revolution long enough to protect the constitutional convention of 1787 against the plottings of English toryism and an aping American aristocracy. Liberty slumbered in the breasts of the American people until human slavery had dragged its loathsome form almost across the continent. Then there came to the common people of the north a resurrection of the spirit of the forefathers, a revival of the days of 1776. Under that inspiration they fought for the preservation of the Union, the freeing of the slave, the glory of the republic.

"With the close of the war commercialism strength-

The real socialist and the newspaper idea of the socialist.

ened its grasp on a country weakened in the protracted struggle. Slowly, surely and insidiously a new slavery has enthralled a people—a wage slavery infinitely worse than that of human bondage. Brave soldiers, upon whose bodies are honorable scars, received in battle for the abolition of slavery, are to-day in a bondage compared with which the old slave days of the south seem as a pleasant memory.

"This is no figure of speech, no phantasy of words. It is a fact, a hideous reality. A nation has drifted into slavery. The crack of the slave-driver's whip is cringingly obeyed by ignoble slaves. The cruel mandates of the slave-owner are executed without a murmur of revolt from the white slaves of the republic.

"American liberty! American freemen! The free-born American citizen! The spirit of American institutions! What mean these phrases?

"Words with which to conjure the masses. Soft platitudes with which to flatter dupes. Meaningless terms which tickle the ears of fool slaves, who hug to their breasts the delusion of liberty and tamely submit to the lash.

"What is the picture drawn for your edification of the free-born American citizen? A stalwart, bearded workman in the full vigor of a splendid manhood; the protector of a fair wife and the father of happy children. He is an honest workman who looks every one full in the face and fears no man. He is a sovereign freeman, owning allegiance only to his country and to his God. Favors he asks of no man. With his strong arms and clean brain he can wrest from nature her wealth and secrets and bestow them upon his children. A hater of tyrants and tyranny, a lover of law and order, and a respecter of rights of all men. Ever jealous of his rights, watching with vigilance any encroachment upon his liberties, and ready at all times to take up arms in defense of his home, his family or his country. Independent, fearless, honest and ever industrious—such is the picture drawn of the free-born American citizen. Such was the American citizen of the long ago. What is he to-day? Let me sketch a typical American citizen of to-day.

"He is a workman in a great city. Factory labor has bent his shoulders and dimmed his eye. He lives in a rented house, and only yesterday the landlord handed the trembling wife a five days' notice to vacate the premises. He is out of employment. For three weeks he has been begging for work. The factories are closed—his fellow workmen and companions are powerless to lend him aid. The scant hoard saved from irregular toil has been exhausted. He is skilled in his craft and only asks to be allowed the use of his hands and brain. But it is a period of hard times. What shall he do? Take a farm in the undeveloped west? He knows nothing of farming, and there is no undeveloped west. An agent of a charitable institution calls at his home. The good wife suppresses a sigh, looks at the hungry children, swallows her pride and accepts with thanks the food that willing hands cannot earn. He is a free-born American citizen He is a voter. He is one of the nation's sovereigns He is an honest man. He is a slave.

"Another picture. He is a farmer. While yet the nation's lands had not been absorbed by railroad and land syndicates he pre-empted 160 acres of fertile land. As years passed by he sees the price of his grain decrease. He is robbed by railroad pools, fleeced by elevator syndicates, and upon the product of his labor speculators fatten. An iniquitous tariff system enhances the price of every article necessity compels him to purchase. In order to meet his obligations his wife becomes a drudge, and his children work on the farm instead of going to school. A failure of his crop plunges him into debt. He is in the mesh from which there is no escape. In a few years the mortgage is foreclosed. He is now a tenant farmer, a shade above a Russian serf. There are 3,000,000 such farmers in the United States. They are American citizens. They are honest workmen. They are voters, and they are slaves.

"Another picture. He is a merchant—a small tradesman. From his wages as a mechanic he has saved enough to start in business on a small scale. He is honest in his dealings with men. In fairly prosperous times he has enlarged his store, devoting his profits to that purpose. A panic comes. Factories close and his trade decreases. Workmen customers remain away or obtain credit. Rent continues and bills for goods fall due. The sheriff nails a notice over the door, and at the auction sale the agent of a great down-town store buys the goods for a trifle. The execution is satisfied and the merchant is ruined. Not from any fault of his own. He is a free American citizen, but a slave. His number is myriad. To whom are these men slaves? They are slaves to themselves. They are slaves to a system which they have helped fortify and which they have the power to overthrow.

"The people are enslaved because they deserve to be enslaved. Slavery is the natural condition for a people who have lost the very idea of what constitutes liberty. Men who will tamely submit to idleness, hunger and poverty, and accept it as a dispensation of Providence have never tasted liberty. The future has nothing to hope for from such men. Liberty can count no defenders in their ranks. History records the sufferings and the death of men who have devoted their lives to liberty and to the people, but no band of patriots ever slavishly starved in the name of their country and for their country's good.

"The slave must ever be freed; he cannot, he will not free himself. Slavery finds some of its most earnest champions among the slaves. In the armies of the south in the late rebellion were found many black men willing to sacrifice their lives in defense of a system which held them in bondage. A few negroes fought in the ranks of blue and fought nobly, but the great mass remained dormant and took only a passive interest in the battle for their freedom which was waging around them. They had been born slaves and taught that such was their natural condition. Their masters had quoted them passages from the Scriptures upholding the institution of slavery and they accepted their lot without question.

"Thus it is to-day. The poor are taught and repeat to each other that 'poverty is no crime,' that 'some must be poor and some must be rich.' They are consoled by the Scriptures. Christ's saying, 'The poor ye have always with you,' is distorted into a divine approval of poverty. They are taught to believe that there is consolation in the fact that it is 'easier for a camel to pass through the eye of a needle than for a rich man to enter into the kingdom of heaven,' and are coddled into a belief that earthly misery and suffering paves the way for an early entrance into the kingdom of heaven. An insult to the intelligence of the Supreme Being! The industrial slave takes a foolish pride in the increasing affluence of his master. From afar off he is content to gaze at the splendor of his establishment. He is elated at a passing glance from a factory lord, and a nod of recognition from a millionaire fills his simple heart with joy. Is this an overdrawn picture? No. It but faintly portrays an obseqiousness, a smirking humility, which has developed in the last twenty years and more clearly than anything else indicates the decadence of the proud spirit of equality and independence which once marked the citizen of the American republic. Show me an act of tyranny in the last generation at which thousands of its victims have not arisen and defended it! Point to an act of oppression and usurpation in which the oppressed and downtrodden have not kissed the hand which smote them!

"Unscrupulous men have taken advantage of the growing servility of the American people. Outrages against the people were committed in 1850 which would have been avenged in blood in 1800. National disgrace and scandal were glossed over in 1870 which would have plunged a nation into war in 1850. Crimes against the people were sanctioned, maintained by a form of law, and only feebly apologized for in 1893 which in the earlier years of our national life would not have been attempted, much less tolerated for a single day.

"The American people have been criminally patient. Patience with oppression and injustice is not a virtue but a crime—a crime whose penalty is national death.

"Delegates of the people, from out of the free prairies of the west a breeze is wafting, which with the coming of the dawn shall pile into fantastic shapes the now obscuring clouds. The rising sun shall tinge their edges with beauty until, like some enchanted dungeon, they shall scatter and melt into nothingness before the eyes of men. Truth is not dead; reason is not dead. Not until you blot from the human race the attributes of reason and truth shall liberty forever disappear.

"The battle must be fought and won by those who yet are free. Into their hands has been intrusted the fate of a nation founded by free men. The works of the enemy are not so formidable as they appear. Before the coming onslaught the already disorganized ranks of plutocracy will break and run.

"The time in which we live may be designated as the mechanical age. It had its birth in the years between 1800 and 1820 and reached its highest development in the period of 1870-90. Inventions will be made in the future, but as an era distinct in the progress of civilization the mechanical is already on the decline, and this gray old world is awaiting the advent of another and a grander epoch of progress. The mechanical age will make way for the age of government.

"Hail to the coming age, the grandest in the history of civilization! For centuries man devoted his energies to war. The earth shook with the tread of armies and her soil drank deep of the blood of contending hosts. The age of war reached its culmination in the eighteenth century, and with the growing years of the next century went into decline. The mechanical age forever checked war. It perfected death-dealing instruments; it made the destruction of human life a science. War became impossible. Nations dared not go to war. A battle meant death to nearly all engaged. War had become a science and it disappeared. The age of competition—the era of commercial activity and the struggle for business supremacy followed. Competition became a science and it disappeared in the mechanical age. War was dead, competition was dead, man was half-starving, but the machine survived.

"Great was the machine. It supplanted man, dethroned labor and ruled the world. Everywhere there was heard the whizzing of belts and pulleys and the ceaseless clatter of tireless metal. When the machine stopped the pulse of the nation beat slowly; when the wheels again revolved men went about with smiling faces. Great was the machine. By it nature had been subjugated and man enslaved. The enslaving of man was not primarily the fault of the machine, but was a logical outcome of attempting to harmonize the scientific with the unscientific. The machine was scientific. Its environment, the government, was crude and unscientific. In the language of a great philosopher, the introduction of modern machinery into the governmental conditions of to-day is like placing a triple expansion marine engine in one of the old wooden hulks built by the shipbuilders of a vanished generation. The engine was perfect, but the combination was disastrous. The powerful throbbing of the engine is fast shattering the feeble and rotten walls of the old hulk, and the water is pouring into the hole and the crew is in peril. The fault is not with the machine, but with the old hulk—the government. Run the old hulk into dry dock, take out the magnificent engine and place it where it belongs, in an environment fitted to stand the strain of a mechanical age.

"The age of government is the coming age. Progress has touched with its magic wand every science and art but that of government. Music, poetry, philosophy, war, medicine, literature, astronomy, mechanics, navigation have progressed with the advancing years. Government—the grandest study of man—has alone repelled the aid of science and with its eyes fixed on the past and its ears deaf to the higher activities of the present, exists among men to-day, grotesque, antique, incongruous. There is no applied science of government.

Where science and precision should prevail superstition and precedent hold sway. Modern government is a patchwork, handed down from an age of kings and of wars, for the observance of a people who hate kings and wars.

"In the future years earth's greatest heroes shall be its gifted lawgivers. Government will not become perfect from a multiplicity of laws, but the nation will prosper in proportion to the wisdom displayed by the people in the enactment and enforcement of just and simple laws. Government can never be an exact science. The wisdom of one generation is not sufficient to draft laws for a future it cannot read or whose changed condition it cannot comprehend. No age is empowered to enact an unalterable law. None but the criminally egotistic arrogate to themselves the attribute of infallibility. *A true government is one which profits by the lessons of the past, governs for the people of to day, and erects no bars for the generation of to-morrow.*

"Such is the government of the future, and in that day slavery will be dead and man shall live. In that cause I concentrate my energies and my life. Delegates of the people, I accept the responsibility you have reposed in me. Let us bury the past and lift our eyes to the future. Hail to the people! Hail to the coming age—the age of government!"

The ticket was completed by the nomination of Frank K. Foster of Boston, Mass., as Vice-President. Foster was an editor of ability and an orator eloquent and convincing.

CHAPTER XIV.

PRESS COMMENTS.

THE press greeted the work of the convention and Judge John Smith's nomination with comments, of which the following are fairly representative:

"A remarkable speech before a remarkable convention."—*St. Paul Globe.*

"Judge Smith's speech was a strange mingling of rare common sense and rank socialism."—*New York Sun.*

"The platform has the merit of brevity. It will be popular with those who believe that the world owes them a living, but is repugnant to the sturdy good sense of the average American."—*St. Louis Globe-Democrat.*

"At last the Smith family has been recognized. Judge John Smith seems to possess the hard-headed common sense of the Smiths and the inborn courage of an American who dares tell the truth. He calls a spade a spade, and the subjugation of the majority a crime. On this issue the American people are with him."—*New York Recorder.*

"Judge Smith's attack upon the Democratic party is unwarranted. The Democratic party has always stood for the people as against the encroachment of a moneyed aristocracy. The people will conserve their own interests by letting Smith and all such agitators severely alone."—*Atlanta Constitution.*

"The People's party has drifted into socialism. It has affirmed its belief in the odious theory of paternalism in government. Judge Smith is a radical, who disguises his socialism with a pretense of Americanism. The trouble with this country is not a lack but a superfluity of laws."—*New York World.*

"The platform ignores the tariff, free silver, greenbacks and wild-cat money, and all the old issues which have been flailed until the straw is pulverized. It confines itself to an affirmation of a belief in the right of the majority to rule and the right of a citizen to demand and obtain work. This is a new departure in politics and one which will be watched with interest." —*Pittsburg Despatch.*

"Judge John Smith is a politician. He is enough of a politician to take advantage of an issue which the people have been demanding for years and which the old parties, engrossed in the struggle for spoils, have ignored. The right of the majority to rule was affirmed in the declaration of independence and ignored by the constitution of the United States. The People's party may not go to victory on this issue, but they have done the country a service by forcing it to the fore."—*Kansas City Star.*

"Judge Smith's speech was the rant of a socialistic demagogue who is shrewd enough to take advantage of temporary hard times. The people of this country are not demanding paternalism with its state penitentiary system of work and compensation. In spite of Smith and other calamity howlers the people rule—ever have and ever will. His tirade against the constitution of the United States comes with poor grace from a man whom the people of Chicago once honored with an election as judge. It is little short of treason."—*Chicago Tribune.*

"When Judge Smith declared that the right of the majority to govern has been lost he told the truth, and he told it well. All the platitudes of professional patriots and self-styled Americans to the contrary notwithstanding, the constitution of this country does not guarantee the rule of the majority of the people. The performances of the Senate in recent years should be sufficient to prove this statement to intelligent men. This issue must be met. Abuse, lying, subterfuge, and cheers for the old flag will not prevail against cold, hard facts. The majority do not rule; honest, willing men are denied work. The majority must rule; the right of men to work must be granted."—*Baltimore American.*

"The platform is an open attack upon the constitution of the United States. The reforms which Judge Smith and his adherents propose can be accomplished only by the practical repeal of the fundamental clauses of that document. This issue is made plain. The contest is to be between those who believe in the perpetuity of American institutions as bequeathed us by Washington and Jefferson and those who have lost faith in the republic and seek its overthrow. There can be but one outcome. Fanaticism will be defeated and the republic will live."—*Milwaukee Sentinel.*

"Does the majority rule? Have the American people been deluded into a belief that the republic is in reality not a sham? Has a citizen an unalienable right to demand and obtain work? These are questions which must be answered. Judge John Smith, the Populist candidate for the presidency, speaks in no uncertain tone upon these issues. He denounces representative government as a failure and declares that the people can assert themselves only by a direct vote on all great public questions. This is not a novel idea, but is presented in a new light. The campaign will be unique in the history of politics."—*Omaha World-Herald.*

"The sober sense of the American workman will repudiate the Populist platform. His salvation lies not in an assurance of governmental protection and work, but in the tearing down of the tariff wall, which denies him a chance to work in those industries which should compete in the markets of the world. The Democratic party is pledged to the destruction of that tariff, and a little patience on the part of the people is all that is needed. Nothing will be gained by a support of the radical and even revolutionary doctrines advanced by Judge Smith and affirmed in the platform of his party."—*Louisville Courier-Journal.*

"Mark Kimbly and not Judge John Smith is the true friend of the American workmen. Smith has sullied his fame as a judge and developed into a dangerous agitator with the temerity to attack the constitution of the United States. In the coming election the American workman will repudiate the Hilds and the Smiths and the other enemies of protection for American workmen and American homes. The twin foes of American workmen are free trade, represented by Hild and the Democracy, and anarchy, as represented by Smith and the Populists. Hurrah for Kimbly and the old flag! Down with anarchy and up with the stars!"—*Chicago Inter Ocean.*

"In a country where every American citizen is a sovereign voter and a free man there is no room for men like Judge Smith. The government which produced a Washington, a Jefferson, a Lincoln, a Grant and a Garfield cannot be destroyed by any crank or set of cranks howling about majority rule. There is plenty of work in this country for men who want work. There is no room for loafers and agitators who seek to make capital out of the temporary financial distress of the community. If Judge Smith and his colleagues do not like this country they are at liberty to get out of it."—*St. Paul Pioneer-Press.*

"There is the true ring of Americanism in Judge Smith's speech accepting the people's nomination for the presidency. He is an American citizen of that sturdy type that is not afraid to denounce tyranny wherever he finds it. When Judge Smith declares that the constitution of the United States has fostered and perpetuated the rule of the minority he says what every Democrat and every honest man knows to be true. If a belief in the rights and rule of the majority is socialism the great mass of the American people are socialists. Judge Smith has given the people an issue which must be met. He has cleared the political atmosphere and the situation stands plainly revealed. He has done what the Democratic party should have done years ago—affirmed faith in the intelligence of the majority. The fact is that both the Republican and the Democratic parties are under the control of

men who fear the people. They will be found among the stanchest defenders of a political system which in theory is founded on the will of the people, but which in reality holds them firmly in check. Under existing conditions the reign of the majority is a myth; a legend told by designing demagogues and listened and heeded by gullible voters. Unless it shall become a reality American liberty is forever lost. THE TIMES will support Judge John Smith for the presidency and predicts a victory which will sweep from power the enemies of majority rule and inaugurate the reign of the people."
—*Kansas City Times.*

In the short limits of this book it is impossible to give an extended account of the presidential campaign of 1900. It was waged with extreme bitterness. The Republicans and Democrats fought on the familiar old party lines, varied only by an increased attention to the third party. As the campaign progressed the Populists made astonishing inroads on the strength of the old parties. Judge Smith confined himself entirely to the large cities and addressed immense audiences of business and working men. The accession to his ranks seemed divided almost equally between both parties and both claimed the advantage. During the campaign there was little change in the business situation. Some factories were running on half time and wages steadily decreased in spite of the activity of the unions, whose discipline was threatened and eventually ruined by the long-continued hard times. Members with large families rebelled against remaining idle part of the time for the common benefit of the unions and desertion became common. Employers took advantage of this growing feeling of dissatisfaction among trade unionists and as a result a series of strikes followed. The summer of 1899 witnessed the practical disruption of the trade union movement. A writer in a New York magazine thus summed up the causes which led to the downfall of that stupendous organization of workmen:

TRADE UNIONISM IS DEAD.

"Hunger is stronger than discipline. Men will face

the black muzzles of cannon without a quiver, but will tremble and cower before the wail of a hungry child. The trade union movement reached its height in 1898. It enrolled as its membership practically all the wage toilers of the nation. In the boom incident to the war scare there was work for all. The panic which followed did not disorganize the ranks. They apportioned the work among the members, and for over a year maintained their ranks unbroken against the forces of industrial depression. But hunger is a relentless enemy. He works in the weary hours of the night and gnaws at the vitals of his victims, silent and insatiate. Hunger has won. The trade union has fallen. The arguments of industrial economy fell powerless on ears which could not resist the pleadings of half-starved children. At first there were a few desertions. Then men refused to work with the deserters and a strike followed, the employers declaring their intention of repudiating their agreement with the unions and employing whom they pleased at prices mutually satisfactory to those who accepted work. They justified this policy by the statement that alternate periods of work and idleness lessened the skill of the workmen. The temptation to secure steady employment was too strong to be resisted. One concern after another adopted the steady work system, and had little difficulty in obtaining deserters from the ranks of the unions. The faithful members saw their places filled by those whom hunger had weakened. The defection became a stampede and trade unionism was doomed. Probably 55 per cent of the former members are now at work. Their positions are threatened by the unemployed 45 per cent, who do not hesitate to bid against the employed and find justification in the fact that the latter were traitors against a system which insured at least a pittance for all. Under this fierce competition wages are tending lower, and have already reached a point where the man who now works full time receives about the same as he did when he worked half time. It is noteworthy that in spite of this decided decrease in the wage fund the price of manufactured products has not appreciably decreased, although there is a constantly diminishing demand for the products of factory and mill."

No other result could have been expected. The trade union stood alone, as a barrier against that competition which, unrestrained, inevitably forced wages down to a point where men would consent to work—the starvation line. That is the iron law of wages. Under a competitive system in which the workers exceed the demand for work, the starvation line is the one around which wages slightly fluctuate. Men will not work for less than will support life, but that wage which will support a single man is inadequate for the man of family. The stern necessities of the married man therefore limit the point below which wages cannot far tend without a revolt. The trade union recognized the inexorable force of this natural law and stood as a barrier against it. So did the trust. Under free competition between manufacturers and jobbers profits ever tended to decrease until they reached and fell below the line where profit ceased and loss ensued. Any slight industrial depression or congestion forced prices below this line and hundreds of producing concerns failed trom this cause. The trusts opposed a barrier against fhis and by the aid of co-operation and favorable legislation defied the forces of competition and maintained artificial prices. Hunger did not menace the trust. The commercial greed and selfishness of its members occasionally led to brief disorganization, but in 1900, as in 1893, the trust had learned its lesson well and was firmly bound by the strongest of ties, those of self-defense and self-interest.

Trade unionism was dead and the trust survived. The crushing defeat of the unions was gleefully received by certain people who had ever held that the organization was one which checked the independence of the American workman. He had plenty of liberty now and spent most of his time roaming the streets in search of work, pouring into the ears of employers tales of woe, and offering to go to work at any price which would keep soul and body together. Eighteen hundred and ninety-three destroyed one delusion—the people learned under the existing conditions that economy was a failure; that the general saving of money meant general dèpression and distress. This year destroyed another delusion—the workmen learned that no combination of workers could maintain wages under a system of limited production.

The Democrats were badly handicapped in the campaign of 1900. Their ranks had been split by the silver issue and the more progressive of the party had gone over to the Populists. Hild, their presidential candidate, was a skilled politician, but it soon became evident that the fight was between the Populists and the Republicans. The south had rebelled against the bourbons, and the frantic appeals of the fire-eaters were in vain against the victorious march of the People's party. The west was in revolt against both old parties. In the early part of October it was generally conceded that every state west of the Mississippi, with the possible exceptions of Arkansas, Texas and California, would cast their votes for Smith and Foster. It was the south and west against the east, with the Ohio valley as fighting ground. The Republicans made their fight on the gold standard, high tariff and pensions for all soldiers. They raised an immense campaign fund and flooded the country with speakers and literature. The Democrats lacked the advantage of federal patronage and were badly in need of money. As the day of election approached the excitement became intense.

CHAPTER XV.

EXTRACTS FROM CAMPAIGN SPEECHES.

JUDGE SMITH delivered addresses in New York, Boston, Providence, Albany, Rochester, Buffalo, Philadelphia, Baltimore, Pittsburg, Detroit, Cincinnati, Indianapolis, Cleveland, Louisville, St. Louis, Kansas City, Omaha, St Paul, Milwaukee and Chicago. The author has been permitted to select from these speeches—which will shortly be published in full, with the history of the life of John Smith—such extracts as created the most comment at that time.

Extract from speech delivered in New York City, August 14: "No political party or social theory that attacks the right to own property can ever succeed in the United States. I care not how much property a man has acquired under the laws of the United States, he is entitled to that property or a fair compensation in consideration thereof. No system of government or taxation which aims directly or indirectly at the appropriation or confiscation of wealth, honestly acquired by labor, capital, or both, will ever meet the sanction of the American people. The love of property is deeply implanted in the human nature. It is a sentiment not to be uprooted, but to be wisely nourished and cultivated.

"The charge has been made that the People's party proposes to confiscate the bulk of the property in this country under the leadership of a desperate socialist—myself. It is hardly necessary for me to assure the good people of New York that we have no designs on the massive and beautiful buildings which for miles make Broadway the grandest business street in the world. We may look almost with envy on the palaces of Fifth Avenue, but no hand shall be raised against them in the name of the people. Not in our platform, not in the minds of our leaders, not in the great heart of the people exists there a thought of taking by force or theft that which can be duplicated by labor. We claim—and when the will of the majority shall vest us with authority shall demand—that every citizen of the republic again be clothed in that God-given and man-denied right to work and earn a living for himself and for his children. We intend to beat down the obstructions which skilled politicians have interposed against an expression of the voice of the people.

"None of the rights of property is in peril because of these demands. The owner of the great factory may rest secure in his possession. The people can duplicate his factory. The landlord with his thousand tenement-houses need not fear the uprising of an indignant and rent-racked population. The people can build houses. The man with the little home and plot of ground has naught to fear. The people desire not the fruits of his labor. The capitalist with his bonds and mortgages, his accumulated stock of gold and gold-bearing securities, need fear no invasion of modern Goths and Vandals. The people cannot eat money and their willing hands can produce all that money can buy.

"But the people cannot produce land. The labor of a million generations cannot produce a continent. Land existed before man, and with water and air will survive when man shall be no more forever. Land is not property. Concede the right to monopolize land and you affirm the justice of human slavery. The people must have land and they will have it, but so long as my voice shall prevail it will not be acquired by confiscation. Unwise laws handed down from past ages have made land a legal property and its holders are entitled to just compensation for any land which passes from them into the hands of the people. The government—the people—possesses the right of eminent domain. A railroad, under the same right exercised in the name of the people, cuts its way across a continent, condemning property and reimbursing its owners in proportion as justice may direct. The people have that same right and existing laws empower them to use it. We affirm the right of the people to exercise eminent domain and acquire such lands as public policy may from time to time direct, paying therefor a fair and honest compensation. More than that the people do not demand; less than that they will not accept.

"I am aware that vast tracts of land have been acquired from the government by favoritism, bribery and fraud. Some of this land still remains in the hands of those who wrested it from the people and some has passed into the possession of innocent purchasers. They have paid for it and should be protected. No man should be defrauded out of a dollar of the money he has honestly invested, be it in land or in property. But the people will demand their own. They will condemn and purchase under the right, not alone of eminent domain, but under the higher right—the right to live—all lands held for speculative purposes, all lands which the present generation cannot occupy, and will hold it as a sacred trust for the children of the future. There are many who urge that all such land should be confiscated without the payment of a dollar in return, and while such a procedure would result in no injustice to thousands of dishonest speculators, it would wrong some innocent people. Nationalism seeks to work injustice to no man.

"The people demand only that land which the present generation cannot use. That they will have, and all the forces of wealth and prejudice shall not prevail against them.

"Upon some of the land thus acquired the government will erect shops and factories, confining itself at the start to those industries most indispensable to the actual needs of the people. Farming and mining land will be developed on such an industrial plan as the people may elect. So long as a human want remains unsatisfied, so long will there be employment. Those who work will receive the profits of their toil.

"We have in contemplation no plan of socialism or communism in which the products of an industrial community are to be equally apportioned among its members; no scheme by which the dull and the proficient, the weak and the strong, the lazy and the energetic shall work on a common plane. There may be advocates of such a policy, but they are not delegated to voice the principles of the People's party.

"We contemplate the establishment of a system of industry in which the government shall hold in trust certain property in the interests of the people. No man will be compelled to work for the state. No effort will be made to destroy or ruin the various industries which exist to-day. We simply propose that the government shall ever retain in its possession enough of the tools and means of production to insure remunerative employment for all who demand it. If, under the management of the United States, the people cannot produce enough to support themselves, starvation is the only alternative. No such calamity will ensue.

"Give the people a chance to work and this country will witness a prosperity unexampled in the history of the world. Look at what we propose to do. There are to-day not less than 5,000,000 men out of work. Upon these men 10,000,000 people are dependent. Fifteen millions of people are, therefore, living on charity. So far as the community is concerned, they are a burden. The wealthy must support them. For years the rich of the United States have been supporting by taxation and charity a number of people sufficient to form a powerful nation. The People's party proposes to take this burden from the shoulders of the rich.

"We propose to make these 5,000,000 men producers and not paupers. Each one of them can earn $2 a day and add that amount to the national wealth. Ten million dollars a day, $3,000,000,000 a year; twice the amount of the national debt. Every dollar of this is added wealth. Every dollar of that enormous sum represents a necessity and comfort which is now denied.

"Such is the policy of the People's party. It is not

socialism. It is common sense applied to affairs of state. Government has too long been conducted on sentiment; it is time that accepted business principles were applied."

EXTRACT FROM SPEECH DELIVERED IN BOSTON, AUGUST 18.

"Stunted production is the curse which is afflicting the nation. If the combined products of American manufactories were divided equally among the 70,000,000 people of the United States, we should be a shabbily dressed, poorly shod and half-starved people. The general prosperity of a nation can exist only under two conditions, viz., an adequate production and a comprehensive system of distribution. We have neither. In this respect our country is not more unfortunate than other countries, but that is no argument. The United States should be an earthly paradise as compared with any of the densely populated, land-starved nations of Europe.

"Does anybody pretend that in this country an average man by the unrestricted exercise of his labor is unable to create enough to support life? No. And yet men are denied labor. It is almost impossible to obtain accurate statistics of the numbers of the unemployed. I doubt if in the last thirty years there have been twelve consecutive months in which there was work for all who wanted it. In various places at divers times there has been a demand for labor which the immediate community could not furnish, but idle men cannot travel from Chicago to San Francisco in search of work which may not last more than three months. The percentage of the unemployed has steadily increased. Forced idleness begets loaferism. The discharged mechanic of to-day is the tramp of the future.

"All wealth is created by labor. The United States to-day is worth just what the men who have toiled with hands and brains have created. The man engaged in useful toil counts in the assets of to-day. He is valuable to the nation just in proportion as he is productive.

The idle man, be he rich or poor, idle from choice or idle from necessity—the idle man counts in the schedule of liabilities. He consumes without producing. When an idle man dies the liabilities of the country are reduced. When one of them goes to work the country is a distinct gainer.

"It does not cost the country much more to support an idle millionaire than it does to support a tramp. The millionaire can eat so much food and wear out so many clothes. The tramp eats three meals a day and wears out old clothes. Both the idle tramp and the idle millionaire consume products for which they render no return. The millionaire cannot eat his houses, his lands or any of his property. He holds them while he lives and they remain in the country after he is dead. The community has simply been compelled to feed and clothe him during his lifetime. He is enabled to leave $1,000,000 behind for the simple reason that in his lifetime he could not consume it if he tried. True, he could squander it, but property squandered, lost in gambling or in speculation, is not lost national wealth. It has simply changed hands. I desire to make this point plain, and therefore repeat that in spite of all the cry about bloated bondholders and millionaires eating up the substance of the country, the hungriest millionaire cannot eat more than twice as much as the hungriest tramp.

"But the idle millionaire is of some use to the country and the idle workman and the tramp are not. The millionaire pays taxes and the idle workman does not and cannot. It is said that labor pays all the tax. As a rule that is true, but there comes a time when the burden is shifted to the shoulders of the rich. In periods like the present, when wages have reached the lowest point at which men will work, labor pays no taxes. The idle millions must live. Some die of starvation and as the result of long continued privation, but the majority live, and live at the expense of the rich. Charity must be extended or revolution and riots follow. Public charities depend upon taxation, and private charities are founded by the rich. The moneyed class is therefore interested, or should be interested, in the abolition of idleness.

"Chicago has given the world two examples of what can be accomplished by pressing into service the idle workmen of a nation. In 1871 the great fire swept $200,000,000 worth of property out of existence and in two years the bulk of that property was reproduced. The idle workmen of a hundred cities flocked to Chicago and upon the smoking ruins erected palaces which stand to-day the admiration of the world. Did this influx of workmen to Chicago absorb the surplus of unemployed? Did Boston or New York or Philadelphia suffer for want of workmen while Chicago was being rebuilt? Not at all. A year later and a panic swept over the country and 2,500,000 men were thrown out of work. Even the burning of Chicago could not check the coming of a panic caused by an overproduction.

"When Chicago built the Columbian Exposition it required the constant vigilance of the local trade unions to prevent the idle army of the country from moving on Chicago. Even while 20,000 men were at work in the grounds and 50,000 were engaged in preparing exhibits, Chicago had 25,000 men looking for work. An insignificant fraction of the idle army reared in a little over a year the grandest group of buildings the world has ever gazed on. The rapidity with which the great exposition was built is one of the wonders of the age.

"Like magic an enchanted city grew from a swamp in a little over a year. Trained contractors and architects were no less astounded than laymen, and watched giant palaces grow almost in a night. And this sublime task was pushed to completion by a single regiment of the grand army of the unemployed.

"Had the romancer or the political economist predicted that which actually happened at Jackson Park he would have been denounced as wild and visionary. One one-hundredth part of the idle men of America built in a little over a year the peerless white city, the sublime realization of the dreams of architect, artist and poet; the matchless wonder of the world.

"The people of the United States, irrespective of party, are seeking a solution of the problem of the unemployed. A few greedy manufacturers may desire a surplus of workmen who shall forever bid against each other for work, but the best brain of the age is earnestly searching for a true remedy. The politicians of the Republican and Democratic parties are not to be trusted. With them it is the same old fight between the employed and the unemployed. The Republicans have a job and the Democrats want it; the Democrats have a position and the Republicans seek it. They whisper into the ear of their employer, the people, delusive promises, and on false pretenses secure a four-year contract. The people are about to dispense with the services of both these corrupt and inefficient workmen.

"The Republican party pities the unemployed and assures the idle workmen that under a protective tariff there is work for all. But we are under a protective tariff now and have been for years. That does not disturb the serenity of the Republican politician. He ascribes the cause to 'lack of confidence in the Democratic party' and to a 'fear of a revision of the tariff.'

"General Grant was President in 1873. He had been elected by a tremendous majority. The tariff was not threatened and protection prevailed in all its glory. But the panic came and millions were out of work for years. I have no patience to discuss the protective tariff. Workmen who yet believe in it deserve to die of starvation.

"Democracy urges free trade. Free trade is logically right, but it does not guarantee work to the citizens of a nation. We had a condition approaching free trade before the war, but it did not prevent the panic of 1857. England has had free trade for nearly a century, and while the nation has grown rich, her artisans are out of work during long periods in which the suffering is intense. England makes the world work for her capitalists. The crowning ambition of some of our statesmen is to shape a policy so that 'English gold will be invested in the United States.' We are told that if we are good, English millionaires will send task-masters over here and put us to work. They will hire us to build railroads in the United States for England and Belgium and Germany—that is, if we are real good and don't scare them away. The advocates of free trade assert that under it America can compete in the markets of the world.

"We are told that under free trade the United States will manufacture for the world all the cotton and woolen goods, the iron, steel, agricultural implements, knives, watches, and in fact all manufactured products. What a glorious prospect! We shall become the hired girl of nations, the tireless, faithful drudge, working from year to year for the people of England, Germany, France, Holland, Spain, Italy and Russia. That may be the ambition of some statesmen, but it is not mine.

"Here is the policy of the people: The first duty of the United States is to manufacture enough of those products the raw material of which nature has lavished upon us for the people of this country. It should then produce and sell abroad a surplus sufficient to purchase from the continent and the orient those necessities and luxuries which are produced abroad and not at home. And when that demand is satisfied—stop. Reduce the hours of labor and take life easier. What sense is there in impoverishing a country of its resources of timber, iron and fertile soil merely that a people slave themselves with work to pile up gold that cannot be legitimately spent?

"Workmen of America, how much longer will you be deluded by these false issues of protection and free trade? How much longer will you stupidly follow some ass who tells you that free silver or paper money is the one thing needful? You want work. You have votes. You are in the majority. Your liberty of voting has not been taken from you. By those votes vest the government with authority to guarantee work and the products of that work to every man who demands it.

"Cease your railing against the millionaires. Their property is not hurting you. The idle millions of American workmen can create more property in a week than the combined possessions of the richest men in the world. The United States is a vast tract of fertile land filled with inexhaustible mines and is sparsely populated. It is capable of a demonstration by figures that the workmen of America can in twenty years more than duplicate all the tangible property in the United States.

"They can reproduce on a grander scale all the great cities, towns and villages, the farmhouses, barns and fences, the 175,000 miles of railroad and its rolling stock, depots and properties, and every colossal project which labor and capital have created from the Atlantic to the Pacific, from the Gulf of Mexico to the British line.

"The imagination cannot grasp the tremendous possibilities of modern methods of production. That which required the labor of thousands of men for months forty years ago is now performed by children in a day. In machinery we have summoned into existence a genie which threatens us with destruction. Whisper a word into his ear and he becomes an obedient slave What is that word? Co-operation."

Appended is an extract from a speech delivered by Mr. Smith, candidate for President. It was at a Philadelphia meeting held August 25, and this is what the speaker said:

"I am in receipt of a letter from the president of your board of trade, in which I am asked 'whether I am in favor of honest money.' While this is tantamount to asking me if I prefer the right as against the wrong, all things being equal, I shall take no offense and unhesitatingly answer the gentleman in the affirmative.

"The money issue does not appear in the platform of our party. The men who framed that platform did not consider the question of sufficient importance at the present time to force it to the front. Money—honest, dishonest, silver, gold and paper—is an issue between the debtor and creditor class of this country.

"The unemployed workmen of this country belong to neither of these classes. They have nothing to lend and no one will extend them credit. Just at present they are endeavoring to take such political action as will guarantee them work. When they obtain that work they intend to retain the products of that work after paying their debts and their fair share of the expenses of the government. They have assumed that it will not be a difficult task to arrange some system by which the products of their toil can be exchanged.

"The president of your board of trade may rest assured that whatever may be the medium of exchange adopted by the people—when they shall have established their right to work—it will be an honest one. I very much doubt if any considerable portion of the people will devote their time to the mining of money.' If it shall be found necessary, as it doubtless will, to mine gold and silver for use in the sciences and arts, Mother Nature will be called upon for such resources, but we shall not devote valuable time or waste muscular tissue in delving the soil for a medium of exchange.

"Let us imagine an inhabitant, say, of Mars, upon which planet they had a system of finance and exchange strange to us. Let us imagine this visitor from Mars making a trip here for the purpose of writing for our heavenly neighbor a book on his 'Impressions of America.' He lands in Colorado and Senator Wildcot shows him around the Centennial State. They proceed to Leadville or Aspen and inspect the great mines.

"'This is the greatest silver and gold mine in America,' explains the senator. 'Three thousand men are digging these treasures from the ground. Sixty-five per cent is silver and thirty-five per cent is gold.'

"'Oh, yes. It is very interesting. Is it hard work?' asked the gentleman from Mars.

"'Rather hard, but it is good pay.'

"'What is gold used for, may I inquire?'

"'Money.'

"'Excuse my ignorance, but what is money?' asked the puzzled martial gentleman.

"'Why, money is a medium of exchange. It fixes the price of things, regulates values and all that.'

"'How?'

"'Because there is not much of it. It is hard to get. It represents so much labor. The supply is limited, you see, and it cannot fluctuate much.' The senator appeared ill at ease.

"'I hardly understand. You say it represents so much labor. Then these men have all the money they find. How do other people—'

"'No, no,' interrupted the senator. 'The men who do the work don't have the silver or gold. They are hired to dig it. It belongs to the mine-owners I own several mines myself.'

"'You puzzle me. I cannot understand what fixes the standard. You said labor. Do you always pay the laborers the same price?'

"'No; they form unions and raise the price sometimes.'

"'Are all mines equally rich in minerals?'

"'I should say not. The silver mines are too blamed rich. A few years ago they became so rich that the United States stopped buying silver.'

"'Remarkable system,' mused the visitor. 'Do all the people own silver and gold mines?'

"'Well, hardly.'

"'How do they get gold and silver?'

"'They exchange things for it—boots, horses, wheat, pictures, everything'

"'What do they want of the gold and silver?'

"'Why, it's money, I told you--a medium of exchange. They have to have it' The senator was perspiring.

"'But you said that three years ago the government refused to purchase silver because there was too much of it. What do they use now?'

"'Gold.'

"'Suppose you should mine so much gold that the government would not buy it, what would the people then do for money?'

"'Damned if I know,' said Senator Wildcot. 'Let's go back to the hotel.'

"'They had such a system as that on the moon,' said the traveler from Mars, 'but they outgrew it 8,400,000 years ago.'

"The power to issue money should be vested in the general government and in that alone. The United States government is to-day the richest property-owner in the world. Uncle Sam schedules as assets:

"Seventy millions of people, 30,000,000 of whom are or should be producers.

"Vast tracts of land.

"Hundreds of thousands of miles of roads and thoroughfares.

"More than $200,000,000 invested in public buildings.

"A public-school system, a postal system, an army and navy with vast stores of ammunitions.

"Can you place a money estimate on that property? Would ten billions or twenty billions of dollars cover it? In commercial transactions a man's note is good for at least half of his unimpaired assets. Uncle Sam is in debt a trifle over a billion of dollars, and under any reasonable system of finance and production could pay that in two years. I hold that the credit of the United States is good for any obligation that the people care to assume. We are told that the United States cannot purchase the railroads. If the people have created something greater than themselves, if the railroads are more than the state, this assertion is true.

"The unit of money should be based upon the average productivity of an hour's or a day's labor, and its credit should be based on the resources of the government and its fundamental right to levy taxes. Gold has no more right to govern as a standard of value than have undressed hides or peacock feathers. The fact that it is accepted as a standard, and that it has been so accepted for thousands of years, is the strongest argument why it should be abolished.

"I am not authorized to forecast just what will be the form of the currency adopted by the people, but it requires no prophetic instinct to assert that it will not be silver or gold. If the people in their wisdom decree that it will be safe to advance money with silver or gold as security they will do so. If they elect that the government be authorized to issue a currency, accepting as security houses, lands, imperishable manufactured products and available and convertible property of whatever kind, such will be a part of the financial policy of the future. And any money thus issued will be 'honest money,' and will pass current among the people as a medium of exchange, convertible at all times into any product that labor can create or any service civilization can render. And when that time comes, and whatever form the currency may take, I have an abiding faith that a way will be found to exchange American wheat for English woolens and American sewing machines for Chinese teas, even though the gold standard prevail in every heathen and semi-civilized nation on the face of the globe."

EXTRACT FROM SPEECH DELIVERED BY JOHN SMITH AT CINCINNATI, SEPT. 2, 1900.

"In recent years we have heard a great deal about 'confidence.' If the papers are to be trusted—and they fairly reflect what the public believes to be the truth—the prosperity of the country is entirely a matter of 'confidence.' You pick up your morning paper and here is what you read:

"'The business interests in every part of the country are less sanguine and the tone of trade is less confident.'

"'An increase of the tariff on soap and scissors would greatly tend to restore the confidence of the business world.'

"'The rates on money still tend upward, and there is no decrease in the feeling of timidity among bankers and capitalists. The unconditional repeal of the tax on walnuts would speedily brighten affairs.'

"'Bohmer & Co. failed to-day for $362,000. Mr. Bohmer ascribes his embarrassment to the prevailing business depression and lack of confidence.'

"'Not until confidence is fully restored will business assume its normal proportions,' etc.

"All of which is perfectly true. Under the business, mercantile and productive systems which the last fifty years have developed, everything is more or less regulated by 'confidence.' Not of the entire community—not by any means. It makes little difference whether the man who works has 'confidence' or not. He does not count. It is the man of money, the banker, the merchant, the manufacturer, who alternately burns with a fever of speculation or chills with a lack of confidence. When confidence is abroad in the land work is plenty, vast workshops resound with the din of industry, and at evening long processions of tired but happy workmen wend their way homeward. When the business world has lost this cud of confidence, this magic wand or potent incantation, depression reigns, industry is paralyzed, children beg on the streets, and poorhouses and prisons are crowded to their doors.

"How tenderly the financial high priests and commercial quacks nurse the new-born babe of confidence, the stunted infant of hard times born in travail and agony! Its feeble life is preserved for a time, but loud lamentations arise when, after a few years of miserable existence, the pale youth passes away.

"What is business confidence? Where does it come from? Why is it necessary and what can be done to perpetuate it? These are questions which should be answered. Let us analyze the situation.

"Business is conducted for profit. Manufacturing is in the hands of men who have invested money and expect some return for it. So long as a steady demand exists for goods produced, manufacturers, jobbers and retailers are assured of profits, provided they exercise reasonable business discretion and economy. But a time comes when the demand for products decreases. Then is when the business world begins to lose confidence. They have their hand upon the public pulse. It may be a false alarm and the demand may again resume a normal stage. Sooner or later the symptoms reappear. Trade falls off, the manufacturers take alarm, the shops shut down, confidence is lost, and hard times are on. Confidence in what? In the people; in the power of the consumer to keep up with the machinery of production. The reservoir is full to the top and threatens to run over. The engines of production are shut down.

"Money is a coward, and gold is the greatest coward of all. Money is not only a coward, but it is an ignorant, blundering coward, whose head is devoid of brains and filled with timidity. Money does not know when it is in danger, and as a rule is most timid when there is nothing to fear, and assumes a bravado when there is real danger. Money never created hard times. When the keen-eyed manufacturer perceives that he has produced more than enough to meet the demand, the country, ignorant of that fact, is yet in its normal condition. Money knows nothing of the manufacturer's secret, and likely enough is at that very moment duplicating the great factory which is about to close its doors. The factory shuts down. Gold trembles. A bank shuts down. Bankers raise their rates of interest and call in loans. The people become alarmed, a run on the banks ensues, every one secures all the money he can and locks it up. The panic is on. Gold has locked himself up in a cage and the chattering of the teeth tells of his pitiful cowardice. But gold did not precipitate the panic. The manufacturer made the panic and gold did the running. A period follows in which gold refuses to leave his cage. Three or four months pass and finally he ventures out. He is not harmed and loses some of his fears. Money flows back into the banks. The rates of interest fall. Money becomes a drug in the market. The manufacturers cannot use it. They are not ready to start up their shops. The surplus of manufactured goods yet remains unsold. Such was the experience in 1893 and such was the experience in all preceding panics.

"The panic of 1893 was made the subject of more partisan misrepresentation than anything which ever occupied public attention. In their attempt to make political capital and to secure a temporary partisan advantage out of a great national calamity public speakers and writers lied about the causes of the panic or knowingly and maliciously distorted the facts. Every thoughtful business man, banker or manufacturer, every student of political economy, and every intelligent citizen of the United States knew in August, 1893, that the panic was caused by an overproduction of manufactured goods. The factories began to shut down in the latter part of 1892, when the country was enjoying almost unexampled prosperity. Hundreds of them had closed down before the general public were aware of it. There suddenly developed a demand for the repeal of the silver bill. Republican and Democratic papers, Republican and Democratic orators, Republican and Democratic partisans declared that the factories were closed down because the banks would not advance money to the shop-owners. This assertion was made again and again and never refuted. It was absolutely false. The manufacturers did not want money. They did not close down on account of a money stringency or a money panic. A financial panic and a stringency followed because the factories closed down. The factories were the cause and not the effect.

"The people did not know this. They were told that work would be resumed just as soon as the banks had money to lend. They believed this. When the panic fwas past money began to pour into the banks, but the factories did not resume work. What was the matter? The predictions of the politicians had not come true. The Sherman silver bill had been repealed, money was plenty, but the hard times continued worse than ever before.

"Money never created an industrial depression and never averted one.

"Politics never created an industrial depression and never averted one. Manufacturers do not allow politicians to interfere in business affairs and the demand of the manufacturers fixes the rate of interest at the banks.

"When the factory shuts down, the banker knows that there is trouble ahead. He therefore lends no more money. He begins to prepare for the inevitable run on the bank. During the panic money cannot be had. The banker does not know who is in danger of failing. After the scare is over depositors return their money and the banker waits for men with security who want money. The factory-owner has plenty of security, but he does not need money. The banker has plenty of 'confidence,' but it availeth nothing without the 'confidence' of the manufacturer.

"A day finally comes when the mill owner decides to open the doors of the shop and put his men to work. He does not ask the banker when to resume. He has been examining the shelves of the retailers. They are empty. The surplus has been consumed. He borrows the necessary money and the wheels of the great factory again revolve. Another factory does the same thing. The bank raises the rate of interest. Good times have come. Everything is on the boom. Money prances around and builds new factories and the rates go higher and higher.

"A few years roll by and again the manufacturer shuts down, a panic follows, and the same performance is repeated.

"The kingpin, therefore, is the manufacturer. He shuts down not because he wants to, but because he has to. He watches the consumer. The banker watches the manufacturer and such of the statistics of trade as he can reach. He 'obtains confidence' and 'loses confidence' in this way. The system is simple and amusing.

"It has been politically impossible to successfully assail the Chinese wall of protective tariff. Manufacturers who close on account of overproduction have lyingly told their workmen that the reason for their so doing was either a lack of sufficient tariff or a fear that the existing one was about to be reduced. Lying editors have backed up this falsehood. Some factories have curtailed their production for fear that an immediate reduction in the tariff would find them with a stock of goods on hand which might have to be sold at a slight sacrifice, but these cases are rare. Not all of the workmen have been fools enough to believe what protection editors have told them, but the forces of ignorance in a close election are powerful and too often have prevailed.

"We therefore witness in this country a remarkable phenomenon. We have a country of unsurpassed natural resources as yet hardly touched. We have a strong, willing and industrious population, intelligent on all subjects save that of government, and the greatest inventors on the face of the earth. They are attempting to exist under a social, business and producing system so highly nervous in its organism that an inquiry about its health is likely to bring on a state of extreme depression. Business is a bed-ridden invalid, covered with fever sores, the victim of political quacks who grow rich by applying nostrums which aggravate the disease.

"Clear your brains for a monent, voters of America, and indulge in the luxury of a thought unclouded by bigotry, custom or prejudice.

"Suppose that the people of America should wake up one of these beautiful autumnal days, when the glorious old sun shines down on field and meadow, on forest and mine, on lakes, bays and rivers, glinting the sails of commerce; when warm breezes waft into waves vast fields of grain, until a continent from the Atlantic to the Pacific, rich beyond the dreams of the fabled Crœsus, lies bathed in sunlight, awaiting the coming of the harvester and inviting the toil of the workman—suppose that on such a morning the people should take old lady Business out of her chamber, hustle her decrepit limbs into God's sunlight, throw the sick bed and its foul linen from the window, open the doors, and air out the house. What do you suppose would happen? Would the old lady die of the shock? No. Would the people all perish of starvation? No. But how the quacks would rush around with smelling bottles and restoratives!

"Suppose that the people of the United States should suddenly determine to exercise in government that common sense which inspires them in business, in mechanics and in their social relations with each other. Suppose they should abolish the United States Senate, wipe out of the statute-books all laws designed to choke the majority, elect officers by majorities, pass laws by majorities, and repeal laws which worked injustice by majorities. Suppose that the people should determine to intrust the welfare of the nation to the common good sense of the majority. Suppose that they should place tools in the hands of idle men and endow them with a chance to work for a living. Suppose they should at one stroke abolish every tariff law on these statute-books and declare that, as the grandest country on the face of the earth, with the grandest soil, mines, forests and resources, peopled by the grandest people now in the full possession of their faculties, they feared not the pauper labor of any downtrodden country. Suppose they should do that. Would the world come to an end? Would the rivers run dry, the grain wither in the shock, and the arms of strong men become palsied? A thousand times no. What reason is there why the people should not do this?

"I hear some weakling whisper that it is not practical. There exists in this country a class of human beings who call themselves practical men and who believe that poverty is practical, that idleness is practical, that the rule of the majority is impractical, that tariff robbery is practical, and that any man who assails an acknowledged wrong is a crank and impractical. Such men encumber the earth and are permitted to exist in a civilization whose glories are bequeathed by patriots, philosophers and inventors whom the apes of successive ages have termed impractical, have derided and vilified, and whenever possible have crucified.

"I give you a sentiment: 'Long live the reign of the majority.'"

EXTRACTS FROM SPEECH DELIVERED AT INDIANAPOLIS, SEPT. 12.

"I shall speak to-night of paternalism. Paternalism. You have seen and heard that word frequently in recent years. 'Paternalism in government,' 'believers in paternalism,' are phrases generally coupled with a well-worded sneer. Those simple-minded but well-meaning people whose political beliefs are hand-made and who dare not trust themselves to form opinions of their own have been made to believe that paternalism is something awful, which if not checked may sap our national existence.

"A republican orator will talk himself red in the face defending the protective tariff and then launch into a tirade against farmers who want the government to advance them credit on wheat, denouncing it as 'a paternalism which no intelligent people will subscribe to.' Another will extol the glories of the public school system and wind up by urging every American citizen to assert his own individuality and frown down the rising tide of paternalism.'

"What is this paternalism, who introduced it into the country, and how can we frown it down?

"I may as well confess at the start that I am a paternalist and prepared to defend myself on any charge which may be brought against me. A paternal government is one which is watchful of the interests of its subjects, one which stands ready to aid its people, a government which holds itself to an extent responsible for the personal comfort and happiness of its subjects. It is the antithesis of anarchy. Of all the words in the dictionary the true anarchist hates paternalism worst.

THE SOUP HOUSE

ANOTHER GOVERNMENT SLAVE.

A GOVERNMENT SLAVE.

The government of the United States and our various states and cities have many paternal features. Here are a few of them:

"The public school system.

"The post office system.

"The pension system.

"The protective tariff.

"The government land system (now obsolete).

"Public waterworks.

"Fire department.

"Street-lighting system.

"All of these are examples of paternalism. Anarchists and a great many other people do not believe in such institutions. They believe that individuals and private corporations can render better service than the government. They prefer private schools, and object to being taxed for public schools, and denounce the system as an odious paternalism. They assert that private corporations would improve on the postal service. They rail against pensions. They are opposed to the protective tariff. I plead guilty of entertaining an opposition to the protective tariff form of paternalism

"The paternal features of our government are the ones which save it from a complete and lamentable failure. The splendid service which the state renders to the people through the school, post-office, and the various municipal departments partly atones for the ignominious failure to legislate in the interest of the people. Eliminate these paternal features of government and little remains but official corruption.

"A government is directly responsible for the personal comfort and happiness of its people. If the mass of a people are in financial distress the fault lies with the government. If an honest citizen starves to death the government is a murderer. Deny this proposition and you renounce your faith in government.

"If the government is not responsible who or what is? In this city of Indianapolis to-day there are 6,000 men out of work. They are good, honest, industrious men, capable of earning a living, but there is no work for them to do. They have families dependent upon them. Their means of support is cut off. Who is responsible? The men who own the great factories? No. They are under no obligations to give these men work. They are at liberty to close down any time business policy so dictates. Your wealthy citizens are not responsible and are not compelled to feed these men or keep their families from starvation. The men themselves are not to blame. The United States government is responsible. It is the fault of some evil system that honest men are denied work. In some way the machinery of the government is defective or this thing would not have happened.

"Here is this idle workman. He is an American citizen, a voter and a tax-payer. He fought to protect his country and has ever been a law-abiding citizen. He has ever defended the constitution and laws of his country. A day comes when the factory in which he works is closed down. Other factories are closed. It is impossible for him to obtain work. In other parts of the country the same holds true. This man has been swindled. *The government of the United States has obtained money for taxes from him under false pretenses.* Instead of protecting his interests it has brought about a condition of affairs ruinous not only to himself, but to his employer. Why shall he not hold the government responsible? Is not the government responsible for the lives of its subjects?

"As a believer in paternalism, as a believer in the responsibility of a government, I declare that any honest citizen of this country, when denied employment in private workshop and mill, has the right to demand and obtain from the government work and compensation. I hold that any government which refuses such a demand invites revolution and anarchy.

"American workmen do not want charity. Charity breeds revolutionists and criminals. A public soup-house will make more criminals in one week than all Johann Most's ravings can in a year.

"An American workman desires a chance to work

and earn a living. He cannot supply himself with work. The watch factory with its 3,000 operatives and wonderful machinery has taken the place of the patient, plodding watchmaker of the olden time. The age of machinery has robbed the workman of his individuality. He is nothing but a 'hand.' The factory is part of his life. He answers to the ring of a bell, the sound of a whistle, and willingly obeys the petty rules of tyrants that he may earn a living. Shut down the factory and he is lost. He is not to blame for that system. It grew up around him and unconsciously he became a part of it. He is helpless to release himself from it. He is a small and not very important part of the machine, and one very easily replaced, and when the machine stops he stops. Whom shall he look to in this his day of distress?

"I say he should look to the government, and I make the assertion that no government can long exist which sits idly by and watches its faithful subjects subsist on the bread of charity or sees them forced into pauperism or crime.

"*The day is at hand when the American republic must choose between paternalism and anarchy.* The day is at hand when the American government must either protect its people or go down in revolution and blood. There is no middle ground. We must either have a government of the people, for the people, and by the people, or have no government.

"*I have an abiding faith in government, in the will of the majority, in wise paternalism, in scientific nationalism. I believe in the people. I believe that the great heart of the people is kind, loving and unselfish. I believe that we can trust in the good common sense of a people who are permitted to express their opinion unhampered by restraints. I distrust the individual. He is selfish. He is often dishonest and corruptible. He is easily misled and influenced. But you cannot long deceive the whole people; you cannot corrupt the whole people. I believe that it is the duty of the government of the United States to immediately establish industries which will give employ-*

ment to everg idle man in America. The government has or can command the capital and the people are eager to supply the labor. This plan is perfectly practical. It solves the most difficult problem which ever confronted civilization. It should have no opposition.

"But it will be fought by those who are opposed to a strong government and to paternalism, by those manufacturers and capitalists who fear the competition of the government, and by a lot of idiots who believe that a do-nothing policy is conservatism.

"The strongest argument made against paternalism, against any comprehensive extension of the functions of the government, is that it will create an army of government officials and workmen who will perpetuate themselves in power by means of an enlarged political machine. It is stated that the power of political patronage is already too powerful, and that any extension of it is unwise. This argument is worth answering. It contains a foundation in fact. Patronage is abused, but let us examine into the purely paternal features of our government and see to what extent this patronage is wielded for political effect. The two purest examples of state paternalism are found in the public school and the post-office. Both could be carried on by private enterprise and both have competitors backed by enormous capital. There are private schools and there are wealthy express companies. The official patronage of the public school system is enormous. How often does the school-teacher meddle in politics? How often is his political belief made a test of his employment? When have the school-teachers been enrolled as a political factor in this or in any other country? Care is even exercised in the selection of schoolbooks, so as to preclude the introduction of teachings which tend to fortify religious or political doctrines. The public school, with its army of 250,000 teachers and officials, cannot be cited as an argument against paternalism.

"The post-office system is another pure form of paternalism. It is but slightly tainted with the curse of political patronage. The high officials are generally

A flagrant example of paternalism.

selected by the party in power, but the civil-service rule is enforced without protest. In Chicago, New York, Philadelphia, and in all the large cities of the country political changes do not impair the discipline of the force. Even high officials, with authority to employ and discharge hundreds of men, are not disturbed by meddlesome politicians in the exercise of their duties. There may be rare exceptions to this rule, but these exceptions prove the rule. The vast numbers of postal clerks and mail carriers are selected by a civil-service examination, and an efficient and faithful workman can hold his position for life even under the existing corrupt and partisan system of politics.

"The United States government has immense navy yards and government workshops filled with great machinery and employing thousands of mechanics and laborers. Surrounded as these institutions are at present with an environment of fierce partisanship and corruption, these great industrial concerns are conducted on a business basis. The mechanic is seldom selected for his political belief or disbelief. In workmanship the government workshops rival any private corporation in existence. Any thoughtful man who inspected the government exhibit at the Columbian Exposition must have been impressed with this fact. The superb exhibit was not a Democratic argument, it was not a Republican argument. It was a triumph for the distinctly paternal features of our government and a glorious contrast to the partisan exhibit which was being displayed at that very time in the senate chamber of the United States capitol at Washington. The splendid exhibit of the fish commission which is filling our lakes and rivers with game fish at the expense and under the direct management of the government; the distribution of seed to farmers and the scientific development of new fruit and food products; the equipment and extension of the signal and life-saving systems; the eradication of fruit and grain destroying insects; the perfection of precautions against cholera and other contagious diseases—these are a few of the paternal features of the government which were displayed at Chicago in the splendid exhibit of the United States.

"The paternal features of the United States are the ones which have saved it from destruction; the ones of which the people are proud; the ones which reflect the progress of our civilization. The great mass of the people are in favor of these paternal features, but they meekly join in a chorus of condemnation when some fool politician or editor warns them against 'paternalism,' as if it were something little less than a crime.

"The postal system of the United States and the fire departments of several of our large cities are not only the finest illustrations of paternalism, but they are the most superb illustration of mechanical and scientific progress in the world. There is nothing in private enterprise that can approach them. They are in acute touch with the progress of to-day. They are ever ready to test any promising improvement and to adopt it if it proves of value. They are not conducted for profit, but for the benefit of the whole people.

"While the people of the United States have been stupidly listening to the denunciation of paternalism, the monarchies of the old world have been putting into operation many wise plans for the betterment of the people. Germany has adopted a pension system by which the faithful workman, after serving a term of years, receives from the government a stipend sufficient to support his declining years. In this country we send him to the poorhouse.

"Australia has abolished the private monopoly of railroads and telegraph lines, and given to the people the finest service in the world. In France and even in Spain the spread of paternalism has been noted.

"It has remained, however, for Glasgow, the leading municipality of Scotland, to give the world an example of what can be accomplished by wise paternalism. Under the leadership of local statesmen that city, ten years ago, began to undo the blunders of former years. It has taken charge of its street-car lines and given the people a splendid service. It dispenses with the private gas and electric lighting companies and furnishes its citizens with these necessities at half the monopoly prices. It has established a public telephone service at reasonable rates, and from these and other enterprises it derives all needed revenue and has abolished local taxation.

"Is there anything wild or visionary about this? There is not the slightest reason why New York, Chicago, Indianapolis, and in fact every city in the United States should not take immediate steps to follow Glasgow's example. They should own and operate street-car lines, gas and electric lights, telephones and other great public enterprises. They would derive enormous incomes from these paternal features and their citizens would be relieved of the immense tax now paid into the pockets of stockholders.

"The triumphs of paternalism in the United States have been achieved in the face of tremendous odds. They have approached perfection in spite of the fact that they have been surrounded with an atmosphere of hostile partisanship, and menaced by corruption and the greed of private competition. Unscrupulous partisans have attempted to use them; corrupt officials have stolen or diverted the funds which should have gone to them, political bigots have railed against them; economists like Homan of Indiana have cut down the appropriations which rightfully belonged to them, but they have survived and grown more beautiful—a lily in a quagmire, the one redeeming feature in an age of political degeneracy.

"Wipe out this corrupt political system, which protects the individual official in the robbery of the public.

"Give the people the power to elect their officers by majorities and to remove them when unfaithful to their trusts.

"Invest in the people the right to pass laws for their improvement and the last argument against the scientific development of paternalism shall be swept away. The school, the post-office, the government workshops, and all other paternal industries will then be planted in a friendly soil and thrive as never before.

"I am not advocating a paternalism or a nationalism which shall subjugate the individual—which shall establish a monopoly of production and of labor. I believe that the government should assume the exclusive right to maintain an army and to issue money, and own and manage the great interstate railway lines. More than that it does not require. To those who demand competition the government will act as a competitor. If private enterprise can safely and economically carry letters and perform postal service permit them to do so and let the government compete with them. The fittest will survive. If the government can manufacture guns and sewing machines and fairly compete with private enterprises the government should engage in such enterprises. If the millions of idle men in this country can find remunerative employment in the government manufacture of agricultural implements, boots and shoes, cotton goods, woolens and clothing, no private enterprise has a right to protest.

"*If private enterprise cannot compete in any given industry against the government but one conclusion is possible—the government should undertake that industry. If the government cannot compete in any given industry against private enterprise but one conclusion is possible—the government should abandon that enterprise and devote its attention to something else.* There need be nothing unfriendly in this competition. If the government shall undertake, let us say, the manufacture of shoes, and in the competition which follows a certain shoe manufacturer finds it impossible from any cause to compete successfully, the government should stand ready to purchase his plant at an honest price and resume work where he left off.

"Under such a system injustice could be done no man. The government would produce, manufacture and sell its products a shade above cost price. It would sell to the community at large. The government could lose nothing and the producer would be able to buy back the products of his labor. The private competitor would be compelled to meet government prices. If his means of production, management and economy were equal to that of the government his profits would be in proportion. In so much as he excelled the government he would increase his profits. If he could not compete—the logic of events has simply demonstrated the superiority of government control of that industry. In such a system ambition would not be checked and the spirit of invention would not be stifled. Well-managed private enterprises would survive and flourish, and wages would ever hover around the point at which the laborer could buy back the products of his toil. Private capital would ever be ready to embark in new and promising industries or to develop new inventions. The inventor who desired to sell or develop an invention would find in the government an active competitor against the private capitalist."

EXTRACT FROM SPEECH DELIVERED AT ST. LOUIS, SEPT. 19.

"The declaration of independence was written by a statesman; the constitution of the United States was drafted by politicians. We look to the declaration for inspiration, to the constitution for political trickery. The country is governed by the constitution, and the declaration is for use only on the Fourth of July.

"The politicians who represented the petty and jealous colonies in the constitutional convention had a hearty hatred of majorities and a fear of the people, but it is unfair to their memories to intimate that they contemplated a constitution whose enforcement would result in the existing subjugation and degradation of the majority. They could not have anticipated a band of protected freebooters ready to combine in a common raid on the people. The men who drafted the constitution did not knowingly erect the political machine which has turned out a Tammany in New York and a 'blocks of five' system in Indiana and Ohio.

"It is idle to talk of reform under any such political system as now prevails. If the history of the last 100 years has demonstrated anything it is the absolute failure of representative government. Do not talk to me about the glories of this country. Its glories and triumphs have been achieved in spite of the constitution and not because of it. No system of misgovernment can entirely ruin this country. The existing one has gone the entire length of imbecility and the country triumphantly survives.

"No maladministration of affairs, however criminal, can entirely eradicate happiness. Some modern philosopher has declared that there is happiness in hell. He must have made his discovery at the time when American citizens, hungry and panic-ridden, were going around with smiling faces with a United States Senate in session at Washington. The American citizen in recent years has developed a patience and a smile under discouraging circumstances, which breeders of mules would give a fortune to successfully imitate.

"A returning board swindles the majority of the people out of a presidency, and after pouting over it a few days they regard the steal as a huge joke.

"A street-car syndicate steals fifty miles of streets from a city, and the citizens poke their alderman under the ribs, slyly wink, and ask him how much he got. This is so good a joke that the alderman buys the drinks.

"Twenty-five thousand idle men parade the streets with banners demanding work, and the next day every newspaper paragrapher in town has a joke to the effect that what the men needed most was a bath. At this excruciating bit of humor a great city laughs until its sides ache. But the day for laughing at these things is past. Good humor and cheerfulness is an excellent thing when it is not accompanied by asininity.

"This country has attained a degree of prosperity because unwise laws and thieving politicians were not potent enough to overcome natural advantages. The pioneer who drifted into the west laid the foundation of a fortune without the aid and without the restraint of any form of government. He became rich because he could not help it. Every newly developed country has been prosperous before the blighting influences of our so-called civilization became fastened upon it. Look at the state of Illinois to-day. With its imperial city of Chicago and all its wealth the standard of happiness is lower than it was fifty years ago. The burdens which now rest upon the country can never be removed until the people are given a voice in the management of their political affairs.

"So long as the people permit themselves to be deluded into a belief that they are governing, so long will they be robbed. So long as they cherish the shadow, and refuse to grasp the reality which is in their reach, so long will they be robbed, and so long will they deserve to be robbed. The people have had just the kind of government they deserve. Their criminal carelessness, stupid patience with wrong-doing and inane complaisance with steadily encroaching tyranny, has had the inevitable result and they are paying the well-deserved penalty.

"Representative government is a failure. It is wrong in principle and criminal in practice. It should have been repudiated fifty years ago, when its defects were discovered, but instead of boldly denouncing the mistakes of the founders of the constitution the people have been led by wily politicians into a defense of the very things which struck down their liberties.

"Man is naturally honest. He is born that way. He learns dishonesty. Naturally a man will do the right rather than the wrong thing. Where he is not directly interested he will decide fairly between right and wrong. Thrown into a contest where he is compelled to struggle with others for a living or for advancement, he becomes selfish. This is natural. His natural sense of fairness and inherent honesty becomes dominated by self-interest. Few men escape the action of this general law. A representative system of government is one in which a number of people delegate to one of their number or to several of their number the power to pass laws and transact business in which all are interested.

The men they select as representatives are also interested. The theory of a representative system is that the best men in the community will be selected. In practice this does not come to pass, and even if it should it would not save the system from failure.

"Only in rare cases is a representative elected on a specific issue. Take a state election. Eighty members of the lower house are to be elected. In different parts of the state various issues are being forced. There are such issues as mining reforms, eight-hour laws, taxation of corporations, the method of electing senators, etc. The people elect representatives to decide these issues. No representative can reflect the will of his constituents on all these questions. He does not even know what the majority of his constituents desires. More than that, he does not care. But all the people have decided views on all of these questions. The eighty representatives proceed to the state capital and for months the hotels are filled with lobbyists from all parts. These questions are decided in defiance of the known will of the majority and the only recourse the people have is the right of petition. The same is true of municipal councils.

"The history of state legislatures and city councils in this country is a history of revolting and openly paraded corruption, in which the property and sacred rights of the people have been bartered and sold with as little compunction as brokers buy and sell wheat and hogs on a board of trade. There is no need to particularize. The record is a shame to civilization and the people should have wiped out the iniquitous system a generation ago.

"In no monarchy or despotism, ancient or modern, have the people been so robbed by corrupt and insatiate officials as in the United States. From the Alaska seal-thieving syndicate in the United States Senate to the petty thief who steals postage stamps in a country town the taint of corruption is spread. The people do not even have the power to depose an official when he is detected in rascality. They have given their authority for a term of years to an agent they are powerless to discharge or discipline. He can serve his term and draw his salary in spite of the people, unless by process of law they succeed in landing him in the penitentiary.

"The people should not be compelled to surrender their rights to a representative. It may be policy to transact certain routine work by means of a representative body, but on all laws, issues and large expenditures of money in which the whole people are interested, and by which they must be governed, the people should cast the vote, yes or no, and the minority should abide by the result without appeal to any higher authority.

"There should be, there is, no higher authority than the people. Laws have created many such higher courts of appeal and they have ever decided against the people. These petty monarchs, these usurping rulers should be deposed, and the laws creating them should be abolished.

"The Supreme Court of Illinois has overthrown every law in which the farmers and wageworkers of that state have directly interested themselves.

"The people passed a law providing for a weekly payday. The Supreme Court declared it unconstitutional.

"The people passed a law against the crime of child labor in factories, mines and stores. The Supreme Court declared it unconstitutional.

"The people passed a law against the iniquitous system of truck stores. The Supreme Court declared it unconstitutional.

"The list might be continued indefinitely. In every instance where a newly passed law operated to the advantage of the workman as against that of his employer the Supreme Court promptly and enthusiastically declared that law unconstitutional, and the people were forever checked from obtaining legal redress for their wrongs.

"The right of the majority to rule will be secured only after a fearful struggle. The issue of majority rule will be fought inch by inch by every great corporation, thieving syndicate, money shark, office-holding politician, and by the combined forces of those whose supremacy would be imperiled by the rule of the majority.

"For one hundred years privilege has been rearing a wall against the people. They are intrenched behind this wall with its thousands of court decisions in favor of monopoly and against the people. They have able advocates who will tell you that it is not wise that the people should have a direct vote on laws; that it is un-American and contrary to the spirit of American institutions; that people who advocate any such measure are attempting to overthrow the work of Washington and Jefferson, consecrated by Lincoln, Grant and Garfield. They will call you anarchists, socialists and revolutionists in an impartial and indiscriminate manner. They will thereby convince a great many men that the people are not safe rulers for themselves. They will spend untold millions of dollars in an attempt to defeat popular rule. They will spend this money foolishly and in vain--foolishly for the reason that the people will, when successful, in no way encroach upon their rights or attempt to confiscate their property; in vain for the reason that the people are no longer to be kept away from their birthright."

EXTRACT FROM SPEECH DELIVERED AT ST. PAUL, OCT. 14.

"Under our present industrial system we are dependent on the wages of the man who runs the machine. Capitalists and the independent classes are small in numbers. The farmer cannot consume the total products of his fields. He looks to the workman in the city as his customer. When a thing is produced it must be sold or permitted to rot. If 4,000,000 men are working in factories and new machinery throws 3,000,000 of them out of work the wages of the remaining 1,000,000 must be nearly sufficient to purchase the same amount of the product of the factories as was formerly bought by the wages of the 4,000,000. Otherwise a surplus is inevitable. The non-producers depend on the wages of the producers. Stated broadly, therefore, the wages of the wokman must be sufficient to purchase back the increment his labor has added to raw material after a fair profit has been deducted by the capital employed in manufacture.

"The logical and theoretical end of the development of machinery is one vast machine, manipulated by one workman, and owned by one capitalist—the workman the sole wage-earner and the capitalist and the workman constituting the consuming class. They would pay all taxes, support the government, and maintain a police and standing army to preserve the peace. The wage-earner would receive the lowest rate of wages at which any efficient workman would consent to run the machine, and would go on a strike whenever he could organize himself. The machine would run until a surplus was created, which would be in about fifteen seconds. An industrial depression would then ensue until the workman, capitalist, and the several millions of idle workmen, paupers, criminals and tax-eaters had consumed the surplus, when business would revive and a new panic and depression follow. We have been rapidly approaching this beautiful condition of affairs for thirty-five years, a condition disastrous to every member of society, and one which can be commended by no man possessed of one grain of common sense or actuated by that political horse sense which is the best kind of patriotism.

"Look over the United States to-day. There are great factories filled with machinery so perfect that it can almost think. It stands idle and the corroding touch of time is frosting the delicate mechanism with rust. Strong and willing workmen look wistfully through the windows and watch in vain for a wreath of smoke from the great chimneys. In the warehouses are manufactured goods for which no purchaser calls. A million people are in need of these necessities of life which swift-moving machinery has so easily fashioned.

The capitalist paces through the deserted rooms of the factory and looks sadly at the decaying machinery. Taxes, insurance and perhaps rent are eating their way into his pocket and destroying his capital. The morning paper says that the stock in that factory dropped three points on the exchange the day before. Twenty-five thousand hungry men march through the streets of a great city. A reformer timidly suggests that something is wrong in our industrial system. Four thousand editors and 2,000 preachers pronounce him a crank and a fool, who cannot understand the spirit of American institutions."

CHAPTER XVI.

THE WILL OF THE MAJORITY.

A STATESMAN had lifted a party from obscurity and made it a power in politics. The People's party, as it existed in 1888, '90, '92 and '93, had passed away, and only its name survived. No longer a coterie of greenbackers, trade unionists, debt-ridden farmers and political faddists, it had been transformed into a political party of the sternest American type, American in its platform, its leaders and its methods. Self-interest had been eliminated from its platform and statesmanship substituted. Its orators fearlessly demanded the rule of the majority, and with that as a battle cry they carried the fight into the very strongholds of the enemy.

In Boston a "Majority Rule Club" was organized. The idea spread like wild fire. Majority rule clubs sprang up everywhere, and embraced in their membership all classes of citizens. Not since 1828, when the people of the United States repudiated President Adams —who had served a term after being elected by a minority vote of 105,000, as against Jackson's 155,000—and a second time triumphantly elected and inaugurated Jackson, had such a political revolution swept the country.

For twenty years the people had been waiting to break away from the old parties. They had waited long and patiently for a man and an issue. There had been third parties, but neither their platforms nor leaders commanded general respect.

For twenty years the political discontent of the people manifested itself in an unmistakable manner. Like a caged panther they paced the short limit of their cage, reversing again and again, only to be confronted bp the same old iron bars and prodded by the same old trainers. In 1876 they repudiated the Republican party and elected Tilden by a popular majority (not plurality), but were counted out by the party in power. In the four years of Hayes' administration the financial depression eased and Garfield obtained an election on a minority vote. Hard times again returned and the people wanted "a change." They elected Cleveland and in four years more repudiated him and took the back track. One term of the old Republicanism was enough to again sicken the people and they demanded and obtained another change. Cleveland was again elected by sweeping pluralities.

One year after his election the Republicans swept the country on the issue of hard times. The same men who voted against Blaine and Harrison on account of the then prevailing hard times voted in 1893 for McKinley and Jackson and other Republicans on the same issue.

But the panther was becoming more restless. He threw himself against the bars more recklessly. In 1890 Chicago went Republican by 10,000 majority. In 1892 it went 35,000 Democratic. In 1893 it went 7,-500 Republican. Six months later it went 1,500 Democratic. In 1892 New York State went Democratic 45,-000, and a year later it went Republican 75,000.

What good did all this do? The people were simply electing one set of men and repudiating another. In 1893 hundreds of thousands of disgusted citizens remained away from the poles and no pleading could persuade them to vote. The result was received with apathy except by a few dupes who imagined that in some way the country would be benefited. Free trade has been rebuked, they said. In that election there had not been a man elected who had any voice in deciding on tariff or any other national measure. A few men had secured political jobs, and the people had been accorded their annual privilege of "voting."

Affairs were changed in 1900. Old party lines were obliterated. From one end of the country to another the people demanded "a change" which would amount to something. In vain protection orators addressed themselves to workingmen; in vain old-time Democrats protested that the Democratic party was the repository of the hopes of the people. There was a new south, a new west and a new northwest. Bourbon politics retained its hold only in the east and along the Atlantic coast and in the extreme south. Early in the campaign the Republicans abandoned all hope of carrying Kansas, Nebraska, Iowa, Minnesota and the Pacific coast states. They realized that Illinois and the central northwestern states were in danger and poured money into them without stint. They made their stand in New York, Pennsylvania and Ohio, and with a corruption fund exceeding $5,000,000 conducted a campaign which will never be forgotten in American politics. They had able speakers and writers. They organized a literary bureau and buried the country under a flood of pamphlets. The autumn sky was red with fireworks, and processions of men paid for the purpose paraded the streets of Chicago, Cincinnati, Philadelphia, Pittsburg and New York.

Every trick of the politician was brought into play. The manufacturers, capitalists and business men were scared into giving liberally, and the day of the election found the Republicans with an enormous campaign fund on hand. It was used. In large and small cities bribery was openly practiced. In a subsequent investigation it was ascertained that in New York City alone 30,000 votes were bought and delivered.

The Democrats were handicapped and disorganized. The south was in revolt The new generation of the south was tired of hearing the war talked about. That splendid section was held back by existing conditions, and the southern voters refused to follow the old-time leaders. The new party cut the Democrats in two in several of the pivotal states, and early in the campaign it became apparent that Hild was defeated.

Judge Smith closed the campaign in Chicago, holding his last meeting in Manufacturers' Hall on the lake front. One hundred and fifty thousand people crowded in and around the great building The meeting was a surprise to the local politicians, but they were not prepared for what followed.

Election day passed quietly and an immense vote was cast. The afternoon papers claimed everything for their respective sides, but the people patiently waited. In the evening the streets of Chicago were blocked by a surging mob. The newspaper offices were the points of interest. The first bulletins were of the usual vague, speculative nature and varied with the politics of the newspaper men at the opposite ends of the wire. Here are some of the early bulletins which set the crowd howling:

"The *Sun* estimates that Hild has carried New York State by 45,000 majority."

"Kimbly has carried Ohio by a large majority."

"Ten precincts in Burlington, Vt., give Kimbly 903, Hild 840, Smith 648."

"Who is Smith? Seems as if I have heard the name before."

"Texas has gone Democratic by from 150,000 to 200,000 majority."

"South Carolina is Democratic by the usual large majority."

"The Cincinnati *Commercial-Gazette* claims Kimbly's election by a large popular majority."

The first authentic news from New York State came over the wire about 8:20 in the evening. It read:

Two hundred and twenty-seven precincts give:

Hild	28,427
Smith	25,812
Kimbly	12,713

A roar went up from the street which brought every busy writer in the newspaper offices to the windows. While the cheering was still in progress the bulletin disappeared and this one flashed across the street:

Four hundred and ten precincts in Philadelphia give:

The last rally before election.

Kimbly	41,318
Hild	33,917
Smith	50,428

The wildest excitement prevailed. In the clubs and in the Republican and Democratic headquarters the assembled politicians refused to believe the news until private telegrams confirmed the report that in the cities Smith was running even or ahead of Hild and Kimbly. Judge Smith received the returns at the People's headquarters on Adams Street. Out in the streets the cheering mob yelled itself hoarse. Here are some of the bulletins displayed before 11 o'clock:

Chicago—Twenty-nine precincts give:

Hild	2,172
Kimbly	1,841
Smith	5,374

New York City—Seven hundred and twenty-nine precincts give:

Hild	71,118
Kimbly	35,021
Smith	85,490

Smith's plurality, 14,372

The New York *Herald* estimates that Smith has carried New York by from 25,000 to 30,000 majority.

Chairman Matt Quinn of the Republican national committee claims New York State by 15,000 majority.

Seventy-two cities and towns in Connecticut give:

Kimbly	48,121
Hild	17,433
Smith	46,207

Charleston, S. C.—Charleston has gone Populist by not less than 5,000 majority. The Populists are claiming the state by 40,000 majority.

Burlington, Iowa—Smith and Foster have swept Iowa by not less than 85,000 majority.

San Francisco, Cal.—Judge Smith has carried San Francisco by 30,000 majority. Chairman Potter estimates Smith's plurality in the state at 150,000.

Burlington, Iowa (11 o'clock)—Nine hundred and eighty towns and precincts in Iowa give:

Smith 173,640
Kimbly.. 55,924
Hild.. 37,683

Smith's plurality 117,716.

St. Paul, Minn.—Scattering reports indicate heavy Populist gains. The Republicans claim the state by a small majority.

Pittsburg, Pa.—Pittsburg gives Smith 28,000 majority. The Populists claim the state by a good majority. Returns are coming in slowly.

New York City—Returns are coming in very slowly. The Populists have probably carried New York City and the state by large majorities.

New York City (11:15 o'clock)—The Associated Press reports indicate the election of Judge Smith as President of the United States.

Cleveland, O. (11:35 o'clock)—Governor Kimbly concedes Judge John Smith's election and has just forwarded him the following telegram:

"CINCINNATI, O., Nov. 5, 1900—To Judge John Smith, Chicago, Ill.: Permit me to congratulate you on the most stupendous popular victory ever attained by an American citizen. Accept my sincere congratulations.

"MARK KIMBLY."

In the exuberance of their joy men laughed and cried. Frenzied crowds paraded the streets all night. Men who had voted the Republican and Democratic tickets joined in the popular victory. The landslide was so sweeping that party ties were sundered and every one seemed to go with the victors.

The day after the election brought no subsidence of the excitement. As the returns came in the victory appeared more sweeping. Here are a few editorial comments:

New York *Herald*—The People's party has swept the country. The west and the south, with the possible exception of Texas, have cast their votes for Smith and Foster. New York State has gone Populist by not less than 50,000 majority. Pennsylvania for the first time in forty years has repudiated a Republican presidential candidate. The HERALD has no comment to make on the result. None is necessary.

Chicago *Inter Ocean*—Governor Kimbly's election is in doubt. The result is a surprise and can be accounted for on no other grounds than that the people want a change. There was a decided falling off in the Republican vote. Thank God, the Democrats did not win anyhow.

Louisville *Courier-Journal*—The Democratic party is dead and no smirking Republican is alive to follow the hearse. In the face of the popular uprising of the people the COURIER-JOURNAL has no invidious comments to make. The star-eyed goddess of reform is safe in the company of Judge John Smith. As Democrats we take off our hats and shout: "Long live the reign of the people."

New York *Mail and Express*—The latest advice indicates the temporary triumph of anarchy, lawlessness and Judge Smith The Republicans have not yet abandoned all hope. The Democratic party is wiped out of existence. There is some consolation in that.

Bangor *Express*—Maine was true to her traditions and is still in line. We cannot realize that the country has departed from its time-honored traditions.

Wednesday the returns from New York State gave Smith 48,000 majority Thursday's figures cut this down to 32,000. The following day it was announced that owing to mistakes in the count this figure would be considerably reduced In three days Smith's majority in Pennsylvania decreased from 70,000 to 15,000, and in Ohio from 35,000 to 8,000 Saturday afternoon the Chicago *Tribune* displayed a bulletin claiming Kimbly's election. Scenes of wild excitement followed. Newspaper offices were besieged by mobs of people and all manner of exciting rumors prevailed.

There was a scent of bribery everywhere. A Chicago paper published a dispatch from New York giving the details of a Republican-Democratic conspiracy to steal the election. In later years the details of that account were verified. Tuesday night, when it became evident that Smith had carried practically everything except the Atlantic states, a meeting of New York politicians was hurriedly called. Messengers were sent in different directions, and at midnight in a room at the Hoffman House the plans were laid. Tammany agreed to deliver New York to the Republicans and a representative of the Pennsylvania political syndicate agreed to take care of the state. The people had few election clerks or judges, and the task was not a difficult one.

The returns were withheld and falsified in New York, Pennsylvania, Massachusetts, Ohio and Michigan. In the latter state eight electoral votes were needed and would have been obtained had not a Grand Rapids newspaper man discovered the conspiracy. As it was, six districts were successfully manipulated. For this job thirty men were subsequently convicted and sentenced to long terms in state penitentiaries. But they had done their thieving work well. After 28,000 votes had been stolen in New York State, 33,000 in Pennsylvania, 40,000 in Ohio, 20,000 in Massachusetts and 31,000 in Michigan the official count gave the result indicated in the table on the opposite page.

According to the constitution of the United States there was no election and it devolved upon the House of Representatives to select a President. The mere fact that Smith had carried twenty-seven out of the total of forty-five states and had received twice the vote of any opposing candidate and a majority of all the votes cast, made not the slightest difference. The 305 votes of New York State, representing the stolen plurality, cast thirty-two votes in the electoral college and offset the thirty-two electoral votes of California, Minnesota, Kansas and Montana with their 650,000 majority.

The rage of the people knew no bounds. In New York a mob sacked Tammany Hall and burned the building to the ground. Several of the Tammany chiefs who were under suspicion were roughly used, and but for the intervention of leading Populists would have been killed. In Boston, Philadelphia and Chicago wild mobs paraded the streets and in several instances

STATES WITH REPUBLICAN PLURALITIES AND THEIR ELECTORAL VOTES.

States.	Kimbly....	Hild....	Smith...	Kimbly's plurality over Smith.	Electoral vote.
Conn	68,714	43,103	61,823	6,991	6
Me.........	58,327	23,604	44,982	12,345	6
Mass.	201,781	58,728	198,320	3,461	15
Mich.......	122,644	48,623	118,742	3,902	7
N. H.......	43,618	16,241	36,820	6,798	4
N. J.......	146,388	75,911	138,161	8,227	10
N. Y.......	509,622	427,213	509,317	305	36
Ohio.......	306,121	297,681	301,280	4,841	23
Pa.........	415,849	274,303	402,111	13,638	32
R. I........	28,326	17,812	19,641	8,685	4
Vt.........	32,416	7,293	26,313	6,100	4
Totals.....	1,932,803	1,290,512	1,857,510	75,293	147

STATES WITH DEMOCRATIC PLURALITIES AND THEIR ELECTORAL VOTES.

States.	Kimbly....	Hild ...	Smith...	Hild's plurality over Smith.	Electoral vote.
Dela.......	11,398	16,291	16,103	188	3
Texas......	23,814	225,747	218,614	7,133	15
Virg.......	62,212	136,614	135,590	5,024	12
S. Car......	4,822	47,815	46,812	1,003	9
N. Car.....	43,662	192,218	182,741	9,477	11
Mo........	141,600	238,101	236,418	1,683	17
Mar'ld.....	63,817	92,281	84,512	7,769	8
Total......	331,354	949,067	916,790	32,277	75

STATES WITH PEOPLE'S PARTY PLURALITIES AND THEIR ELECTORAL VOTES.

States.	Kimbly....	Hild....	Smith....	Smith's plurality.	Electoral vote.
Ala	....	65,728	188,321	112,593	11
Ark........	23,814	41,914	108,648	58,734	8
Cal	82,119	76,416	239,937	157,818	9
Col	12,555	....	109,412	94,857	4
Fla.........	....	14,818	29,747	14,929	4
Ga.........	....	81,684	178,814	97,130	13
Idaho	6,714	....	15,746	9,632	3
Ill	238,396	228,864	374,101	135,705	24
Ind	122,399	141,428	357,848	216,420	15
Iowa.......	86,401	58,063	373,717	287,316	13
Kan	86,682	....	329,146	242,464	10
Mich.......	62,417	52,241	188,446	86,019	7
Ky.........	32,446	133,192	238,430	105,238	13
La.........	....	28,742	116,318	87,576	8
Minn,......	108,559	53,918	295,422	186,863	9
Miss...	....	15,843	57,319	41,476	9
Mon, ...	7,767	....	73,982	66,215	3
Neb..	36,422	....	213,431	177,009	8
Nev........	1,480	....	12,617	11,137	3
N. Dak....	12,902	....	47,588	34,686	3
Tenn.......	32,726	61,717	212,464	150,747	12
Wash	15,616	....	88,992	73,376	4
W. Va.....	27,411	43,929	138,820	94,891	6
Wis........	108,883	101,828	209,862	100,979	12
Wyo.......	6,223	....	26,141	19,818	3
Ore....	22,373	....	64,914	42,541	4
S. Dak.....	19,822	....	83,617	63,795	4
Totals.....	1,145,127	1,200,725	4,373,866	2,771,866	222

RECAPITULATION.	Kimbly.	Hild.	Smith.
Republican states	1,932,803	1,290,512	1,857,510
Democratic states	331,354	949,067	916,790
People's states	1,145,127	1,200,725	4,373,866
Totals	3,409,284	3,440,304	7,148,166
Smith's plurality over Kimbly			3,738,882
Smith's plurality over Hild			3,707,862
Smith's majority over Kimbly and Hild			298,578
Smith's electoral vote			222
Kimbly and Hild's combined electoral vote			222

attacked Republican newspaper offices. Nothing but the coolness and patriotism of Judge Smith and other party leaders saved the country from revolution and anarchy.

Nov. 21 Judge Smith issued an appeal to the members of the People's party and to the voters of the country, urging them to maintain order and respect the laws of the country. In this address he said:

"The 7,000,000 men who voted for the People's electors can afford to wait yet a little time longer. While the written laws of this country proscribe majority rule no clique or conspiracy, no bribery or corruption can stand against the people and their overwhelming verdict as recorded at the polls the ninth day of November. Privilege dies hard, but it has received its deathblow. We have carried the House of Representatives by a small but probably safe majority. Let us with patience await the results. Refrain from lawless demonstrations. This is a revolution not of force, but of intelligence. I earnestly appeal to every American citizen to maintain the peace and with calmness await the coming session of Congress.

"JOHN SMITH."

This appeal effectually put an end to riots, but excitement ran high. It was rumored that the Republicans and Democrats had combined and by bribery had secured one or more electoral votes from the Populists. Congress convened in January. The Vice-President, in the presence of the Senate and House of Representatives, broke the seals and read the results. The vote as cast was: Kimbly, 147; Hild, 75; Smith, 222. Necessary to a choice, 223. The Vice-President announced that there was no choice and that the election would go to the House of Representatives.

The mob sacks the Senate Chamber.

CHAPTER XVII.

A GOVERNMENT OF THE PEOPLE.

THE last session of the House of Representatives does not illumine with glory the pages of American history. The American people have vainly attempted to forget it, but the record is there, sad and shameful. The author prefers not to enter into the details of the conspiracy by which a popular verdict was twice set aside under the form of law. It is sufficient to say that through bribery, open and flagrant, enough votes in the House of Representatives were secured by the Republicans and Kimbly was declared elected as President of the United States. That honest and honorable gentleman was not a party to the conspiracy, and in a dignified address to Congress and the people of the United States firmly declined to serve either as President or Vice-President. The details of the plot were made public in later years. The leaders of the conspiracy had been advised by both Kimbly and Reeve that they would not accept an election secured by fraud, but they refused to believe it and went ahead with their damnable work.

Washington was in the hands of a mob. When the result was announced to the thousands on the outside of the capitol building nothing could restrain their fury. They broke through the lines of police and soldiers and poured through the marble hallways of the great structure. Doorkeepers and sergeants-at-arms were swept aside like chaff and 50,000 enraged men adjourned Congress. Three of the Populist representatives who betrayed their party were shot down in the great chamber. A score of representatives were badly injured, some of them being hurled from the windows of the capitol by the mob. The President ordered out the troops, and after a determined fight the mob was repulsed and dispersed. He also issued a proclamation warning the people against riotous demonstrations and counseling moderation. To this no attention was paid.

Anarchy prevailed. Business was completely suspended and, in fact, had been since the day of election. The victory of the people's Party had precipitated a business panic, and stocks of all kinds sank to the lowest points ever recorded. Factories were closed down, their owners declaring that it would be suicidal to continue work under the existing "unsettled state of affairs." Judge Smith's appeal for law had quieted the people for a time, but the news from Washington broke down all restraint.

The country was on the verge of a revolution. In Chicago the great business houses were closed and heavily guarded. From every great city in the country there came appeals for state militia and government troops. Bread riots were of daily occurrence.

In Kansas the state militia refused to protect property, and the President sent three companies of regular troops into the state. In the fight which ensued several citizens were killed. The state militia came to the aid of the mob and in the fight the regulars were repulsed with some loss and compelled to retreat. The general government was powerless and the country was rapidly drifting into a state of absolute anarchy. This was in the early days of December.

In the prevailing excitement little attention was paid to some very startling rumors from Alaska. In October it was reported that important gold discoveries had been made in that country Wild stories of fabulous gold deposits were in circulation and there was a stampede from California and the coast states for that northern territory.

December 7, 1900, the steamer W. R. Baker landed in San Francisco having on board $48,000,000 in gold. In spite of all precaution the story leaked out, the secret being disclosed by a sailor. The facts were not made public until the miners had secured several million dollars' worth of railroad and other property in consideration of the yellow metal. The Alaska gold mines were practically inexhaustible. With crude methods of mining twenty men had secured over $40,000,000 worth of gold ore in less than three weeks.

Almost simultaneously with this came equally startling news from the Witwatersrand gold fields of South Africa, where gold deposits estimated at the current value of $75,000,000,000,000 had been discovered—enough for a per capita of $50,000 for every man, woman and child in the world. Gold was demonetized. It was of no more value than iron. Gold-bearing securities were worthless. The national debt of the United States was wiped out in a day. Europe was in a panic. Men worth millions woke up to find themselves penniless. But nothing had been destroyed. No real property had been wiped out of existence. Houses and railroads and all forms of improvements yet remained. Nothing was lost but an artificial standard of measurement Silver went to an enormous premium. But this financial revolution did not affect the hungry millions of American people. They could not eat silver or gold.

Such was the chaotic condition of affairs Jan. 15, 1901, when a number of men met in Judge Smith's office in Chicago and issued a call for a national conference of the people at Omaha, to convene Feb. 2. The call briefly set forth the condition of affairs, the peril of the country and imperative need of action. The people were requested to select one delegate from each congressional district and invest him with power to act. These elections were held Feb. 21, and two weeks later the 350 delegates met in session at Omaha. There was none of the enthusiasm of a political convention. Every man seemed to feel the responsibility resting upon him. Judge Smith and other national leaders were heartily applauded as they entered the convention hall. R. C. Brewster, a St. Louis business man, occupied the chair and called the convention to order. A temporary organization was perfected, credentials examined and approved, and the temporary organization made permanent. Judge Smith was called for and amid great applause thus addressed the convention:

"MR CHAIRMAN AND DELEGATES OF THE PEOPLE: The time for oratory is past. This is a day for action. We are called together to-day to take the initial steps in the correction of abuses which have been patiently borne by the people for over a century. If any man has come to this hall with a selfish nature, if any delegate is inspired by a thought other than that of the highest welfare of the whole people, his place is not within these walls. Let us proceed with our work inspired by a patriotism which seeks naught but the common weal.

"The government of the United States, after a century of existence, has failed in its duty to the people. It has been found lacking and inoperative when confronted by a condition which its founders could not foresee or provide against. It is not necessary that we shall go back 100 years for a precedent or an inspiration to urge us on. If precedents for the action we are about to take are needed we may go back to the illustrious patriot who penned the declaration of independence and repeat the glorious words of Jefferson in that immortal document, in which it is declared that the people not only have the right—nay, more than that—that it is their duty to abolish a bad government and institute a new one. The spirit of Thomas Jefferson is with us to-day.

"No republic can exist in name alone. An avowed monarchy or despotism is perferable to a state in which the people are deceived by a pretense of liberty and freedom and cunningly enslaved by their own political action. The republic of to-day is not the one of which Jefferson dreamed. That republic must be made possible, and we are assembled to-day for the purpose of laying the corner-stone of a government which shall be of the people."

Judge Smith urged the appointment of a committee

empowered to draft a constitution which should be submitted to the conference at a subsequent meeting. He suggested that the delegates discuss in a general way the outlines of a new constitution, and that two weeks be given the committee in which to submit their reports. On motion the delegates from each state were empowered to select one member of the constitutional committee. The committee retired and organized by electing Judge Smith chairman. The conference then devoted three days to a general discussion, a full record of which was preserved by the committee. The conference adjourned until Feb. 20, at which time the constitutional committee was instructed to submit its report. Before adjournment the following proclamation was issued to the country, signed by every member of the conference:

PROCLAMATION.

"TO THE PEOPLE OF THE UNITED STATES, GREETING: We, the delegates of the people, by virtue of authority vested in us by the majority vote of our constituents, do respectfully address the sovereign citizens of the United States.

"We solemnly reaffirm our allegiance to the truth contained in the inspired words of Thomas Jefferson and incorporated in the glorious declaration of independence, and with him declare that 'all men are created equal; that they are endowed with certain inalienable rights; that among these are life, liberty and the pursuit of happiness. That to secure these rights governments are instituted among men, deriving their just powers from the consent of the governed; that when any form of government becomes destructive of these ends it is the right of the people to alter and abolish it and to institute a new government, laying its foundations on such principles and organizing its powers in such form as shall seem to them most likely to effect their safety and happiness. Prudence, indeed, will dictate that governments long established should not be changed for light and transient causes, and, accordingly, all experience hath shown that mankind are disposed to suffer, while evils are sufferable, than to right themselves by abolishing the forms to which they were accustomed. But when a long train of abuses and usurpations, pursuing invariably the same object, evinces a desire to reduce them to absolute despotism, it is their right, it is their duty to throw off such government and to provide new guards for their future safety. Such has been the patient suffering of these colonies and such is the necessity which constrains them to alter their former systems of government.'

"Such has been the patient suffering of the people of the United States, and such is now the necessity which impels them to revise the existing system of government.

"We declare it to be a self-evident fact that the majority of people of any republic have rights which any minority, however fortified by wealth, influence or power, must be compelled to respect, and declare that any laws which defeat the plainly expressed will of the majority must be erased from the statute-books.

"We declare it to be the first duty of any government to so shape its laws and regulate its affairs that the humblest citizen shall have the opportunity to obtain employment at such a compensation as will enable him to live comfortably and maintain a family. Any country or community in which this right is denied is without government, and the senseless forms which exist under the guise of constitutions and laws should be swept away by an outraged people.

"It is not necessary to lodge formal and specific indictment against the existing government or to fix the responsibility for the crimes which have been committed under the name of law and so long tolerated by a deluded people, who have been taught that it is more patriotic to submit to a wrong than to arise and resist it. In the name of the people national honor has been sacrificed. Under the protection of the law public lands have been wrested from the people and bestowed on corporations; snobbery has been extolled and honest labor insulted. Justice has been made to pour with one hand wealth into the laps of avaricious affluence, while with the other she has taken bread from the hand of starving families. Under the malign influence of such conditions brutish instincts have been so developed that it has become only a question of a few years, when, unless a reform be instituted, civilization shall relapse into that barbarism from which it came.

"A corrupt government has fallen without a blow being struck against it. Over its ruins the people must erect a new government, avoiding the mistakes of the past and profiting by the experience of a century of national life. In a few days there will be submitted to the people for their approval or rejection a constitution which shall embody a true republican form of government. The men who draft that constitution have in contemplation a republic in which the people shall make and unmake laws, in which the people shall elect and depose officials; in which the will of the people is supreme. They have in contemplation a republic which shall enable its people to secure the greatest possible share of those blessings which multiply with an advancing civilization. We have an abiding faith in the wisdom, justice and sound government of any people in whose hands is lodged the untrammeled exercise of a ballot.

"Mindful of the rights of the minority, the framers of the constitution will care that their opinions be respected, their rights, property and legitimate privileges preserved inviolate. They aim to encourage the desire for the accumulation of property and believe with the philosopher that 'property communicates a charm to whatever is the object of it. It is the first of our abstract ideas, it cleaves to us closest and longest. It endears to the child its plaything, to the peasant his cottage, to the landlord his estate.'

"Governments long established should not be changed for light and transient causes, and not without the consent of a large majority of the people to be governed. It has, therefore, been decided by the delegates of the people, and is hereby affirmed, that no clause of the constitution about to be submitted shall be adopted or in force until it shall have received three-fourths of all the votes cast. We appeal to the people of the United States to go to the polls on the day fixed for the constitutional convention, and with a full realization of the responsibilities resting upon them, vote as their conscience and their duty dictates.

"Respectfully submitted to the people of the United States this sixth day of February, in the year of our Lord nineteen hundred and one.

"JOHN SMITH."

"And 340 Members of the Conference."

Congress was in session, but the people paid little or no attention to its proceedings. The Populists had a small majority in the House of Representatives, but were powerless to do anything. In fact, there was nothing to do. The government was dead. There was no system of finance. Silver had been demonetized several years before. Alaska and Witwatersrand had demonetized gold. One-third of the members of Congress went home after the second week of the session. In the later part of February the plot by which Judge Smith was defrauded of an election was exposed by the confessions of two New York politicians. Governor Kimbly issued an address to the American people asking them to support Judge Smith and pledging his own hearty co-operation.

It was a peaceful revolution. The mayor of Chicago called a conference of citizens in extraordinary session. A relief committee was formed and clothed with practically unlimited powers. They were backed by the credit of the city and authorized to purchase, or seize if necessary, provisions and other absolute necessities of life. The latter expedient was not required. The great packing-houses, the wholesale grocery-houses, flouring-mills, and other food-handling concerns placed their resources at the hands of the relief committee and accepted scrip currency in payment. Other cities followed the example. The country was practically under localized provisional government without a central head at Washington. Production, with the exception of farm products, had almost ceased. The excitement died away and the people patiently awaited the report of the committee on constitution

The conference reassembled at Omaha Feb. 20, and after a three days' session ratified the following constitution of the United States of America and arranged for its submission to the voters March 2, 1901.

CONSTITUTION OF THE UNITED STATES OF AMERICA.

"We, the United people of America, in order to preserve to ourselves and to posterity the blessings of civilization, to maintain the republic, to establish justice, insure domestic tranquillity, provide for the common defense, secure and guard the rights of the majority, and to guarantee to every citizen a fair opportunity for a livelihood, do hereby ordain and subscribe to this constitution of the United States of America.

ARTICLE I.

"Section 1. The executive power shall be vested in a president of the United States of America. He shall hold his office during a term of four years unless recalled during that time by a majority vote of the people. He shall be elected by a direct vote of the people, and must receive a majority of all votes cast If at any election no presidential candidate shall receive a majority of all votes cast a second election shall be held and a choice made between the two candidates receiving the highest number of votes in the preceding election.

"Sec. 2. No one shall be eligible to the office of president unless he shall have been born in the United States and shall have attained the age of 40 years.

"Sec. 3. A presidential election shall be held once in four years on the first Tuesday in November. The vote shall be canvassed by a returning board in each state and the certified result forwarded to the secretary of state and presented by him to the house of representatives, which shall convene on the third Tuesday of November—two weeks after the day of election. If no candidate has a majority a second election shall be held on the fourth Tuesday of November and the result announced by the secretary of state in the house of representatives on the second Tuesday after the fourth Tuesday of November. The president shall take possession cf his office January 1, unless that date shall fall on Sunday, in which event the president shall take possession the Monday following.

"Sec. 4. In case of the death, resignation, disability or removal for any cause of the president, the secretary of state shall act in his place until such time as a special election may be called according to law as may be hereafter provided. In the event that the death, resignation, disability, or removal for any cause of the secretary of state prevents him from acting as president, the secretary of the treasury shall be called to the presidential chair. The line of precedence shall be: President, secretary of state, secretary of treasury, secretary of war and navy, attorney-general, secretary of the interior, and superintendent of education.

"Sec. 5. The president shall be commander in chief of the army and navy of the United States and of the militia of the several states when called into the actual service of the United States. He shall have power by and with the advice and consent of his cabinet to make treaties provided two-thirds of the cabinet consent, and he shall nominate and by and with the consent of the senate shall appoint ambassadors, other public ministers, and consuls, judges of the Supreme Court and such other officers of the United States as he may be authorized by law to appoint. From time to time he shall give the people information of the state of the country, may recommend to their consideration such measures as he shall judge necessary and expedient, and he may on extraordinary occasions convene the house of representatives.

ARTICLE II.

"Section 1. At the presidential election the people shall also select by popular vote a secretary of state, secretary of the treasury, secretary of the army and navy, secretary of the interior, attorney-general, secretary of census and statistics, superintendent of education, secretary of foreign commerce, and chiefs of departments of agriculture, transportation, mechanics, and mining, the last four constituting a bureau of industry of which the president shall be chief. These twelve officers shall form a presidential cabinet for the advice and guidance of the president in the administration of the affairs of the country.

"Sec. 2. No person shall be eligible to a cabinet position except he shall have been a citizen of the United States for twenty-one years and shall have attained the age of 30 years.

"Sec. 3. Cabinet officers shall be elected in the same manner as the president and may at any time be recalled by a majority of the people.

"Sec. 4. The duties of the secretary of state, secretary of the treasury, secretary of the army and navy, secretary of the interior, and attorney-general shall be the same as those which have devolved on these officials in the past, subject to such new regulations as the president and his cabinet may from time to time direct.

"Sec 5. The secretary of the census and statistics shall collect and make public such statistical information as may be demanded by the president or required by the bureau of industry.

"Sec. 6. The superintendent of education shall have charge of the public school and university systems.

"Sec. 7. The chiefs of the departments of agriculture, transportation, mechanics, and minings shall systematize and supervise the work of their various departments. They shall appoint by and with the consent of the president and his cabinet such subordinate officers as the people shall provide by law.

"Sec. 8. The secretary of foreign commerce shall be the custodian of such surplus manufactured and other products as may be placed at his disposal by the bureau of industry. He shall be authorized to sell such products to foreign purchasers and make such exchanges as the president and his cabinet may direct.

"Sec 9. The president, cabinet officers, and their subordinates shall receive such compensation as the house of representatives may direct, subject to the approval of a majority vote of the people.

ARTICLE III.

"Section 1. All legislative power shall be vested in a majority vote of the people, subject to such exceptions and regulations as the people may formally direct.

"Sec. 2. Each federal state shall be divided into congressional districts on a unit of representation obtained by dividing the whole number of inhabitants of the United States by 200. Upon the adoption of this constitution the secretary of census and statistics shall make an enumeration of the inhabitants, and congress shall divide the several states into districts. There shall be no fractional representation, each state being allotted such a number of districts as will be obtained by dividing the whole number of its inhabitants by the unit of representation, the remainder being apportioned among the districts thereby obtained. Any state not entitled to a district under this law shall be merged into such adjoining state as a plurality of its voters may select.

"Sec. 3. A census shall be taken and congress shall make a re-apportionment of districts once in four years, said apportionment being made and put into effect within sixty days preceding the presidential election.

"Sec. 4. Each of the districts thus obtained shall be represented by a congressman, the 200 composing the house of representatives. A congressional election shall be held once a year on the first Tuesday in November, and congress shall convene at the national capitol on the first day of January immediately following its election. On extraordinary occasions the president may convene congress in special session.

"Sec. 5. No person shall be eligible to an election as congressman except he shall have been a citizen of the United States for fourteen years, and shall have attained the age of 30 years.

"Sec 6. On the vote of fifty members of congress any question pending before them shall be submitted to the people for a final decision. Congress shall have power to make its own rules and define its powers, subject to the approval of the people. It shall not be empowered to finally pass upon any act of legislation in which the whole people are directly interested. In all questions of national importance, such as the levying of taxes and the enactment of important legislation, they shall draft and prepare such bills as shall seem to them fitted for the government of the republic and submit them to the vote of the people for approval or rejection, at such times and in such manner as may hereafter be provided by law. Any law thus passed by the people shall be in force and effect from the time of its passage, and there shall be no appeal from it. Congress shall be guided in its deliberations by the opinions of the Supreme Court and the attorney-general, to whom all important measures shall be submitted for an opinion. Congress shall not be bound by this opinion, and may submit the law as drafted and the opinion to the people for approval or rejection.

"Sec. 7. No person shall represent a district unless he shall be an inhabitant of the state in which that district is situated.

"Sec. 8. Congressional representatives shall receive a salary for their services to be fixed by law and paid out of the treasury of the United States.

ARTICLE IV.

"Section 1. The judicial power of the United States shall be vested in a Supreme Court and such inferior courts as the people may from time to time establish.

"Sec. 2. The Supreme Court shall consist of a supreme judge and four associate judges, to be appointed by the president and indorsed by the people.

"Sec. 3. The Supreme Court shall be the final court of appeal, and shall be clothed with power to decide all cases affecting ambassadors, other public ministers, and consuls; to controversies in which the United States shall be a party; to controversies between two or more states, between a state and a citizen of another state, between citizens of several states, and between a state and citizens thereof. The Supreme Court may pass upon the constitutionality of laws passed by federal states, counties, townships, or cities, but it shall have no jurisdiction over laws passed by the people of the United States. It shall, when asked, examine any law under consideration by congress, and shall at such times furnish congress an opinion containing such advice and suggesting such alterations or amendments as will in their judgment more strictly conform to the spirit of the constitution.

"Sec. 4. Upon the recommendation of the president and a majority of his cabinet, or upon the recommendation of a majority of the house of representatives, the question of the retirement of any United States judge or judges may be submitted to the people, and upon a majority vote of the people such judge or judges shall be retired and a successor appointed or indorsed.

"Sec. 5. The judges of the Supreme Court and of all inferior courts shall receive a compensation to be determined by law and to be paid out of the treasury of the United States.

ARTICLE V.

"Section 1. The United States shall issue a currency and bonds of such denomination, volume, and upon such a basis as is specified in this constitution or as the people may hereafter enact by law.

"Sec. 2. The secretary of the treasury shall be empowered to issue a currency of a volume authorized by the president and his cabinet, based on the credit of the United States and redeemable in such products, labor, property, services, assets, or valuable compensation as shall be in the possession or at the disposal of the United States government. The treasurer of the United States is authorized to issue bonds bearing interest not exceeding $2\frac{1}{2}$ per cent, payable in currency of such a volume and for such purposes as the cabinet, congress, or the people may direct. The treasurer of the United States is authorized to issue currency or bonds to federal states, counties, townships, cities, private corporations, or individuals, accepting as security such tangible assets as state, county, township, or city property, or upon unincumbered and valuable property, lands, or convertible and negotiable products of labor, provided that in no case shall bonds or currency be issued in excess of half the value of the securities pledged to the redemption of this currency.

"Sec. 3. These bonds and the currency of the United States shall have as a unit a dollar, the said dollar standing as the representative of the average productivity of one hour's work, the said unit to be an approximation of the average benefit the community receives from one hour devoted to mental, manual, physical, and supervisory employments and positions.

"Sec. 4. The secretary of the treasury shall be empowered to issue such an amount of bonds and currency as may be necessary to defray the debts and expenses incurred by the government. The government may at its discretion refuse to sell, exchange, or dispose of any property or privileges except on payment therefor of such an amount of its own currency or bonds as may be mutually agreed upon.

"Sec. 5. Bonds and currency of the United States shall be printed or stamped in such a manner and upon such material as the secretary of the treasury may direct, provided that no article or substance which is of rare value or utility in mechanics or the arts be thus employed.

"Sec. 6. Counterfeiting the bonds or currency of the United States shall be a crime punishable by death, and any person or persons convicted of knowingly handling or passing such counterfeits may be adjudged guilty of treason and punished accordingly.

"Sec. 7. No federal, state, county, township, municipality, individual, or combination of individuals shall be permitted or authorized to issue a currency or a medium of exchange which shall conflict with that issued by the government of the United States.

ARTICLE VI.

"Section 1. The United States shall possess and is authorized to exercise the right of eminent domain, but this right shall be employed in such a manner as to work no injustice to any citizen of the United States or to the citizen of any other country.

"Sec. 2. The United States is authorized to preempt and occupy all unoccupied and all unused lands, taking possession of such land in the name of the people of the United States and holding them in trust for the citizens of the present and the future generations. The government shall proceed to acquire such land in a manner prescribed by congress.

"Sec. 3. The United States may purchase and acquire under the right of eminent domain such railroads, canals, telegraph and telephone lines, and such other inter-state and national mediums of transportation, communication and exchange as the people may by a majority vote direct.

"Sec. 4. The United States may upon the recommendation of the bureau of industry acquire by purchase under the right of eminent domain such lands, mines, forests and other property as may be deemed necessary to general production and the prosperity of the nation.

ARTICLE VII.

"Section 1. The United States, through its president, cabinet and congress, with the indorsement of a majority vote of the people, is authorized to undertake and supervise any of the forms of industry and production which may be deemed necessary to the welfare of the people, retaining such a share of the products thus created as shall be sufficient to retire the bonds and indebtedness incurred by the government. When such indebtedness shall have been retired the government shall withold none of the profits of production from those engaged in it.

"Sec. 3. The United States shall levy taxes for the general expenses of the government, but no tax shall ever be levied against the products of labor.

ARTICLE VIII.

"Any section or article in this constitution may be repealed, revised or amended by a majority vote of the people of the United States. Any proposed amendment shall be submitted to the people sixty days in advance of the date of election for its consideration.

PROVISIONAL.

"This constitution shall be submitted to the people March 10, 1901. It shall be voted on by sections, and no section shall be adopted unless it shall have received three-fourths of all the votes cast. The adoption of this constitution, or any substitutes, alterations or amendments, shall repeal all other constitutions, statutes, or laws conflicting with it.

"The first presidential election shall be held March 24, 1901, at which time the people shall elect a president, twelve members of a cabinet, and a provisional congress consisting of one representative from the congressional districts as now constituted. The president shall take possession of his office and congress shall meet in Washington April 4, 1901, the first presidential term expiring January 1, 1905. A presidential election shall occur the first Tuesday of November, 1904, in the manner as set forth in this constitution.

"It shall be the duty of the attorney-general, acting with the Supreme Court, to proceed immediately with the formation of a code of laws in harmony with the spirit of the constitution as finally adopted. The president and his cabinet are empowered to form such a provisional government, appoint such officers, and execute such a policy as the immediate needs of the country may dictate. The provisional congress shall remain in session until such time as it may decide to suspend the provisional government, at which time the constitution shall go into full force and effect."

Before adjourning the conference issued a call for a presidential nominating convention March 7, and a general election March 24. There was some debate on this question, several delegates claiming that the call should not be issued until after the constitution had been passed on by the people, but the majority urged that valuable time would be wasted, and that in the event of a rejection of the constitution the call for the nominating convention could be annulled. The call for the convention provided for two delegates from each congressional district. The primaries were held March 1, and March 7 the convention met at the Auditorium in Chicago and was held amid scenes of enthusiasm and joy. John Smith was nominated for President and a full ticket placed in the field.

With few exceptions the constitutional election of March 10 was held under the regular forms of law as a special election. In New York, Boston, Chicago, and in all the large cities the representatives of the Omaha conference went before the election commissioners and secured the calling of a special election. In small towns and villages the regular polling places were used by common consent. The People's party always insisted on having one judge of election, though the result proved this to be an unnecessary precaution. In most states the election was held under the Australian ballot system.

The agitation against the adoption of the constitution was confined mainly to the old-time bourbon Democrats of the south and their few northern sympathizers, who protested that it subjugated the federal states to the general government. These honest, but antique statesmen found themselves allied with the anarchists of New York and Chicago, who issued proclamations and addresses without number denouncing the proposed constitution as a "paternalistic outrage," a "contemplated governmental monopoly," a "villainous conspiracy to subjugate the minority."

The only difference between the bourbons and anarchists was in their methods and in their numerical strength. In 1893 there were about a thousand anarchists and about 50,000 bourbons in the United States, but they made noise enough to make up for their numerical weakness. Ninety-five per cent of the people of the country believed in a government. Bourbonism and anarchy make no distinctions in government. There is no such thing as "good government" with them. The anarchist wanted no government, and the bourbon fairly detested the word and regarded a government of any kind as a more or less necessary evil. For the numberless wrongs resultant from existing conditions the anarchists had a theory and a remedy which few people could understand and which no two anarchists ever explained in the same way. The bourbons had no remedy, and when prodded hard mumbled something about Thomas Jefferson or old Andy Jackson or the Darwinian theory of the survival of the fittest.

This interesting faction of the American people made a fight against the new constitution. There were a few who protested against what they termed "fiat money," and wanted to return to a silver basis. England, France and Germany had adopted a silver basis, gold having been demonetized, and some financiers urged that unless the United States did the same this country would never be able to make a living. They, therefore, talked against and probably voted against the currency features of the constitution.

March 10, 1901, the American people, by a popular vote of 14,490,000 against 1,324,000, ratified the new constitution. March 24, Judge John Smith was almost unanimously elected President of the United States, and on the 4th day of April was formally inaugurated at Washington amid scenes of popular rejoicing unparalleled in the history of the United States. In his inaugural address in the presence of 500,000 people President Smith said:

"No executive or administration in history ever was confronted with a problem so complex and momentous as that which demands solution at the hands of those the people have to-day intrusted with power. The years of our national life which have passed into history have not chrcnicled the failure of popular government. The mistakes of the past cannot be charged against the people. The long train of abuses which culminated in the unparalleled distress of our people sprang not from the popular branches of our government, but from those monarchical traditions incorporated in the constitution by certain of our forefathers who had not shaken off the superstitions which bound them to the throne of England. They gave to the country the name of a republic, and to its people the constitution of oligarchy. They so framed that document that while its preamble and spirit proclaimed popular rule and majority rights, its context made the people subject to any clique or cabal of men wealthy, daring and unscrupulous enough to take advantage of its provisions. That the country has advanced in wealth and that its people have secured a fair share of prosperity testifies not to the wisdom of the constitution, but to the glory of the citizen who has risen superior to unjust laws. The true American citizen looks not with envy upon riches honestly obtained, but he demands for himself and his children the opportunity to live and to contribute his share to the commonwealth of the republic. No government which permits this right to be subverted can long survive. Upon the ruins of a government which fell because it was not of the people let us erect a new government, 'laying its foundations on such principles and organizing its powers in such forms as shall seem to the people most likely to effect their safety and happiness.'

"This country is not ruined. Anarchy has prevailed for a period, but no permanent loss has been inflicted.

Financial distress and business depression have stopped the smoke from factory chimneys and dulled the fires in forge and mill, but the country is solvent. The United States of America is the most magnificent piece of property which nature ever lavished upon the children of men, and the operations of no systems of unwise laws can destroy its inexhaustible stores of natural wealth. Nature knows no politics. She yields up her treasures alike to Democrat and Republican, Prohibitionist and Populist, anarchist and socialist. She only demands the tribute of labor and brains, and the financial cyclone which swept across the country has not seriously impaired the brawn of the workman or the brain of the great captain of industry. The land lies smiling before us. Willing arms are eager to work. Let no man again say that the country is poor so long as land yields its wealth to labor.

"In the name of the people this administration assumes control of the government. In the name of the people and by virtue of the power vested by the people in the President and his cabinet, I now declare a provisional government to be, and to continue in effect until such time as Congress shall install in power the constitution passed by the people. It shall be the policy of this administration to so administer the immediate affairs of the government as to secure at the earliest moment the greater good to the greater number of people. Private interests and private rights and property will be conserved and protected, but no individual or combination of individuals shall in this emergency stand between the government and the welfare of the people. This administration will act in the capacity of a receiver for a valuable but mismanaged estate or corporation until such time as a majority of its stockholders, represented by Congress, shall terminate that receivership.

"I appeal to every American citizen to do his full duty and loyally support the administration in the stupendous task now before it. Selfishness must be put aside and patriotism act in its place. Not in a day or a week or in a month can the vast machinery of this country be put in perfect motion. Years of semi-idleness have incased with rust the working parts of our national mechanism, but under the magic touch of labor friction will disappear, and like a great engine abandoned for a time by its makers will the nation throb with a higher and more perfect activity."

CHAPTER XVIII.

THE RULE OF COMMON SENSE.

PRESIDENT SMITH and his cabinet, after a long and earnest conference, decided to take immediate action looking to the restoration of industry. Production had been suspended almost entirely for six months, and for over two years had been carefully restricted and curtailed to the lowest possible point. The demonetization of gold and the startling political revolution had paralyzed everything. Silver and silver certificates were used as money, and in Chicago, New York and other large cities the local governments had issued scrip in payment of food and other necessities purchased by the relief committees and distributed among the people. The secretary of the treasury was authorized to issue $1,000,000,000 in paper currency and bonds, the said issue to be considered as a temporary expedient and to be retired and replaced by a permanent system at the earliest possible date. This currency and the bonds were based on the credit of the government, and had as a precedent—if one were needed—the issue by the government of several billion dollars in greenbacks during the war of 1861-65. The administration had already determined on a permanent financial system, and Treasurer Childs lost no time in organizing and perfecting his department.

Agriculture, of all the industries of the country, was saved from the wreck which had overwhelmed the nation. As a rule the farmers had planted their usual crops. Chief of Agriculture Moulton, the day after his installation into office, issued an address to the farmers urging them to increase thei r acreage of crops to the greatest possible extent, and offered, on the part of the government, to supply any reasonable quantity of seed corn or grain of any kind. Thousands of requests were made, and Secretary Moulton made large purchases of grain from elevator companies in Chicago, Minneapolis and Duluth, paying for the same in the new currency and bonds. Some of the elevator men protested and accepted the crisp new bills with poor grace. They had no alternative, however, and contented themselves with denouncing the "fiat stuff" and proclaiming that they had been robbed in the name of the law. The banks and merchants at first refused to accept the new money except at a heavy discount. This was just what the enemies of the administration had predicted, and they took a grim satisfaction in the realization of their doleful forecast.

Chief of Mechanics Browning took possession of the great manufacturing industries of the country. In a circular addressed to the owners he outlined the policy of the government as follows:

"It is imperative that the industries of the United States be restored at once to their fullest possible activity. The supply of manufactured products is so low that the whole people are threatened with want. The government desires the earnest co-operation of factory-owners in this stupendous task. I am authorized by the President of the United States to take temporary possession of your factory in the name of the people and for the common welfare. The government will hold itself responsible for all damages done your machinery, all losses by fire, and other losses during its occupancy. You are earnestly requested to act as the agent of the government or to appoint a representative to act as your agent during this period. You will co-operate with an officer of the department of mechanics, whose duty it shall be to jointly keep with your aid an accurate account of the value and quantity of materials used in production, the rate and quantity of wages and such other data as properly come under the department of book-keeping. Our representative, acting on your advice, will fix a scale of wages conforming as nearly as possible to the average which prevailed in the fairly prosperous years of 1879 and 1891. For any material employed in production, for your own services, and for any other expenses which may be incurred or losses which may follow the temporary occupancy of the government you will be reimbursed by the payment of government bonds or currency. The government officer will pay the wages of the men and all other expenses which may be incurred, and turn over the finished product to the government. The department of mechanics trusts that you will find it to your interest to co-operate with the government at this time. An immediate answer to this communication is requested."

In response to this fully 65 per cent of the manufacturing establishments of the United States notified the department of mechanics of the appointment of an agent. Secretary Browning appointed government representatives for the larger establishments, and in the smaller ones trusted for the time to the books of the concern. Where manufacturing concerns ignored the government address the department took possession of the plants and resumed work. There was some little trouble, but the firm stand of the government soon convinced the most stubborn factory-owner that opposition was not only futile, but foolish. Every workman in the country was pressed into service. They had an abiding faith in the administration, and did not hesitate to accept the government scrip.

President Smith issued a message to the people, warning holders of the new currency or bonds against accepting any discount from merchants or bankers unless forced to by the direst calamity. He informed the people that the government was establishing distributing retail stations in every city of the country, at which government money would be accepted at a shade below the labor cost of the article purchased. Bondholders were also assured that their securities were of the highest order, and were advised to hold them for a time rather than sacrifice the new bonds for silver at a loss. This address had a slight reassuring effect, but for the first thirty days the government currency was either refused or accepted at a heavy discount by the banks, merchants and retailers. The new bondholders accepted President Smith's advice and held on to their securities, and with more or less faith awaited the result.

The first government distributing system was established in New York almost simultaneously in twenty places in the city. Agents of the government had no difficulty in renting for a short term many of the large unoccupied buildings, into which there began to pour the products of thousands of factories. In Chicago, Cleveland, St. Louis, Kansas City, St. Paul and all the great cities of the country such depots were in operation before the end of April. At the outset these distributing depots contained the simplest necessities of life, such as flour, sugar, cheap clothing, meats, coal and wood. But the prices caused a sensation and precipitated a small panic among private retailers, and even among wholesale merchants. The average rate of wages then being paid in the government shops was about $2.50 a day, but with this the workman was able to purchase from the "gov. shops," as they were termed, twice as much as the same wages had formerly commanded. The government prices were experimental, it being possible at the start to ascertain only approximately the cost price. As a result the government found at the end of a month that it had lost heavily on some articles and gained on others, but the average was a fairly accurate measure of the cost of production and distribution.

The effect of the introduction of the government shops was magical upon the private retail and wholesale trade of the country. The wholesale merchants had a considerable stock of goods on hand and were compelled to meet the government prices. The retailers not only had to meet the same prices, but were compelled to accept the new money in order to do business. The government shops accepted silver and silver certificates at par with the government currency. As fast as silver coins and the silver certificates were paid into the depots they were forwarded to Washington and retired from circulation.

The government shops had forced the credit of the government money. By the middle of May, less than six weeks after the inauguration of President Smith, the inexorable law of supply and demand had established the solidity and credit of the fiat currency. Every dollar which had been issued from Washington represented a fixed value and had something substantial back of it. The money advanced to the elevator companies for seed grain was represented by growing fields of grain. The money advanced to the factory-owners and to the 6,000,000 men already at work was represented by the vast stores of products now in the possession of the government stores and exchangeable at their cost value for this very currency.

"The moment $1 or $100,000 was transferred from the treasury department at Washington to a private individual it was represented by and based on a property or commodity now in the possession of the government. The holder of the currency could purchase back from the government all but a fraction of the property on which that currency was issued. The credit of this currency depended not upon the fluctuating intrinsic value of stored-up quantities of silver or gold, at the mercy of any bold or lucky developer or discoverer of mines. Its value was enhanced by every advance in civilization or discovery in science, invention, art or skill

Commerce with England and other foreign countries for the first two months was carried on by means of silver, vast quantities of which were stored in the treasury vaults at Washington as security for the silver certificates. The government coined into silver dollars all of this bullion and purchased abroad such commodities as sugar, wool, woolen manufactures, chemicals, coffee, flax, hides, fruit, tobacco, india rubber, tea and other necessities and luxuries. June 16 Congress demonetized silver, and the secretary of state informed the nations of the world that on and after July 1 the

United States government would refuse to accept any consideration other than its own currency. Europe refused to believe it.

Shortly after the passage of the act demonetizing silver the representative of an English grain syndicate called on Secretary of Commerce Field to negotiate for the purchase of 4,000,000 bushels of wheat, large quantities of which had been exchanged by farmers to the government in consideration of currency and stored in elevators leased by the department of commerce. Mr. Field and the syndicate representative agreed on the price of 73 cents per bushel.

The Englishman tendered the amount in silver, and was astonished to have it refused.

"Why, sir," said the English gentleman, "silver is the standard coin, don't you know. It has a ratio of 114½ to 1 as against gold. It has been accepted as the standard by the monetary congress of Europe."

"I am aware of that," said Mr. Field, "but, really, we have no use or demand for silver at present. We are not even working our silver mines, and have a large quantity of silver we would like to dispose of."

"No use for silver? Why, bless me, man, it is money!"

"Not in the United States," said Mr. Field. "If you desire to buy any wheat from the government you will have to pay us in United States currency."

"But we have no United States currency; it is not good in England, don't you know. Our merchants won't accept it, and all that sort of thing, don't you know. How am I going to get it?" asked the puzzled syndicate representative.

"That is not a part of my department," answered Mr. Field. "Secretary of the Treasury Childs can inform you as to that. The United States accepts no money other than its own."

The Englishman called on Mr. Childs and was informed that the United States could not assume the risk of accepting silver in payment for wheat or any other product of the soil or of labor.

"We can mine enough silver in two years to flood

the world," explained the kindly secretary of the treasury. "For all we know, there are other such mines in the world. Any day may bring the news of the discovery of a new and prolific silver mine. That would find us with several hundred tons of white metal on our hands which is valueless even in the arts. We can take no such risk. We will accept any good securities on bonds based on land or safe and imperishable property. If you have no such system of currency or security you would beter make an arrangement with Mr. Field to exchange certain English products for the wheat you desire. If your firm is responsible I may accept their note for the amount, provided it so reads as to be negotiable for English products at current rates governing the exchange of such products. But we will not accept silver. Perhaps Mr. Field may make a bargain with you for copper or tin. I understand he is in the market for tin. Otherwise, you will be compelled to furnish me with some absolutely safe security, in exchange for which I will give you the desired amount of United States currency or bonds."

The Englishman returned home without making the purchase. He vainly attempted to buy wheat from Chicago capitalists, but they would not accept silver, the government having retired it from circulation. For nearly three months the commercial relations between the United States and England were in a peculiar condition. The United States continued to purchase from England, paying their debts in silver, but steadily refusing to accept silver in payment for anything. The commercial contest was too one-sided, and England surrendered and made terms for United States currency.

That was the opening wedge which eventually forced the credit of American money upon the world and finally established a new international financial standard. For ten years the United States continued to unload silver upon Europe and the rest of the world, receiving in return every product of labor from the poles to the equator. These foreign products were placed on sale at the government depots, and the people of the

United States were not compelled to pay any McKinley or other tariff as an added price to the cost of purchase and transportation. The pauper labor of Europe did not seem to bother the administration, and whenever Mr. Field could make a good purchase of any commodity needed by the people he did so regardless of the cost of production in the United States.

In a few industries it was found that the United States did not possess natural advantages which enabled it to produce at the labor cost abroad, and it was the policy of the government to gradually curtail and eventually close such industries, employing the resources and the labor of American workmen in other directions and buying the required products in the cheapest market. The production of sugar and wool was practically abandoned, these necessities purchased abroad, and the capital and labor formerly unprofitably invested in them was employed to better advantage. The tariff question ceased to be an issue and was relegated to history.

The government took immediate possession of the railroads, and Chief of Transportation Jeffery assumed the control of the 175,000 miles of railroad. The great railway trusts and pools had simplified the work of this department. The railroads had already been merged into four or five great trusts. The officers in control were not disturbed at first, and as a rule were made agents of the government under Chief Jeffery. The stockholders and bondholders were assured that their property rights would be respected and protected by the government. In this stupendous industry the peaceful revolution was effected without the slightest friction and without the loss of a day's usefulness. The railroads accepted, of course, the new currency, and this had a tremendous influence in establishing the credit of the government. The inter-state commerce commission operated with the government, and the great railroad presidents lent valuable assistance to the administration. Many of them had for years been in favor of the national control of railroads and had foreseen that such was the inevitable trend of events. It was not necessary to issue government bonds to the owners of railroad property, the administration pledging itself to recognize, at the proper time, all lawful issues of stocks and bonds.

The wages of the 850,000 railroad men were paid by the government, and under the efficient management of Chief Jeffery revised rates were put into effect and the vast system operated as a private corporation for the benefit of stockholders and public alike.

President Smith assumed personal supervision over the most difficult, complicated and delicate problem confronting the administration, that of taking possession of unused and unoccupied land. A land commission was formed and the work subdivided among the several states. The title to every acre of property in the United States was examined into and properly classified. Speculators had subdivided their holdings in anticipation of this action of the government and rendered the task a more difficult one. In mining lands the commission allowed to the owners an acreage equal to thirty years' average development of the mines then in operation, taking as the standard of measurement the highest production in any given year. In mines, as well as in forest and other property, recent transfers made with an evident intent of defeating the policy of the government were ignored.

The vast undeveloped tracts of land in New York, Pennsylvania and the central states which had been held for years by home and foreign speculators were condemned and purchased and their holders paid a fair profit on their investment. The work of the commission was rendered more easy by the action of Congress, which in September levied a heavy tax on all unoccupied or unimproved land, which had the effect of destroying its speculative value. It was many years before the land commission completed its work, which, while of great importance to the future of the country, was not of such vital consequence to the people of that time. The United States eventually found itself the owner by purchase, condemnation, and forfeiture by reason of non-payment of land taxes, of over one-half of the fertile, productive land of the United States, and of not less than 85 per cent of the coal, iron and other mining lands.

CHAPTER XIX.

PROVISIONAL GOVERNMENT.

UNDER the provisional government the people were enjoying a prosperity such as had never before come to a nation, and on every hand was expressed the hope that the administration would make no change. But President Smith was eager for the day when Congress could safely declare the provisional government at an end, and the President and his cabinet bent every energy in that direction. In the latter part of June, Treasurer Childs had perfected the permanent system of finance, which consisted of:

1. United States paper currency of denominations of $1, $2, $5, $10, $20, $50, $100, $200 and $500, and a fractional currency of 1-cent, 2-cent, 5-cent, 10-cent, 25-cent and 50-cent pieces, stamped on aluminium, a cheap and light metal.

2. Agricultural certificates of the same denominations as the currency, and issued upon standard farm products sold to the government.

3. State certificates issued to a federal state by the general government on the credit of the state, and of the same denominations as the currency.

4. Municipal certificates issued to an incorporated city by the general government on the credit of the city, and of the same denominations as the currency.

5. Manufacturing certificates issued to owners of factories and manufacturing plants by the general government in consideration of the purchase of said plants by the government. These certificates were in denominations of $50, $100, $200, and $500, and $1,000, $2,000, $5,000, and $10,000.

6. Railroad, telegraph, and general bonds issued to the owners of railroads, telegraph, or other corporate

stocks or bonds of denominations of $100, $200, and $500, and $1,000, $2,000, $5,000, and $10,000.

The government currency and agricultural certificates were intended as a general circulating medium for the payment of wages and for the general use of the people. The government was authorized to issue a sufficient volume to meet all the demands of production. The secretary of the treasury was authorized to issue agricultural certificates upon such standard grains as could be easily stored and for which the world always had a market. He was also empowered to determine from time to time the certificate value of such grain or standard and ever negotiable farm product.

State and municipal certificates were issued to federal states and cities for public improvements, and were redeemable after stated terms of years in national currency raised by the states or cities from the revenues of such public improvements or by taxation.

Manufacturing certificates were issued by the government in the purchase of manufacturing plants, being a full payment for such property on terms mutually agreed upon by the government and the owner or owners of such property. These certificates were exchangeable at any time by the government into currency.

The most important issue was that of railroad bonds. The railroad capital of the United States in 1891, according to the report of the inter-state railroad commission, was $9,437,343,420, divided as follows:

Railroad stock	$4,409,658,485
Funded debt	4,574,576,131
Miscellaneous debt	453,108,804
Total	$9,437,343,420

"Of this," says the report of the commissioners, "the bonds or funded debt represents the certain or bed-rock value of the railway property, while the stocks represent their speculative value."

The dividends on this stock and payments of interest on the bonds amounted to an annual dividend, interest or profit, of 3.35 per cent. In no year after 1891 had the railroads shown an equal prosperity, and the statement of that year was accepted as a fair basis of settlement. The railroad property of the United States was appraised by Congress at $5,400,000,000, and bonds for that amount were issued to the stock and bond owners, the said bonds bearing interest at the rate of 4 per cent, or $216,000,000 annually, a sum exceeding that formerly paid in dividends and interest, except in the more prosperous years. These bonds bore interest for a term of thirty years and were so numbered that one-thirtieth of the total amount, or $180,000,000, was retired each year by the government, both interest and principal being paid in currency. The cancellation of the face of the bond did not impair its interest coupons, which were payable each year. The government therefore stipulated to pay to the railroad owners the sum of $396,000,000 annually for a period of thirty years, or a total sum of $11,880,000,000. These figures fairly staggered the people and many declared that it could never be done.

In answer to this criticism, which amounted almost to a protest, President Smith in a message to the people said:

"The reason why it can and will be done will be found in the fact that it has been done for years under the most distressing financial circumstances and even when the whole nation was staggering under the handicap of restricted production and general business and financial depression. The people of the United States have created nothing greater than themselves. They have always paid by their patronage all dividends which have accrued to the stock and bond holders, and have annually added to the railroad equipment a value of not less than $200,000,000 a year. The $216,000,000 fairly represents the earnings of the roads, which will be vastly increased under the management of the government. The $180,000,000 applied to the purchase of the roads divided among the 75,000,000 people of the United States amounts to $2.40 per capita, or to less than $10 a year to the average head of a family. The decreased cost of products to the consumer incident to a lessened rate of transportation will more than thrice offset this trifling sum."

This was strictly true. The consumer and the producer had always paid not only the stock dividends but the interest on the bonds. Every day, when the citizen of the United States seated himself at the breakfast or dinner table, he paid a small tribute to the railroad stock and bond holders. From across the broad Atlantic the long arm of the English, Belgian, German and Holland bondholder reached out and collected its tax. Every dollar of this represented the product of American labor. It meant that the American workmen were compelled to annually produce $500,000,000 worth of grain, boots and shoes, lumber, cotton goods, knives, etc., the proceeds of which went to pay the dividends and interest of the railway capital. The burden was not increased by the government purchase of these roads. The sum stipulated was enormous in the aggregate, but under a system which permitted the people to produce to their full capacity the $15,000,000,000 was a mere trifle.

Even under the provisional government over 3,000,000 formerly idle men had been placed at work. This was in excess of the number which had at any former time been employed in production. Their work was a clear gain to the community. It was more than that. Formerly the community had to support them in idleness. Each of those 3,000,000 men created a product of value not less than $3 a day, or $9,000,000 a day and $2,700,000,000 for the 300 working days in a year. These 3,000,000 idle men, unaided by the 20,000,000 other producers of the United States, were therefore able to cancel the entire debt to the railroad stock and bond holders—a sum of $15,120,000,000—in the short space of five years and eight months.

To put it in another way, the obligation assumed by the government was annually met by the labor of 560,000 men, less than one-ninth of those who had formerly been forced into idleness. The 5,000,000 men who were idle in 1893 could produce every mile of railroad, every car, bridge, and the entire assets of the railroad companies of the United States in less than eighteen months. They could do even better than this. The railroad values were based on labor performed by the clumsy processes in use in former years before the time of steam dredges, shovels, and all the magnificent equipments of the present.

Had it been necessary the United States could have duplicated the railroad property in a year without the slightest strain on the national resources.

This is a striking illustration of the waste of production permitted in the years before the reign of common sense. The United States railroad bonds became the finest securities ever placed on the market of the world. They were based on the actual railroad property and backed by the credit of the United States. Their annual interest amounted to more than had ever been paid in dividends and in interest on bonds and was payable in a currency which could by no possibility depreciate. They had a life of thirty years—a generation—with interest paid in some cases for twenty-nine years after the face of the bond had been redeemed. This system worked exact justice to every holder of railroad property. It would have been manifestly wrong for the government to have taken possession of the railroad property and forced the acceptance of non-interest bearing bonds in full payment. This would have deprived investors of a steady income for a term of years—a consideration they were clearly entitled to, and one which was recognized by the government.

The new railroad bonds commanded a high premium, and were eagerly sought after by European investors. The manufacturing certificates were also accepted abroad as a perfect security, being represented by improved and steadily enhancing property.

The administration proceeded, after the adoption and installation of the permanent system of finance, to organize its industries on a solid basis. Up to this time the government had been acting under a provisional form, in which the administration had for the time annulled all laws, though aiming to work injustice to no private interest. In this President Smith and his cabinet had succeeded even beyond their fondest expectations. The liberal treatment accorded manufacturers and capitalists had won to the administration thousands of powerful friends, who rendered valuable aid in the permanent introduction of the government workshops. Congress placed at the credit of the department of mechanics the sum of $2,000,000,000 to be expended in the purchase and extension of manufacturing plants and machinery.

Chief Browning devoted a considerable part of this sum to the erection of machine shops near Philadelphia, New York, Chicago, Cleveland, St. Louis, Cincinnati and other manufacturing cities. Large forces of machinists were placed at work in the production of standard and special machinery About one-half of the appropriation was expended in the purchase of fully equipped plants. Large agricultural manufacturing plants were located at Omaha, St. Paul and Kansas City, giving employment to about 30,000 men. In Michigan and Wisconsin the department rapidly developed the lumber industries.

In his report to Congress January 1, 1898, Statistician Wright reported that the government had purchased 6,223 manufacturing plants at a price of $876,485,000 and had invested in 551 new plants the sum of $423,000,000. He estimated that the 551 new establishments, then under construction, would, when completed, exhaust the $2,000,000,000 appropriation, each plant representing an average investment of $2,000,000. There were employed in the purchased plants 439,420 workmen and in the new government enterprises a total of 396,718, a grand total in the employ of the department of mechanics of 836,138. The average rate of wages was $2.98 a day, the minimum wage being $1.75 and skilled workmen receiving from $3.50 to $10 and, in exceptional cases, $18 and $20 per day. The cost of direct government supervision had been 1.3 per cent of the total product, this sum representing the proportional expenses of the national government, the salaries of government officials and inspectors directly in charge, and other general expenses. The products of these industries had been sold to the customer at an average excess of $9\frac{1}{4}$ per cent over their cost price. This represented the expenses of transportation, retailing, and losses from various causes. Statistician Wright stated that this percentage could be materially reduced.

In his report to congress Chief Moulton of the department of agriculture set forth that his department was ready to rent or lease farming lands, and in a few weeks would be able to co-operate with the department of mechanics and enable occupants of government land to secure, upon proper security, such farming tools and machinery as was necessary. His report showed an average crop throughout the country, only a small portion of which had been sold abroad.

Chief Skiff of the department of mining reported that little had been accomplished in his department, owing to the lack of mining machinery and the necessary caution of the land commission in proceeding with its work. The government had purchased and acquired by condemnation valuable iron mining lands, and work on such lands would be hastened as rapidly as possible. The forced development of the mines under the management of the government had reduced the price of ores until it was possible, if advisable, to export large quantities to England and other countries. The chief made no recommendation on this point.

Attorney-General Burke submitted a long report, detailing the work and proceedings of the inter-state legal convention, called for the purpose of forming a code of laws in conformity with the new constitution. The secretary of the interior and superintendent of education reported that no material changes had been made in their departments, the postal and school systems having been well nigh perfected under preceding administrations. Superintendent Ely recommended the founding of great universities in New York, Chicago, Denver and San Francisco, modeled after the Columbian Exposition held at Chicago in 1893.

CHAPTER XX.

DOWNFALL OF THE MIDDLEMAN.

APRIL 4, 1902, exactly one year after President Smith's inaugural, Congress declared the provisional government at an end and decreed the constitution as adopted by the people in full force and effect. The day was one of great rejoicing, tinged with a slight feeling of apprehension among the hundreds of thousands of workmen who for a year had been retained at work by the authority of the government. There were fears among the timid that many of them would be discharged or their wages reduced, but the majority had faith in the future, and the first anniversary of the new government was celebrated with parades and great public demonstrations. In his annual message to Congress and to the people President Smith paid a tribute to the capitalists and great manufacturers of the country. In his message the President said:

"The administration is under deep obligations to the manufacturers, railroads, and other capitalists of the United States, who have loyally aided the government in the stupendous task of repairing the losses inflicted by years of idleness and depression. With but few exceptions they have voluntarily placed the entire resources of their great producing plants in the hands of the administration and have generously co-operated with us in the work of the last twelve months. Such of these factories, mills and plants as have not been purchased by the government are now placed in the full possession of their former owners. With but few exceptions the government has made a satisfactory settlement with the owners for the use of their plants and in payment for materials, and all disputes which have arisen have been submitted to arbitration, the verdict of which will be accepted by both parties.

"Every industry of the country is now in full operation, and from the Atlantic to the Pacific, from the Gulf to the British line no American workman is idle by reason of a lack of opportunity to work. A reference to the accurate reports submitted to Congress by the secretary of census and statistics shows that the total output of manufactured products for the year more than doubles that of 1891, which was considered a prosperous year, and quadruples that of the corresponding period of 1900, the year preceding the adoption of the constitution of the United States.

"It will be the policy of the government in the second year of its existence to extend the industries now in process of construction, and to add to their number and scope as rapidly as the prosperity of the people will permit. The government now enters into a friendly competition with the private capital and manufacturing interest of this country, but none of its powers will be exercised to secure an unfair or unnatural advantage. Railroad rates will be made uniform, all departments of the government paying into the department of transportation such freight and other rates as that department may establish, which rate shall be the same as those made to private users.

"No system of taxation shall be proposed or adopted which shall operate against private interests, and whatever influence the executive or the present cabinet possesses will be urged against any discriminating legislation. It is but fair that private capital and the private machinery of production should bear its fair share of the common expenses of the government, and to that end it shall be the policy of the administration to urge the adoption of a system which shall bear lightly upon actual property, and to place the heaviest burdens upon lands held for purely speculative purposes."

The provisional government came to an end and the constitution entered into effect without the slightest friction or disturbance of the affairs of the country. The government officers were withdrawn from private factory and mill. The thousands of workmen applied for work the next morning and with hardly an exception were assigned to their former positions. There were some slight modifications of the wage scale and a few men were discharged. Such men applied at the government shops and, if capable and worthy, were placed at work. The changed condition had no effect on the government industries, and the bureau of industry steadily increased the force of workmen, drawing upon the private concerns for its extra men. Under this stimulus wages rose slightly, the manufacturers being compelled to meet the government prices in order to retain their workmen.

The first congressional election was held Jan. 10, under the new apportionment of districts as prepared by the preceding Congress. Of the 200 congressmen nearly two-thirds were selected from the membership of the provisional Congress, which had been in continuous session for a year.

The newly elected Congress assembled in Washington Jan. 28. The most important question before it was that of immigration. A long debate on this problem ensued. Immigration had almost ceased in 1896, but the prosperity of the country under the new government brought thousands of more or less desirable emigrants from the old country. Many citizens were in favor of absolutely prohibiting immigration, and others urged that this was not only unwise, but impolitic.

At the close of the debate Congress submitted three propositions to the people for an informal expression of opinion. The first provided for a restriction of immigration to 300,000 a year for a period of five years, the second provided for the absolute restriction of immigration, and the third for no restriction or limitation of immigration. The people by an overwhelming majority indorsed the second proposition and Congress enacted it as a law.

It is interesting to note that the people made a mistake the first time they decided a great popular question. For years many of the evils of the country had been charged against immigration. It was a curse under such conditions as prevailed in 1870-1896, but those conditions were changed. There was a demand for workmen. Production had increased to such a point and work was so plentiful that Chicago, New York and other large cities found it impossible to employ men to work on the streets. Farmers could not obtain hired hands. In all departments where hard or distasteful labor was required it was impossible to employ men except at very high wages. The government found it impossible to hire all the men it required. Six months after the passage of the law prohibiting immigration the people repealed it and substituted a law providing for the admission of 450,000 foreign workmen a year, with strict provisions against the admission of criminals or paupers. In 1904 this law was repealed and all restrictions taken from immigration. The country was then in a position to take care of any number of industrious men, and what was more, the overthrow of the German and Russian empires had opened to the people of those countries vast tracts of crown lands which were taken possession of by the newly formed republics and leased to the land-starved people. In Germany over one-third of the most fertile land in the empire had been reserved by the king and the nobility for hunting preserves.

Congress submitted to the people a system of taxation providing for a tax on land, by which house lots, and home property owned by the occupant was exempt from taxation. All rent and income-producing lands were slightly taxed, as were farm lands under cultivation. Unoccupied and unused lands, whether held for speculative purposes or otherwise, were heavily taxed.

The first four years of President Smith's administration were years of prodigious effort on the part of the government. Not until the latter part of 1904 could the government industries be considered as being upon a permanent basis. These were years of construction in which vast amounts of labor were expended on buildings, mines and forests, and nature was levied on for much of her prolific treasure. President Smith was elected to a second term in 1904.

Four years before, John Smith, a plain American citizen, with good, honest common sense which went as far as to consider government a matter of business and not of sentiment—John Smith found himself President of the United States and in a position to put into practice those business principles which the "patriotism" of 1893, '94 and '95 denounced as visionary and its advocates as cranks.

In those four years the nation had almost doubled its wealth. John Smith entered upon the first presidential term at a time when the United States was actually starving to death. The country was constitutionally built on the lines of a turtle, which when turned on its back has no power to right itself and miserably starves surrounded by plenty. Every panic turned the clumsy creature on its back.

President Smith's first term witnessed the decline of the middleman. The middleman came into existence back in the centuries and reached his highest development in the later years of the nineteenth century. He flourished as a wholesaler, jobber, retailer, petty tradesman, peddler, fakir, agent, and had a thousand branches and ramifications. The middleman was the direct product of a false system of industry. He existed by manipulating the products of others. Like any institution founded on false principles, the structure raised by the middleman was doomed to destruction.

The middleman was in his glory in 1893. Take a hat, for instance There was the manufacturer who made the hat and the people who wanted to buy and wear the hat. It would seem a simple transaction, but it was far from it. The manufacturer sold his hats to a jobber, the jobber purchasing them in large quantities at a small margin. The jobber in turn sold them to the wholesaler, who kept hats and caps and many other specialties. The wholesaler sold them to the retailer at a profit, and the retailer sold them to the customer. The manufacturer had, therefore, presumably, made a profit, the jobber had made a profit, the wholesaler had made a profit, the retailer had made a profit and the customer was permitted to buy a hat.

This beautiful system was defended in 1893 and in other years by people who were fearful that the trusts or something were menacing the "occupations and usefulness" of the middlemen. The great trusts and the general stores ignored the middlemen and kept eating up the little retailers, and people denounced the trusts and all other comprehensive and scientific systems of handling productions.

Great retail stores in Chicago and similar enterprises in other large cities bought directly of the manufacturer and ignored both wholesaler and jobber. The little retailer could not compete with them, and many people who reason with a substance which takes the place of brains condemned the great stores and passed laws against any concerns which attempted to carry on the business of the distributers of products in a scientific manner. The trust, with its national policy, its conformity to the laws of business, of supply and demand, and to every natural law of production and distribution, was condemned by law; state legislators and Congress were appealed and petitioned to destroy the one valuable product of modern commercialism.

But all the man-made laws in the world could not destroy the trust. Its birth was inevitable. It came as a prophecy of something to follow. The trust did not conform to the age in which it survived, but that was not the fault of the trust, but of the age. The trust was not an unselfish affair and was not intended for the benefit of the people, but it was scientifically perfect and was the fittest to survive. It crushed down competition—the foolish, petty haggling among small merchants which went by the name of competition—and absorbed small rivals as a snowball grows in volume as it rolls down-hill. The general store and emporium was formed on economic lines, and thousands of small retailers were forced by it out of business. It was hard on them, but they were members of a class whom progress had marked for slaughter. They were going the same way as the old stage-driver, the old mail-carrier and the ferry-boat man.

But some foolish people wanted to stop the wheels of

progress because the job of the retailer was threatened. The "job" was the thing in 1890-96. The great problem was to furnish "jobs." It made no difference to the political economist whether the job was a productive one or not. The capitalist or philanthropist who would set 100 men at "work" hauling stone up the street and then hauling it back again indefinitely was considered a public benefactor. He had given men "work," a "job." The retailers had a "job" and it was generally as non-productive as any occupation well could be.

In 1893 the retailer was nothing but a wageworker. His importance to the community had lessened year by year. Slowly but surely he was being forced to the wall by the powerful and well-equipped general stores. In the great cities thousands of them were forced to the wall by the panic of 1893, and on distinctively retail streets the doors of stores were plastered with sheriff's notices. The advent of a great department store, backed by unlimited capital, meant the certain downfall of from 1,000 to 5,000 retailers. The general store sold better goods at cheaper prices. It could afford to and yet make a profit. One clerk in a great store easily did the work of a dozen in a small retail shop. It was but another illustration of the development of the machine. The department store was modern, scientific and labor-saving. The retail store was antique, unscientific and labor-creating. It fostered useless labor. It ran on useless errands. It was the old stage coach pitted against the compound locomotive with its record of 100 miles an hour.

The retail store was doomed in 1893—surely and inevitably doomed—but its fate was deplored by a certain class of alleged thinkers, who wanted the obsolete system of petty retailing continued because it made "work." These same men would have destroyed a valuable machine because it saves "work." They hated a trust because by a system of production and distribution it made profit by doing away with "work."

But a day had come when the people wanted not "work," but rather the products of work, and the problem was to derive the greatest results with the least expenditure of toil.

In 1893 a great invention was a curse. It did away with work.

In 1903 a great invention was a blessing. It did away with work.

In 1893 a great fire was a blessing. It destroyed the products of work and created a demand for labor. In 1903 a great fire was a national calamity. It had destroyed the products of labor and decreased the actual wealth of the nation.

The government had not extended its scope so as to include all of the forms of industry. Such was not its policy. The administration confined its attention to the production of the actual standard necessities of life and left to private capital the development of the hundreds of specialties which increase with civilization. But in all commodities for which there was a general demand, and in which it had been possible for trusts to assume a monopolistic control by reason of vast resources and good management, the government became an active competitor.

Among the great government industries against which private capital competed, these may be mentioned: Cotton and woolen manufactories, flour milling, stock yards, and cattle raising, the production of standard grocery and drug articles, standard articles in the hardware line, coal, coke and wood, lumber, agricultural machinery, planing mills—in a word, the government engaged in the production of the actual necessities of modern life and ignored the thousands of specialties and luxuries for which the demand is more or less limited. But the government made and had on sale enough of the standard products of civilization to support the people independent of outside production, and its competition with private capital in these branches forever precluded high and exorbitant prices.

The government extended its retail system on the same plan as that pursued in the perfection of the post office system. Whenever, in the opinion of the department, it was advisable to locate a distributing retail depot in any given locality, a site was selected and a building purchased or erected of such a capacity as the present or future needs of the adjacent district seemed to warrant. The location of such a depot would, of course, threaten the supremacy of the local retailers, who usually found it impossible to long compete against the government shops. It was the policy of the administration to offer such retailers advantageous terms for their stocks of goods on hand, a proposition which was generally accepted.

Thus the old-fashioned retailers of meats, boots and shoes, dry goods, coal and wood, lumber and other commodities gradually disappeared without loss of anything but his "job," a much kinder fate than that which befell the old stage drivers on the advent of the unsympathetic but superior railroad company. In certain specialties the retailer survived and so did the wholesaler and jobber, but as a class the middleman gradually faded out of existence and joined the other discarded rubbish stowed away in Father Time's attic.

The great army of retailers easily accommodated themselves to the changed conditions. The more progressive found profitable employment as heads of departments in the government depots or in the competing stores of the private industries. The poorly paid retail clerks were happily released from a monotonous life in a dreary store and engaged in the higher activities of the new regime. Their work was more easy and their wages sufficient to enable them to support themselves in comparative luxury. They were no longer useless adjuncts to society, deriving a miserable existence by filling a needless position. They now formed a part of a perfect system of production and distribution. They were absolutely independent, and at liberty at any time to retire from their present occupation and devote their time and energies in any of the numberless activities surrounding them. The line of promotion was ever open. The retail clerk of to-day may be the high-salaried head of a vast department in the coming decade.

The government was a gigantic trust, with the people

as stockholders. It transacted business on a national scale, manufacturing to the best possible advantage. The department of mechanics did not attempt to locate iron mills in New York City or in Chicago when production could be carried on more cheaply at points nearer the mines. It did not attempt to force anything against natural surroundings. It conducted the business affairs of the nation the same as the head of a great corporation manages its affairs for the benefit of the stockholders. Against this vast and scientific system of production the small competing manufacturer who attempted to "go it alone" was inevitably forced under. He was compelled either to combine with other manufacturers and become a stockholder in a comprehensive system of production on lines of scientific economy, or he had the alternative of retiring from business or of selling to the government or to any other purchaser. In order to do business the private manufacturer had to meet the prices of the government. So had the great trust.

It was absolutely free competition, in which the best system or systems survived.

Except in specific and limited industries, the small factory passed out of national existence. There remained the great private industries and trusts and the government industries. Both were supported by the consumers. The government retailed through its own depots and distributing departments. In every city these magnificent stores were established and conducted on the most perfect business systems, with every feature reduced to an exact science, even to a greater extent than prevailed in the post-office departments of former years. In order to meet this competition the trusts were compelled to form a similar system. The little retailer could not compete. The government would sell him goods at the same rate as that charged against the depots, but the margin was so small that living profits were impossible. There was no jobbing trade and there were no jobbers in the great national products. The government and the trusts did their own wholesaling and the private wholesaler sold out his stock and retired from business. Such of those middlemen as had a competency retired and lived at ease. Others connected themselves with the industries of the government or with private interests, and the world moved on as though no back-street clerk had ever sold 5 cents' worth of ribbon over a dusty old counter in a dingy little store.

The middleman, who for a century had stood between the producer and the consumer, demanding and receiving his toll, had been relegated to the past along with other forms of extortion, which the people of former years had accepted and indorsed on the plea that "they always had existed and probably always would"—the helpless wail of a man too lazy to strike a blow at that which oppresses him.

The consumer derived the greatest benefit from this new system. All of the people are consumers. They profited by the competition between the government and the trusts. Prices ever tended to the lowest point at which the government could manufacture, handle and distribute its products. The trusts sold at the same figures, and consequently at very slight margins of profit. All of which was to the direct advantage of the consumer. It was no longer possible for combinations of private capital to monopolize any great industry and force up prices at the expense of the consumer.

The competition between the government and its powerful rivals was inspiriting. Compelled as they were to meet the prices fixed from time to time by the bureau of industry, the trusts and other private interests were forced to seek their profits in superior skill in manufacturing and in handling. The railroad rates were the same to both competitors. It was a contest in which superiority of management, workmanship, inventive skill, and close attention to detail was sure to win. Skilled workmen were in great demand. They transferred their allegiance from one shop to another and received wages in proportion to their fitness and capacity.

It was impossible for the trusts to force the average scale down. The government regulated the wage scale.

It ever stood ready to employ a capable workman at a standard rate of wages in keeping with his skill compared with other workmen. The government had every resource that the trusts had. It was prepared to bid against them for talented managers of industry, and in its employ were many great organizers of industry in receipt of salaries exceeding $20,000 a year. The trust was, therefore, compelled to pay the same wages and to fix the same prices for its products as the government. It had always been claimed that private management was superior to that of the government. The trusts had an opportunity to prove this. Their profits represented their exact superiority over the government, but were not increased either by enforced low wages or monopoly prices for their products. The community, therefore, obtained the benefit of all the good features of combination and competition, without the evils which are ever resulting from monopoly.

The rivalry resulted in a rich harvest to the inventor. The government was always willing to purchase a valuable invention and the trusts were ever prepared to bid against it. The inventor therefore received the full value of his genius. Private capital was in the field to back any promising new enterprise fortified by patents or other privileges, and inventors were protected in their rights by patent laws substantially the same as those of former years.

In 1908 the number of men employed in private industries was 7,638,492, and in government industries 5,429,603, according to the annual report of the secretary of census and statistics. For a period of twenty years the government percentage gradually increased until at present the number is about equally divided.

In 1907 the United States found itself confronted by an actual condition of overproduction in manufactured goods of many kinds. The foreign markets had been supplied and exchanges made until the government stores were loaded with foreign articles and luxuries. In this emergency the hours of labor were reduced from 8 to 6 and some of the surplus energy of the nation diverted to great public improvements in parks, public buildings, and in extension of the railway system. In July and August all government workmen in certain departments had two months' vacation on full pay, and in September and October those who had not been so favored took a vacation on the same pleasing terms. The summer holiday became a regular feature and was extended to three months. This was a simple and by no means disagreeable way of meeting what in 1893 would have caused a panic. In 1893 the factories would have closed down, the men would have been discharged and denied a chance to work, their power of purchase or consumption cut off, and the country permitted to drag out a miserable, half-starved existence for a period of years.

Occasionally a trust would succumb to the severe competition. Some found it impossible to contend with the national industry against which it was pitted. In such cases the bureau of industry conferred with the owners and purchased the competing plant, adding the resources and equipment to the national plant. Such cases were of rare occurrence. It was the policy of the government to encourage competition, and in no industry was a monopoly long permitted to exist.

It was observed that in the absence of competition the efficiency and *esprit de corps* of the industry involved suffered from that cause. Between the heads of departments in trust and nation there existed an earnest though friendly rivalry. The public kept a close watch on the dividends declared by private concerns. A large dividend paid by a trust indicated the superiority of private management, and its long continuance generally led to an overhauling in the government department which suffered by comparison.

Under such a system there was no chance for laziness or incompetency among the workmen or of long-continued inefficiency among heads of departments. It was the policy of the bureau of industry to allow the operatives to select foremen and superintendents, provided the popular choice was possessed of a skill and managerial capacity equal to his popularity. A foreman stood in a direct line of promotion to a superintendency, and from that to the directorship of an industry or a position in the presidential cabinet as a chief of the bureau of industry. The workmen were always able to secure the dismissal or removal of an inefficient or unpopular foreman. No foreman or superintendent was under the slightest obligation to keep an inefficient or disorderly workman.

A discharged workman could be reinstated, upon proper assurances and guarantee of fair conduct, at the discretion of the foreman, but a workman thus discharged had no inalienable right to demand and receive work in that department. He was at liberty to apply for and receive work in some other, and probably less profitable, branch of work, or he could leave the service of the government and find work elsewhere.

Every workman could not be a foreman or superintendent or a chief of a department, but there was always a chance of advancement to a capable and faithful employé. There was none of the slavery that some alleged political economists had predicted would follow the government control of industry.

But the 10,000,000 men employed by the trusts and the government were but a part of the forces of production, and by no means constituted the only avenues open to employment. There were doctors, lawyers, artists, newspaper men, and the thousand and one devotees to professions and occupations not directly concerned in the general production of a nation. The peaceful revolution had not materially affected their status. Their general prosperity had increased with the prosperity of the nation, and in no way had the government abridged in the slightest degree the liberty of any individual.

The press was absolutely untrammeled and at liberty at any time to attack the government or any part of it, a liberty they took advantage of when any responsible government official allowed the work of his department to deteriorate.

Begging was a lost art, and had ceased to be profitable. People had no sympathy for and paid no attention to able-bodied mendicants, and there were plenty of public and private institutions for worthy and helpless unfortunates.

In Chicago, New York and other cities the greatest change was in the long streets, formerly devoted to hundreds of musty little retail shops. These had disappeared, and at intervals corresponding to the density or character of the adjacent population were the magnificent bazaars of the trusts or of the government. Interspersed between these great marts were the more modest shops of dealers in such specialties as art works or the product of some industry which did not enter into general production. But the endless string of alternating grocery stores, butcher shops, drug stores, drygoods stores and hardware stores had disappeared.

There were no long processions of idle men with banners demanding work and bread. There were boards of trades, but no maniac, inspired by a belief that such institutions were impoverishing the people, shot at the noisy throngs of speculators and dealers. Great merchants and capitalists did not find it necessary to maintain guards around their private offices or residences to head off the desperate crank. There were no meetings of anarchist groups to discuss bomb-throwing or murder. No man had lost his liberty. The right of a man to demand and always obtain employment had simply been affirmed and carried out. With this as a condition there was no longer any good excuse for poverty.

There were endless opportunities to acquire wealth. The annual productiveness of the nation had been more than doubled. The wages of the cheapest workman were more than sufficient to support a large family in comfort. Things which would have been deemed luxuries in 1893 were in general demand. The purchasing power of a workman was enormous as compared with the rate which prevailed in 1893-96. Careful estimates indicate that the wages of the average workman in 1910 guaranteed him a daily purchasing power of not less than $15, as measured by the wage scale and prices which prevailed in 1893. In 1893 the workman produced about $7 a day and received less than $1.50 as wages. In 1910, measured by the same standard, the workman produced $16 a day and received not less than $15 of it as wages. The balance went either to the government as taxes or to the trusts as profits.

CHAPTER XXI.

NEW PROBLEMS.

MUNICIPAL governments were made to conform to the theory of the new constitution. Chicago was the first city to fall into line. By a popular vote the people overthrew the old city charter and formed a municipal government in which each ward was represented by a councilman whose powers were limited to the transaction of routine work and who could, at any time, be recalled by a vote of his constituents. The power to vote away the use of streets and alleys to private corporations was revoked. The city condemned, under the right of eminent domain delegated from the state, the various street-car, cable and elevated railroads occupying the streets, and purchased the same from their former owners.

Chicago voted for a loan from the general government, and the cabinet authorized the secretary of the treasury to advance to Chicago the sum of $6,000,000, to be expended in the extension of the intramural railway system. In six years Chicago redeemed this pledge from the profits of the new enterprise, without raising a dollar by taxation. All large expenditures of money were submitted by the city council to the people.

Having been shorn of all opportunity to steal, the aldermen were honest. Politics was no longer a profession. The heads of such departments as the elevated railroad system, telephone system, electric lighting plant and other public enterprises were elected for long terms of years and could be removed during such terms only by a majority vote of the people. The rates of wages paid employés in these concerns corresponded with those paid by private concerns and in the government industries. There was no wild scramble for work, and the position of conductor or lineman under the city administration was no more sought after than was an equally remunerative and responsible position in the great wholesale and retail establishment or in the shops of the Agricultural Machinery Company of America.

There was no political patronage, for the reason that the granting of a "job" was no longer a favor. The American people had reached a point when the right to work was not considered a rare privilege. The press and the public held the officers of the various heads of departments strictly accountable for the efficiency of the service rendered. If a cable road broke down two or three times a week, some official head was sure to fall in the basket. It was not difficult to induce the management to heat the cars in winter or to provide cars enough for the people in the summer. In other respects municipal government remained much the same as in other years. The people always had a chance to condemn inefficient management, and a decided improvement in the police force was soon noticed.

Some cities adopted the Glasgow system and erected municipal dwelling-houses, but the plan was not generally successful, the people preferring to erect their own houses, a task not difficult when steady work and good wages was assured A few cities erected free theaters, but their patronage did not much exceed that of the private theatrical enterprises. It became the settled policies of cities, as of the government, to refrain from interference in those activities and professions not directly connected with the production of standard necessities or in the execution of some public function. The management of street-car lines or of any system of intramural transit was of necessity a monopoly in private hands. It remained a monopoly in the hands of the city. It could be nothing but a monopoly, competition being impossible. The difference was that the private monopoly was for the benefit of the few stockholders and the city monopoly was for the benefit of the entire public.

In a report submitted to Congress in 1912, Secretary of the Census Wright showed that the average productivity of the individual was more than three times that of the year 1894. He ascribed this wonderful increase to the following reasons:

"1. Increased opportunity for profitable and steady employment.

"2. The decided reduction in the percentage of the indefinite and non-productive class.

"3. An improvement in and a systematizing of the methods of production.

"4. Decreased losses from the waste which formerly resulted from overproduction during the periods of depression and crippled consuming power which followed."

In his report Secretary Wright said:

"From 1890 to 1896 not more than one-half of the workmen of the United States were steadily employed. There were more non-producers, middlemen, and handlers and exchangers of products than there were producers. It cost the nation more to sell and protect its products than to pay its workmen. Every dollar taken by the middlemen was deducted from the share which would otherwise have been divided between the capitalists and the workmen. In 1893 the numbers of the middlemen exceeded those of the combined industrial, commercial, professional and independent class, and were exceeded in numerical strength only by the agricultural class, upon whose resources and products they levied a heavy tax. In 1893 not less than 40 per cent of the income-receiving people of the country were non-producers. In 1904 the percentage of non-producers was 28. Four years later it had decreased to 19, and in 1912 less than 10 per cent of the income-receiving people of the United States were employed in the handling, storing, distributing and manipulation of the products of industry.

"With the perfection of the system now in use by the great private industries—copied to some extent from that of the government—I am of the opinion that in a few years not to exceed 5 per cent of the workmen of the country will be required in that necessary work which comes under the classification of unproductive.

"The hundreds of thousands of men once engaged in unnecessary work have been forced into the ranks of the producers. Every man thus transferred has not only taken a load from the backs of capital and labor, but has also added another unit to the total industrial force of the country. This gradual diminution of the ranks of the non-producer has not been made at the expense of the complicated machinery of distribution and exchange. On the contrary, the work of that important department, both in public and private industry, has been made more perfect from year to year.

"In 1894-96 each workman was compelled to support himself, another idle workman, and two non-producers.

"To-day a workman receives the total sum of his products after there has been deducted less than 10 per cent as the necessary expense of transmitting, storing, selling and delivering.

"In other words, in 1894-96 the workman received less than 25 per cent of what his labor had added to raw material, and to-day he receives over 90 per cent. His average productivity has also been enormously increased by improvements in methods of production and machinery, all of which has gone to him after the deduction of a fair percentage to private capital, to the government, and the rewards of inventive genius and superior management.

Among the employments which had disappeared, or in which but few representatives yet remained, were those of the commercial traveler or drummer, insurance agents, solicitors, officials, clerks, etc., book agents, and agents of 100 other kinds. In 1893 there were 300,000 commercial travelers traversing the country at an enormous expenditure of money and energy, and engaged in the task of convincing the retailer of the superiority of a certain manufacture of goods. In 1904 both the drummer and his former customer, the retailer, had disappeared. Three hundred thousand good-looking and bright men were devoting their time and energies to other and more productive work at much higher wages, and 2,500,000 retailers had disappeared as retailers from the face of the earth One clerk in one of the great retail departments, aided by one delivery man, easily did the work formerly done by a score of men.

The government and private retail establishments had certain delivery routes and certain times for the distribution of articles, the same as in former years was the practice with the delivery of postal matter and in the handling of an immense business by the great express companies.

It appears almost incredible now that a time ever existed when forty or fifty rival grocery wagons, from forty or fifty different parts of the town or city, each delivered small quantities of goods in the same block. This was called competition in those days, and the people paid the wages of the forty-eight superfluous delivery men, the feed bills of the forty-eight superfluous horses, the wages of the forty-eight superfluous grocery or butcher clerks, and the profits of the forty-eight superfluous retailers, and protested against any system which would do away with any one of them.

The government did an insurance business and paid all losses incurred. There was no incentive to incendiarism, for the reason that the government stood ready to purchase any property at as high a figure as it would place insurance. In 1893 thousands and thousands of men and millions of dollars in money were wasted in insurance business. Banking was engaged in both by the government and by private capital, but the rates of interest were so low and the demand for money so slight that the business was not a profitable one for private capital. The government was ready to advance money with land or unimpaired improved property as security.

For the first time in American history farming became generally profitable. In preceding years the farmer had managed to live until the mortgage on his farm was foreclosed, when he became a tenant farmer, a tramp, or an unemployed workman in a great city. The stunted production and wage fund of 1870-96 made the farmer dependent on the European market for the sale of the surplus which hungry Americans could not buy, and the price was also fixed by that same foreign market. Lack of profits deprived him of the superb machinery stored in deserted factories, and lack of profits prevented him from being a purchaser in the marts of industry. In the stimuulated industrial era which began under President Smith the consumption of farm products was doubled in twelve months. Wheat jumped from 43 cents per bushel to $1.17. Railroad rates, under the management of Chief Jeffery, decreased. The government ever stood ready to purchase wheat and grains at a shade below the market price, which rose and fell slowly from supply and demand, and not from the manipulation of board of trade operators and gamblers. Secretary Moulton established in several states model farms of from 6,000 to 20,000 acres of land, some of which was purchased and some forfeited by speculative holders. Every modern improvement was employed and the experiment was a success. As a result of this, co-operative farming became a feature throughout the west and south and in many parts of the east. A score or more of farmers would combine their acreage and form a stock company. In some cases a small village would be located near the center of the co-operative farm, and the advantages of closer associations profited by. These farming companies were enabled to purchase and employ every labor-saving device known to invention, and farming became profitable to the advance of civilization, instead of steadily retrograding as in the past.

An event of great importance to the United States marked the present year. At an international monetary congress held in Paris the currency of the United States was accepted by the great nations of Europe as an international standard of value. The fluctuations of silver had been so marked and its decline so inevitable that it was as valueless as gold as a standard. The paper American dollar, based on labor and secured by the inexhaustible stores of wealth of a continent, was unanimously adopted as a standard by which all values could be measured. Based on the average productivity of labor, ever exchangeable in the United States for not less than 95 per cent of the products of one hour's labor, backed by a nation of 100,000,000 people with an ever increasing wealth, it formed the ideal of an "honest dollar."

CHAPTER XXII.

THE PAST AND THE PRESENT.

It is difficult in this year of our Lord 1920 to account for the toleration of abuses which distinguished the American people in 1893. The American of to-day is jealous of his rights. He considers himself a part of the government. There is nothing shadowy or unsubstantial about his citizenship. He makes and unmakes laws; elects and deposes public officials; is an equal factor with any other man in the deciding of the affairs of the nation, state, county, township or municipality. He is not ruled, he rules. He is the government. He is the state.

There is a growing tendency of modern historians which the author must condemn, to ridicule, denounce and hold up to contempt the people of the latter part of the nineteenth century. They were not cowards, as has been alleged by some. They were not fools, as has been alleged by certain writers who were at that time too young to analyze the conditions which prevailed. The crime of the nation in those years was superstition—and national superstition is a national crime.

Their politicians, preachers, writers and schoolteachers taught superstition and labeled it patriotism. That splendid word patriotism came to mean bigoted, partisan, class and caste ignorance and superstition. It was taught in the public schools. The half-starved children of idle mechanics were taught to believe that their country was the greatest and wisest governed country on the face of the earth, the home of liberty, and a refuge for the oppressed of all nations. Intelligent foreigners came from monarchical countries, visited America, and went back across the Atlantic amazed, astounded and discouraged. But the American people firmly believed the fairy tale of their freedom. Hungry workmen year after year drank in the lies of demagogues and ignorant but cunning politicians. They were ready to accept any excuse for their poverty, and with child-like faith grasped at the delusive phantom of hope held out before them. They rallied at the polls, elected men, and men, and men, and were robbed, and robbed, and robbed. And into their ears the public teachers were pouring patriotism, preaching the infallibility of a government, constitution and laws which were defrauding and impoverishing the very men who were preaching patriotism and superstition. Bankrupt merchants, crippled capitalists, idle and despondent workmen, bedraggled and forlorn in the financial storm sweeping over them, would curse the reformer who told them to come in out of the wet. The curse was the curse of time. The constitution of the United States was 110 years old. Therefore it was something to venerate, to worship, to scare little children with. If it had been but ten, or twenty, or thirty years old, it would not have survived the first week of a panic, but would have been cast aside by a disgusted and defrauded people.

Custom has an ascendency over the understanding, says the philosopher Watts, and another great thinker has declared that in the great majority of things habit is a greater plague than ever afflicted Egypt. The people of the United States proved this in the years they submitted to the rule of the constitutional antiquity handed down from the little monarchical colonies which a hundred years before lined the Atlantic coast. John Smith punctured that aged enemy of the people, and the bubble of superstition broke and at the same time the film came from the eyes of the people. Progress has no greater foe than precedent; no grander champion than a true hater of superstition. The path of progress is strewn with broken precedents, and over the shattered traditions of a majority-fearing constitution a free people planted a milestone in history and on it inscribed these words:

"The rights of the majority of a people shall no longer be abridged."

To the Reader:

Are you in favor of Majority Rule? Do you believe that it is of sufficient importance to become an issue in 1900? Do you believe that any reform can be carried into execution by the majority so long as the minority is in control?

Kindly consider the feasibility of forming a Majority Rule Club in your vicinity. The author has no ambition to lead any such movement, and subscribes himself as a volunteer in the ranks. But he is desirous of giving this and other books on the same subject a wide circulation, and would esteem it a favor if the reader will forward his name, with those of friends who may be interested in the reform movement. We must help one another, and by granting this favor you may materially advance a movement which is certain to succeed at no far distant day. Without education there can be no progress. If you regard the suggestions made in "President John Smith" as tending in the right direction, kindly drop me a line and enclose the names of those you would like to have read this book.

Sincerely yours,

Frederick U. Adams.

56 Fifth Ave., Chicago.

Utopian Literature

AN ARNO PRESS/NEW YORK TIMES COLLECTION

Adams, Frederick Upham.
President John Smith; The Story of a Peaceful Revolution. 1897.

Bird, Arthur.
Looking Forward: A Dream of the United States of the Americas in 1999. 1899.

[Blanchard, Calvin.]
The Art of Real Pleasure. 1864.

Brinsmade, Herman Hine.
Utopia Achieved: A Novel of the Future. 1912.

Caryl, Charles W.
New Era. 1897.

Chavannes, Albert.
The Future Commonwealth. 1892.

Child, William Stanley.
The Legal Revolution of 1902. 1898.

Collens, T. Wharton.
Eden of Labor; or, The Christian Utopia. 1876.

Cowan, James.
Daybreak. A Romance of an Old World. 1896. 2nd ed.

Craig, Alexander.
Ionia; Land of Wise Men and Fair Women. 1898.

Daniel, Charles S.
AI: A Social Vision. 1892.

Devinne, Paul.
The Day of Prosperity: A Vision of the Century to Come. 1902.

Edson, Milan C.
Solaris Farm. 1900.

Fuller, Alvarado M.
A. D. 2000. 1890.

Geissler, Ludwig A.
Looking Beyond. 1891.

Hale, Edward Everett.
How They Lived in Hampton. 1888.

Hale, Edward Everett.
Sybaris and Other Homes. 1869.

Harris, W. S.
Life in a Thousand Worlds. 1905.

Henry, W. O.
Equitania. 1914.

Hicks, Granville, with Richard M. Bennett.
The First to Awaken. 1940.

Lewis, Arthur O., editor
American Utopias: Selected Short Fiction. 1790–1954.

McGrady, Thomas.
Beyond the Black Ocean. 1901.

Mendes H. Pereira.
Looking Ahead. 1899.

Michaelis, Richard.
Looking Further Forward. An Answer to *Looking Backward* by Edward Bellamy. 1890.

Moore, David A.
The Age of Progress. 1856.

Noto, Cosimo.
The Ideal City. 1903.

Olerich, Henry.
A Cityless and Countryless World. 1893.

Parry, David M.
The Scarlet Empire. 1906.

Peck, Bradford.
The World a Department Store. 1900.

Reitmeister, Louis Aaron.
If Tomorrow Comes. 1934.

Roberts, J. W.
Looking Within. 1893.

Rosewater, Frank.
'96; A Romance of Utopia. 1894.

Satterlee, W. W.
Looking Backward and What I Saw. 2nd ed. 1890.

Schindler, Solomon.
Young West; A Sequel to Edward Bellamy's Celebrated Novel "Looking Backward." 1894.

Smith, Titus K.
Altruria. 1895.

Steere, C. A.
When Things Were Doing. 1908.

Taylor, William Alexander.
Intermere. 1901.

Thiusen, Ismar.
The Diothas, or, A Far Look Ahead. 1883.

Vinton, Arthur Dudley.
Looking Further Backward. 1890.

Wooldridge, C. W.
Perfecting the Earth. 1902.

Wright, Austin Tappan.
Islandia. 1942.